ON THE CHOPPING BLOCK

A CALLIE'S KITCHEN MYSTERY, BOOK 1

Jenny Kales

Book Layout ©2017 BookDesignTemplates.com

ISBN: 9781520390918

To Jim, thank you for your love and support

"At his best, man is the noblest of all animals; separated from law and justice, he is the worst."
ARISTOTLE

"I think every woman should have a blowtorch."
JULIA CHILD

Contents

One

Calliope Costas' bright blue Volkswagen SUV screeched to a halt in front of one of the most stunning homes in Crystal Bay, Wisconsin. It belonged to her boyfriend, Drew, and it was spectacular. Huge, mullioned windows beckoned, letting in dazzling light and a panorama of the changing seasons. Composed entirely of burnished brick, the house was designed to impress, with majestic neo-classical columns and an envy-producing view of the water. It wasn't on the million-dollar mansion boat tour for the summer visitors, but Callie, as she was known to almost everyone she knew, thought that it should be.

Today, Drew's house looked poised for an autumn photo shoot. The oaks and maples on the property were no longer simply tipped with the caramel and gold shades of fall as they had been the last time Callie visited. Now they were ablaze with red, orange and yellow tones that belonged on an artist's palette.

Glancing at the mirror for a quick check of her appearance, Callie noticed a powdery white substance clinging to her long, wavy dark hair. It had to be either flour or powdered sugar from her earlier baking session at "Callie's Kitchen," her Mediterranean-inspired meals-from-scratch business. Powdered sugar was a key ingredient of the *kourabiethes* she'd been baking. The rich Greek butter cookies were rolled in powdered sugar while they were hot from the oven and the sugar tended to fly out everywhere. Quickly, she tried to brush the white stuff out of her dark hair, but only succeeded in transferring it more securely into her locks. Great: Now it looked like she was graying at the temples. So much for her attempts at glamour. Drew would have to take her as is – powdered sugar in her hair and all.

Callie liked to look her best, but normally, she didn't put quite so much energy into her appearance. Tonight was different. Drew had offered to host her for a rare intimate dinner, not usually allowed by their busy schedules.

An excellent cook, financially secure, funny and dreamy to look at with his green eyes, dark hair and tall, muscular physique, Drew was considered a catch. However, Callie had mixed feelings for the reason behind this particular get-together: Drew's triumph in the first annual Taste of Crystal Bay contest.

Along with a lot of their food-business buddies, they'd both been competitors in what had proved to be a cutthroat cookoff. Even though she had feelings for Drew, it was impossible for Callie to ignore the cold, hard financial facts: Drew's win had shattered her hopes of getting the $10,000 prize.

Going home to get ready after work had taken longer than she thought it would and Callie realized she couldn't keep Drew waiting any longer. As she strode up the paved walkway, she hoped her lateness wouldn't be interpreted as rudeness. Determined to be cheerful and supportive, she put on what she hoped was a happy face and rang Drew's doorbell.

No answer. She waited another minute and rang again. Nothing. "Oh, Drew," Callie whispered under her breath. "Come on. Not today."

Maybe the doorbell was broken. She rapped on the front door. Silence reigned, so Callie continued to hit the door, each knock growing in emphasis and volume. At least her repeated hitting of the massive oak door was good for relieving stress.

Give the guy a break, she thought. Drew was probably on the phone spreading his good news to the world. Just to see if he'd pick up, Callie dialed his cell phone number. No answer: it went straight to voicemail.

Well, why shouldn't Drew tell everyone about his accomplishments? He'd won the contest fair and square. His offer to host Callie for a homemade dinner seemed like a sincere attempt to include her in his victory. She wasn't going to let a business issue interfere with romance. She'd spent enough time alone in recent years, trying to figure out where she had gone wrong in her marriage – and fending off well-meaning advice as well as criticism – from family members. Well, the advice had come mainly from George, her old-fashioned father who she sometimes thought would be happy if she swore off men forever.

Enough. No more negativity. Her best friend Samantha was always telling Callie to "go for it" but Callie went about things her own way, in her own time. And that time was right now. That is, if Drew would ever answer the door.

Once again, Callie picked up the brass door knocker shaped like the head of Medusa, consciously avoiding the abundance of twisting snakes for hair. Drew liked whimsical décor and Greek mythology, something the two of them had in common. Callie listened carefully for the sound of footsteps or Drew's voice talking on the phone. She didn't hear a thing.

As she scanned Drew's elegant veranda with increasing exasperation, she noticed a small hairline crack in one of the elegant Corinthian columns. Callie considered pointing out the tiny flaw to house-proud Drew who liked things just so. Or maybe not. Tonight was starting to look like a true-blue dating disaster.

It was silly to just keep standing there. Callie decided to check the back of Drew's house to see if he was digging in the garden wearing headphones and unable to hear her. He had to be home — she'd already spotted his car in the garage, scrupulously clean and sleekly polished, just like him. However, the white-washed garage was beginning to resemble a Dalmatian print, with patches of dark brown wood emerging from underneath peeling paint. Spending most of his time at work meant that he probably hadn't had time to get it repainted. Success had its price.

The grass was long and scratchy as Callie picked her way across the lawn and onto an immaculate stone patio. She walked over to the windows and tried to peek inside, but the windows were slightly too high. The house had been designed to maximize the view of the water from the kitchen, which was raised above a massive family room with sliding glass doors. The glass doors were locked and the blinds were completely closed. Fortunately, two of the kitchen windows were half-open to the pleasantly cool evening air.

"Drew!" Callie tried to pitch her voice towards the open window. When there was no response, she called his name even more loudly, starting to feel like an idiot.

Strange, Callie thought. He'd been so insistent about having her over tonight – he'd even asked her to leave work early.

As she stood there, about ready to give up and go home, the rich smell of braising meat wafted out the window to her, but underneath was a smoky, unpleasant odor, one she'd already smelled today when her oven overheated. Something was burning. If Drew was cooking, he had to be inside the house. As an experienced cook, he wouldn't leave something on the stove to burn. Frustration turned to concern. What was going on? It was time to find out if Drew was freezing her out – or if he was simply stuck inside of his professional-grade walk-in freezer.

Callie scanned the backyard looking for a makeshift stepstool and spotted oversized pots of mums, so new they still had price tags on them. Carefully, so as not to harm the flowers, she pulled out the packed dirt filled with the herbal-smelling blooms and placed them gently on the patio. The uprooted flowers listed to the side. Carefully, she climbed on top of the overturned planter and squinted to see inside the house, her nose pressed against the glass. How much is that puppy in the window? If Drew saw her now, they could have a good laugh.

As Callie's eyes adjusted to the dimness inside, she did a double-take, stepping back and nearly falling. It looked like Drew was on the floor but she couldn't see all of him, only his jean-clad legs and black high top sneakers. She called his name again and he didn't move. The burning smell was stronger from this vantage point and she didn't want his house to go up on flames. She had to act – and fast.

Callie tried the front door and back side door, but both were locked. She already knew that the sliding doors were locked. Blood began pounding in her temples as she tried to find a nail file or any sharp object so that she could slit the screens and lift up the windows.

Dumping her purse on the ground she dug through lipsticks, her daughter Olivia's emergency asthma inhaler and wallet looking for a nail file or pen. She grabbed her car keys and tried to cut the screen but the end of the key was too dull for the tough mesh. Tears stung her eyes as she kept calling Drew's name with no answer. Callie knew she should call 911 but if Drew needed CPR, she could give that to him immediately. She learned all about CPR when Olivia had her first asthma attack. If she couldn't get in the house five more seconds, she'd retrieve her phone from the grass and call an ambulance.

Adrenaline made her strong – she returned to the window and hurled a heavy stone from the landscaping with all of her might. The glass shattered and she ducked. Grateful that the night had cooled off and that she had a brought a coat, Callie took the garment from her arm and carefully placed it over the window sill. She stepped up onto the overturned flower pot again, her bare feet gripping it for balance, and inched her way inside the window, placing each foot on the hardwood floor cautiously. Finally, she was on solid ground.

Callie screamed Drew's name as she ran to the foot of the stairs. Clenching her jaw, she forced herself to look at what lay on the floor.

Drew was on his back, his wide-open green eyes appearing to look right at her. Not wanting to believe what she saw, it took Callie a few seconds before she registered the large chef's knife that was sticking out of the left side of his chest. A small, dark red circle stained Drew's light-blue Oxford shirt, a recent gift from Callie.

CPR wouldn't be necessary. Drew was dead.

Two

Blood rushed to Callie's head. She tried to fight feelings of dizziness as she sank to the floor, inhaling deep breaths through her nose and out of her mouth. When she could bear to, she lifted her head and leaned over Drew, placing her fingers on his neck. There was no pulse and his skin felt strange, waxen. Recoiling a little bit, she started to grab the knife but whisked her hand away at the last minute, afraid to disturb the scene. Callie stood up shakily, grabbed her cell phone and called 911.

"Someone's been...hurt." Callie stammered to the emergency respondent. She couldn't bring herself to say "dead." "574 E. Hamilton Avenue near the bay. Drew Staven's house. Please, come quickly!"

The operator began firing questions at her. Callie gripped the phone and answered in robotic tones. Yes, she knew the victim. No, he wasn't breathing. And so on, until the room started spinning again.

She sank back down to the floor near Drew's body again, fearful she'd fall over if she didn't. Clutching the cell phone in her hand and answering the 911 respondent in a voice that didn't sound like her own – she'd been told to stay on the line until the police arrived – Callie reached out and touched Drew gently on his shoulder, but of course, he didn't move. *This can't be happening.* She felt numb.

Callie put her head down and waited until the feelings of dizziness and nausea passed, and then slowly rose to her feet, her emotions swirling around inside of her. She knew it was disloyal, but she had to get away from Drew's body. Now.

Still clutching the phone and listening to the calm tones of the operator, Callie wandered dazedly through the house, passing through

Drew's dining room and into his well-stocked kitchen, an oasis of warmth and cleanliness. Stainless steel appliances dazzled like diamonds. Inspecting the range and kitchen island that Drew used as a cooking work station, she saw he had created a *mis en place* for the meal, with herbs and vegetables on a chopping board. His knife block sat nearby, each slot neatly filled.

The burning smell she'd gotten a whiff of outside grew stronger as Callie neared the stove. Bluish flames flickered underneath a large Dutch oven set atop the state-of-the-art range. Dinner. Callie jumped up and searched for a kitchen glove before turning the knob to "off," then inspected the contents of the pot. As she lifted the lid, the luscious smell of garlic wafted out on a cloud of fragrant steam, with the carbonized odor of burning beef underneath. Nearly all of the braising liquid was gone and the food looked dry; it was nearly scorched. An apple tart was already made and sitting on a trivet on the counter. Callie placed her hand above the tart. It was warm. Peering at the floor, she saw it was strewn with garbage, another price tag for mums and a crumpled paper towel.

Wait a minute. The killer could very well still be in the house, watching and waiting. Callie felt a cold chill begin on the top of her head. With silent apologies for not staying in the house with him, she rushed past Drew's body, unlocked the front door and went outside to wait, the voice of the operator assuring her that the police would be there soon.

Callie held onto the front porch rails and tried to stop shivering in the only slightly chilly fall evening. Everything was so quiet that she could hear ducks on the water with the snickering sounds of their distant quacking. Crickets chirped a haphazard concerto. Hugging her arms to her chest, Callie rocked herself back and forth as if to comfort herself but it didn't work. She felt as if she were about to sink through the floor.

Homes in this upscale neighborhood were not placed close together and so far, Callie didn't see any neighbors. She wasn't sure how much time had passed before the faint whine of sirens cut through the calm night air and grew louder as they approached the home. A police car and an ambulance pulled up with a screech and in seconds, Callie found herself in a flurry of activity. Still gripping the phone in a sweaty hand, she told the operator that the police were here and hung up. EMTs rushed into Drew's house

While rattling off her vital statistics to a stocky officer whose name she didn't quite catch, a tall man with a thin face and sad hazel eyes walked up the steps and joined them. His presence made Callie feel on her guard. She stood up a little straighter and waited while Officer Mumble introduced them.

"Detective Sands, Calliope Costas. She says she's a friend of the deceased."

"Ms. Costas," the detective spoke soothingly and surprisingly with a British accent. "I need you to tell me everything that happened here, starting at the beginning," Sands said.

Callie swallowed hard. She told him about her planned dinner at Drew's house and how he hadn't answered the door when she rang. "I stood on a planter and peeked inside his window. That's when I saw him sprawled on the floor, so I broke a window and came inside."

Callie shivered remembering Drew's glazed expression. "He was dead when I found him. I checked his pulse but..." She stopped a minute as a wave of emotion swept over her. "Then I called 911."

"So the window was intact when you arrived?"

"Yes, I saw him on the floor and thought he might be hurt or sick. I don't have a key and there was no other way for me to get in. I thought I might be able to help him because I know some CPR training. I didn't know he was already dead."

"I'm going in the house," Sands said, standing up abruptly. "You stay here."

Callie sat down on one of the cushiony wicker chairs that decorated Drew's spacious front porch. Closing her eyes and trying to stem the tide of nausea that kept washing over her in waves, she found herself thinking about the times she'd visited Drew's home and how happy he'd always been to entertain guests.

The first time she'd ever met him was at a Chamber party and she'd been thrilled at a chance to get a look inside such a beautiful home – not to mention a chance to meet its handsome owner. It was so airy, so majestic, so perfectly decorated. *Of all this I could have been mistress;* a line from Jane Austen, popped into her head and Callie knew she was losing her composure.

Inhaling deeply, she remembered how impressed and flattered she'd been when he'd offered to give her a tour on their fateful first meeting. Polished handrails on both sides of the staircase in the massive living room led to a lofted area highlighted by a large window that framed the changing seasons. The home had gleaming, dark hardwood floors, framed artwork and expensively re-fitted bathrooms. As Drew had led her from room to room, she remembered thinking that it looked like a Pottery Barn catalog: clean, bright, contemporary and somewhat unlived in.

Callie's knees felt weak as she stood up and peered in one of the windows. The uniformed officer was standing guard outside the door and when Callie glanced over at him, he shook his head at her. "You can't go in. Just stay where you are. Detective Sands will be out in a minute."

Callie sighed and sat back down. The sick feelings came back along with a surreal quality that made her feel like she was watching the scene from far away. Callie didn't know how much time had passed before Sands joined her once again on the porch.

"Ms. Costas, I have a few questions for you."

"Of course. Anything I can do to help." She sat up straight, still hugging herself. She felt her arms shaking and hugged herself more tightly in an effort to stop.

"Right. Well, what's with all of the food in the kitchen? It looks like the victim was preparing a meal. It looked pretty good, too. Some kind of stew and an apple pie? Sorry," the detective said when he saw Callie's expression. "I guess I haven't eaten much today."

"Drew was cooking for us tonight," she told Sands, amazed that he could be hungry at a time like this. Her appetite, for once, was completely gone. "I cook all day for work, so he was going to treat me." She sniffed, loudly. Detective Sands pulled a pack of tissues out of his pocket and handed them to her. She thanked him, dabbing at her eyes and nose before continuing.

"I found food burning on the stove so I turned off the flame," Callie said, her breath catching in her throat. She heard the tremor in her voice as she continued her tale. "I didn't want the house to burn down. Drew was an experienced chef. I don't think he would walk away from a hot stove with food cooking on it for more than a minute. I wonder what he was doing by the stairs."

"He might have heard someone come in," said Sands, brusquely. "Have you spent a lot of time here? You seem to know your way around."

Callie blushed. "We've been dating a couple of months and we hadn't seen much of each other lately because of our busy schedules – the food business makes for late hours. In fact, we were supposed to be celebrating tonight because Drew just found out that he'd won the Taste of Crystal Bay."

"I see," said Sands. His hazel eyes seemed to bore right into her. "Did you remain in the kitchen or did you go upstairs?" Sands ran his hand through his hair, making a forelock stand on end. Callie thought it best not to mention it. The sooner she answered his questions, the sooner she could get out of here.

"I stayed downstairs. As soon as I saw Drew, I called 911. I don't know if anything upstairs is disturbed but nothing looked out of place downstairs." Other than Drew's poor lifeless body, Callie thought.

"The bistro business was pretty good to Mr. Staven I take it," he remarked. Obviously, he'd been as impressed with Drew's magazine-perfect house as she was.

"Yes, well, Drew worked hard – he rarely had a day off."

"I work hard too," Sands replied. "But my house is a bit more modest."

"Mine too," said Callie.

Sands gave her a small smile and looked back down at his note-book. "Another question. We didn't find any type of personal electronics in Drew's house. The TV is there but no personal computer, cell phone or any other type of device. Do you know if he had anything like that?"

"Yes, Drew had a laptop and a cell phone," Callie said. "He also had a tablet – he was just showing it to me the other day. You didn't find any of that?"

Instead of answering her, the detective asked another question. "Who is Jane Willoughby?"

"She's the head of the Crystal Bay Chamber of Commerce and she owns the fitness center, Bodies by the Bay. "Enjoy lake views while you whip your body into shape!'" Callie quoted the center's current slogan. "Why?"

Sands looked directly at her. "There was a note on Drew's desk – it said to call Jane Willoughby."

"Oh," Callie said. "That's probably because Drew wanted to talk to her about the competition. They have a newsletter and I know Jane wanted a celebration at the next meeting, after the winner was announced."

"So Ms. Willoughby owns the fitness center, you say? I think I was there once."

"Bodies by the Bay," Callie repeated, slightly dismayed at the double entendre, especially now that there was an actual body by the bay – Drew's. "Uh, you can't miss it. Follow Hamilton all the way around the lake and turn left."

"Fine, we'll talk to Ms. Willoughby too, then. Is she a close friend of yours?" asked Sands. His eyes scanned Drew's porch and the street behind it like a hummingbird, never alighting on any one object or thing for long.

"Jane comes into my shop once in a while with her husband," Callie explained. "I've occasionally worked out at her fitness center." Sands didn't need to know that working out "occasionally" meant "almost never."

"And as I mentioned, we're in the Chamber together. She's more of an acquaintance than a close friend but I admire her. She's a very successful businesswoman."

"Right." Sands said making another note. All at once, Callie felt uncomfortable at being the target of so many questions. Her mind had started to fully grasp the night's events and she felt like she was going to collapse if she didn't get out of there soon. She didn't want the detective to know she was distressed. *Take it easy.* She could fall apart later, in private.

Sands showed no signs of slowing down with his inquiries. "Did Mr. Staven have any enemies? Or, were there any business problems that you know of?" She couldn't read the detective's facial expression and it bothered her.

"I don't know of any enemies or business problems. That's the thing I don't understand. He didn't even get to enjoy his success. He was so excited about the contest," Callie began but stopped. It was too painful to contemplate.

"'Taste of Crystal Bay,' you said." Sands seemed thoughtful. "Interesting. Well, do you know of anyone who would be angry about that?"

"Killing someone over a food contest?" Callie started to scoff, but the steely look in Sands' eyes stopped her.

"Just about everyone would be disappointed, me included," Callie admitted. "I was a contestant, too." The detective's eyebrows rose at that remark, but she continued. "I don't know anyone who was angry enough to kill. I mean, people just don't do that kind of thing around here." Callie realized how silly that sounded and was about to say so when Sands cut her off.

"Well, someone was angry – or passionate – enough to kill him. I have to ask you: Where were you for the last several hours. Can anyone vouch for you?"

"Uh," Callie stammered. "I was at work with my assistant Max, and then I went home after Drew called and asked me over here. He wanted me here about an hour and a half sooner than I arrived – I got hung up at work. Then I went home, showered and changed and came over here. Also, I spoke to my father over the phone regarding childcare for my daughter. But I was alone at home for about maybe an hour and fifteen minutes, total."

Sands folded his arms in front of him. "Right. Do you have a card with all of your contact information?"

"Of course," Callie said, her head beginning to throb. While Callie dug into her purse for her business card holder, Detective Sands produced his crisp white card out of his equally crisp front pocket and handed it to her. "Thank you," she said faintly. Finally, she found her card and gave it to him.

He squinted at it. "Callie's Kitchen. Mediterranean-inspired meals-from-scratch with Midwestern heart," he read. Callie thought Sands looked even hungrier than he had when he was eyeing Drew's unfinished meal on the stove.

As she put the detective's card in her purse, Callie heard a familiar voice coming up the walkway, demanding that someone tell her what was going on. Callie groaned. This could only be Gertrude DeWitt.

Mrs. DeWitt's stylishly-short gray hair seemed to bristle at the unfortunate policeman as he told her that the house was a crime scene and to stay where she was. A lifelong resident of Crystal Bay, now a widow, and a descendant of Crystal Bay College's founding family, Mrs. DeWitt was a well-respected philanthropic fixture at any local event. Her home was on the tourist mansion tour and when she said "jump" the usual answer was "how high?"

Mrs. DeWitt smoothed her tweed skirt and tugged at the fashionable blue scarf at her neck as she kept up her barrage of questions. "What happened? I simply insist that you tell me what's going on. Flashing lights? Police cars? Ambulances?" Mrs. DeWitt's tone suggested these items were as welcome in her elegant neighborhood as a rat infestation.

Suddenly Mrs. DeWitt spotted Callie. "Callie Costas! What are you doing here, dear? Are you all right?" She reached out her arms and hugged Callie tightly to her birdlike bosom. Gently disengaging from Mrs. DeWitt's embrace, Callie noticed that Sands was watching the two women with a stern look on his face. Before Callie could speak, he took charge.

"Your name, please, ma'am," he said, nodding at the older woman.

"Mrs. Gertrude DeWitt. I'm a neighbor of Drew's. What's going on? Isn't anyone going to tell me?" Mrs. DeWitt's blue eyes blazed and her lips pursed in a little bow of wrinkles.

Distressed though she was by the circumstances, Callie eyed this interchange with interest, if only to see how Sands would handle the wealthy philanthropist who was staying true to form, even in a crisis. If she liked you, you were golden – but get on her bad side and watch out!

"There's been a murder, Mrs. DeWitt. You say you're a neighbor? You might have seen something that can help us." Sands appeared to be unflappable in the face of Mrs. DeWitt's demanding words.

Mrs. DeWitt swayed a bit on her feet and looked to Callie for confirmation. Callie took the older woman's arm to give her support and nodded sadly.

"Oh my goodness. Drew!! No!" Mrs. DeWitt wiped her eyes, her long elegant fingers laden with brilliant-cut diamonds and precious gems.

"It's true. I'm sorry," she said to Mrs. DeWitt and placed a hand on her shoulder.

Mrs. DeWitt addressed her statement to Callie as if the detective couldn't hear her. "This is unbelievable. I truly feel like I'm in the middle of a dream." A terrible dream, Callie thought. I wish I would wake up. She sniffled again and noticed that Mrs. DeWitt was looking a bit green around the gills. She held onto the older woman's elbow more tightly.

"Where were you tonight?" Sands asked Mrs. DeWitt.

Mrs. DeWitt appeared to be stunned and a little offended that an actual human existed who didn't know her exact itinerary. "I was working on fundraising activities for the CBC with the financial steering committee for the last couple of hours. I had planned to see Jane Willoughby about the Taste of Crystal Bay celebration we wanted to have, but I couldn't get her on the phone. Someone at her...fitness center...told me she'd left for the day." Mrs. DeWitt wrinkled her nose. She hated the name "Bodies by the Bay" and had told everyone she thought that it sounded like a strip club.

"CBC?" Sands asked.

"Crystal Bay College," Mrs. DeWitt said impatiently.

Sands plowed onward, unfazed by her impolite tone. "Yes, of course. And where, specifically, was your meeting?"

Mrs. DeWitt appeared to be regretting her decision to approach the crime scene. "I was in a conference room with committee members." She glared at Sands as if daring the detective to challenge her.

"The whole time?" Sands wanted to know.

"Not the whole time. I was in my private office, there, as well." Callie patted Mrs. DeWitt's shoulder encouragingly. The older woman had begun to cry, huge silent tears and Callie searched her purse – in vain – for a tissue. She wondered why she – the person who had found Drew -- was relatively calm, when Mrs. DeWitt was so upset. And then she knew: the reality hadn't set in yet. When it did, Callie had a feeling it wasn't going to be pretty.

"Thank you." Detective Sands was saying to Mrs. DeWitt. "Please leave your information with me in case we need to question you further. You're free to go after that."

Glaring at him, her despair beginning to morph into anger at a situation so completely out of her control, Mrs. DeWitt pulled a business card out of her quilted Chanel bag and handed it to him. Giving one sharp nod to Callie, she tromped off the porch and in the direction of her house without another word.

Despite the hellish quality of the evening, Callie couldn't help looking at her admiringly as she departed. She wished she had that kind of gumption when dealing with her ex, Hugh and his pretty but annoyingly cheerful new wife, Raine.

Sands startled Callie with his next comment: it appeared that he was even hungrier than she'd thought.

"You don't make shepherd's pic by chance? At your food business? I'd love a real, homemade shepherd's pie and I'm a horrid cook myself." Food talk? Maybe he was trying to distract her from the horrors of the night.

Callie managed a small smile. Hungry non-cooks were her kind of people. "In fact, we do. My grandmother is part Irish and she swears by her version of shepherd's pie, which she taught to me. Of course, I added my own touches. It's good. Mostly, though, I cook foods from the Greek side of my family, along with some good old comfort food favorites. And yes, I'm Greek." Well, half Greek, but that was neither here nor there at such a moment. Callie's stomach rumbled and she crossed her arms over her abdomen.

Sands didn't appear to notice. "I may just have to stop by some-time. Now, I need you to come along to the station with me. We've got to have your official statement tonight. We'll take your finger-prints, of course. It's routine."

Routine. Wonderful. "Am I a suspect?" Callie asked, realizing that she had begun shivering with fear again.

Detective Sands looked at her intently as if sizing her up. "Ms. Costas, everybody is a suspect until further notice."

Three

C allie awoke the next morning with a headache, her eyes painful and red. Between bouts of crying the previous evening, she'd sipped from a medicinal bottle of ouzo, the strong Greek liqueur that was her father George's spirit of choice. Not a good move, she thought, as she struggled to sit up.

The police station visit the night before had been unsettling. Callie had texted her best friend and local attorney, Samantha, and asked her to meet her there, so at least she'd had some moral support during her ordeal. It didn't hurt to have someone with legal knowledge on hand, either.

Sands had led Callie into an overly air-conditioned room with pale grey walls, where he'd given her a cup of brackish coffee and asked her for her version of events, which he recorded. As she sat there relaying her story, Callie realized that her lack of a good alibi was a problem.

"Don't worry," Samantha had reassured her after the detective had told her she could go home. "Someone must have seen you, or maybe you texted someone, made a phone call, something. We'll figure it out." Samantha, so chipper and loyal, despite the massive black storm cloud threatening her friend, had cheered Callie slightly. Sam had promised to help her any way she could and that was some comfort. Not much, but some.

What was she going to do now? Callie debated, coming back to the present. She felt like pulling the covers over her head but instead, closed her eyes as the horrific memories washed over her. Seeing that her mistress was finally sitting up, if not fully awake, Koukla, her

Yorkie, began her usual morning routine of attempting to dissuade her from getting out of bed. The little dog jumped on her chest and made herself comfortable.

Callie fell back onto the pillows. How wonderful it would be to stay here, cuddling Koukla and forgetting about everything she'd witnessed the previous evening. Not that she could do that if she tried – a picture of Drew's lifeless eyes were burned into her own dark brown retinas. Giving Koukla a gentle nudge, Callie struggled out of bed and made a beeline for the bathroom tap.

While she gulped a glass of water, the idea of going to work seemed more logical by the minute. As much as she wanted to hide, she had a business to run. Koukla made a charming companion, but Callie thought she might go crazy if she stayed home wondering what was happening – both at work and with the investigation into Drew's murder.

Despite everything, her work ethic remained iron clad, no doubt a remnant of her upbringing. Her father George had put in long hours at his diner, The Olympia, and had rarely missed a day of work. In fact, his pride in what he'd built at the diner was so strong that he'd asked Callie to take over for him when he retired. Well, maybe "asked" wasn't the right word. "Commanded" might be more accurate but even so, Callie had declined in favor of starting out on her own. Remembering the arguments that had ensued and the tension that still remained between them, Callie vowed to forget about that for the moment and concentrate on putting one foot in front of the other.

"Mom!" shouted Callie's 10-year-old daughter, Olivia. "Do we have waffles?" With all of the baking her mother did, Olivia was spoiled by homemade foods and thought frozen stuff was a special treat. Callie heard items being shifted loudly in the freezer. Then there was a crash and a yelp from her daughter. "Ow! A chicken just fell on my foot!"

"Just a minute!" She scurried down the stairs, passing through her sunny living room, chock full of soft, cushiony furniture, candles and colorful pillows and into her small but equally sunny kitchen. Olivia was sitting on a stool, holding out her bare foot which was red but not swollen.

Callie picked up the chicken, stuck it back in the freezer, popped some frozen waffles in the toaster and took a closer look at her daughter's foot. She poked it gingerly. "Does it hurt?"

Olivia pushed her honey-colored hair – as yet uncombed this morning – out of her eyes and shrugged. "I guess not, not anymore. Well, maybe a little bit."

"Try standing on it," Callie said as she scooped coffee into the automatic coffeemaker. Olivia stood up slowly, clearly enjoying the attention and drama she'd caused. "Well?" asked Callie, removing the waffles from the toaster, whisking them on a plate and setting them on the kitchen table. Koukla sat at Callie's feet and watched her every move, hoping that Callie would drop a crumb, or better yet, an entire waffle, on the floor.

"I guess I'm OK," Olivia finally pronounced, sounding slightly disappointed.

"Thank goodness," Callie answered, stirring her coffee and adding more milk. "I couldn't handle a trip to the ER today, not after last night." Darn. She could have bitten her tongue. Olivia didn't know yet about Drew. Well, she was going to have to tell her before half of the school told her first.

"What happened last night?" Olivia asked, right on cue, pouring a small lake of pure Wisconsin maple syrup onto her waffles. Frozen waffles with gourmet maple syrup: that made about as much sense as everything else going on right now.

Callie inhaled the steam of her coffee deeply before taking a sip, buying herself some time. She just couldn't bring herself to tell her daughter that Drew had been murdered. Anyway, as far as Olivia knew, Drew was just a colleague. She hadn't told her daughter that she was dating anyone – Olivia had suffered enough and Callie wanted to spare her in case anything went wrong. Boy had something gone wrong. She took another fortifying sip of coffee and addressed her daughter. Keep it simple.

"OK. I have some bad news. You know Drew Staven? He owns that nice bistro in town?" Callie stalled. This was harder than she'd thought. Struggling to keep her voice steady, she forged ahead. "He died. Last night."

"Oh." Olivia looked nonplussed. "I'm sorry, Mom," she finally said after chewing and swallowing a huge bite of her breakfast. "But wait – how do you know? Did Samantha call you or something?"

Her daughter's curiosity was generally considered by Callie to be a bonus, but not right now. "Uh," she stammered and decided to just tell the truth. "I found him, honey. I went to his house and he was dead when I got there so I called the police."

Olivia's eyes widened over the glass of milk she was drinking and when she heard this news, she stopped short and pulled the glass away from her mouth so quickly Callie was afraid she'd choke. Oblivious to her milk mustache, she asked a little too loudly, "What were you doing there, Mom?"

"We had a date," Callie blurted out. Well, she was going to find out eventually. "But listen," she said as Olivia started to make a face of disgust, what was generally known around the Costas home as her "Ewwww," face. It normally only came out when her daughter was told to clean Koukla's leavings out of the yard. Before her daughter could protest, she begged her, "Don't tell Pappou about Drew. Not just yet. Or Grandma Viv. I'll tell them myself. OK?" Thank goodness George had only dropped Olivia off last night and not come into the house. He must have been tired; usually, George would want to sit down and chat.

Olivia shrugged again. What was with all of the shrugging? Wasn't that only supposed to happen with teens? "OK," Olivia agreed. "I'm really sorry, Mom," she said again. "Were you in love with him?" She made that prospect sound as disgusting as picking up after Koukla.

Callie sighed. "None of your business, Livvie. Don't worry about that." She gave her daughter a small smile to soften her words.

Olivia got up out of her chair and stood in front of her mother, looking solemn. Callie hugged her daughter tightly. "It'll be OK," Olivia informed her and Callie looked at her daughter with surprise. Kids were resilient. Then again, could her young daughter really grasp the cold reality of death?

* * *

After consuming copious amounts of dark roast coffee, Callie saw Olivia off to school, fed Koukla her ration of kibble (with a few pieces of waffle thrown in for good measure) and straggled into the shower. The combination of hot water and caffeine had a restorative effect and Callie parked her car nearly a block from her shop, frustrated by the unusual lack of parking spots. A heartbreakingly beautiful blue sky highlighted the changing colors of the leaves. The contrast between bright blue and the brilliant oranges, yellows and reds of fall was so vivid, that Callie was reminded of the construction paper leaf cut-outs that Olivia used to make in preschool.

As usual she peeked inside Minette's Chocolates as she passed by, expecting her college friend and fellow food worker to be bustling around inside the store with her husband and co-owner, Jeff. Instead, Callie was shocked to see Minette's Chocolates dark, no sign of life and the words "Going out of Business" emblazoned in red paint across the front window. Another casualty of the economy? It made Callie's heart ache for Minette and Jeff, since the couple had been her friends for more years than she wanted to count. She'd have to call them later and find out what happened.

Approaching Callie's Kitchen, she saw that she had other, more immediate problems to worry about. There was a line outside the door and people were growing impatient to judge from the jostling of would-be customers as they waited to enter the shop.

"Excuse me, excuse me," she murmured to customers who parted for her with whispers and sideways glances before swarming back into the doorway. Steve Willoughby, Jane's husband, was leaving as she came in. "Hi Steve," she said, but he only patted her shoulder and kept moving, apparently in a rush to get to the office. As she forced her way inside the building, the sight of so many customers lifted her dreary spirits, but only momentarily. The previous evening had thoroughly drained her. Each step felt odd to her, almost as if she were sleepwalking. Nothing seemed real.

Still, even despite her exhaustion and grief, Callie's Kitchen was the same warm and welcoming space she'd worked so hard to create. Geometric chairs in blue and white (in honor of the Greek flag) were paired with gleaming stainless steel tables, while bright crockery nestled alongside chrome and stainless-steel display stands. Her friends and family had contributed wall art including two of her favorites, a painted sign that read: "We'll always be friends: You know too much," (from Samantha) that hung next to a small Greek icon of St. Basil (he was known, among other things, for working in a kitchen). The icon was a gift from George.

Warm smells of honey, cinnamon and frying dough for the Greek doughnuts, *loukoumades*, wafted from the kitchen along with the soul-soothing aroma of fresh-baked banana bread and Greek yogurt coffee cake. Callie inhaled the reviving scents deeply for strength before delving into the fray.

Max was behind the register answering customers' rapid-fire questions in a weary monotone: "I don't know anything about it, no she's not here yet" and versions of the same while simultaneously filling orders for coffee, muffins and breakfast breads. He made a striking figure with his spiky hair, piercing blue eyes, a "sleeve" of tattoos and muscular physique. Callie suspected that much of her female (and a few of her male) clientele were attracted to more than the food Max helped her to create. While she could appreciate his edgy good looks, he was much too young for her. That was why she'd been so happy to connect with Drew, an attractive guy her age who was into food. Drew.

Callie swallowed the lump in her throat and stepped behind the counter to help Max fill his orders.

"What's going on?" she said under her breath while offering a re-assuring nod to her customers. "They heard about Drew," Max whispered back. "And the Taste of Crystal Bay contest. I'm sorry for this zoo in here. They're asking all kinds of questions and I don't know what to do."

Everybody knew she and Drew were competitors as well as col-leagues at the Chamber. Plus, while she'd been able to keep dating Drew a secret from her father and daughter, most of Callie's friends and Max knew that they had been seeing each other. That fact made Callie feel a bit like a 14-year-old with strict parents but she had to at least attempt to protect her privacy from her well-meaning but over-protective father.

"And I thought the crowd was here because you were offering half-price pastries and a date with you," Callie answered with a lame attempt at humor. Max blushed and smiled. "This is crazy. I've never seen anything like it. Not that I mind having a lot of customers, but it's difficult to face so many people today. Maybe I should have stayed home. Besides, something tells me these people are after more than food this morning."

Max continued to look worried while he poured coffee and boxed up Greek yogurt-and-cinnamon coffee cake. Callie noticed that frowning made his eyebrow ring bulge. "The local newspaper called right before you came in," Max whispered out of the side of his mouth. "They said you found Drew. I guess Mrs. DeWitt told them, at least according to the reporter I spoke with. I told them I was only your employee and didn't know anything but they didn't care, so I hung up on them."

"Max, thanks. Hanging up was exactly the right thing to do. Let's just get everybody served and out of here."

"My thoughts exactly."

Not quite able to paste a true smile on her face, Callie thanked her customers for waiting and continued to fill orders as rapidly as her tired bones would allow. Some of her regulars gave her a sad, respectful distance, but others were relentless in their speculation. The hubbub grew in volume until finally, a short blonde woman in a navy tracksuit sidled up to her and lowered her voice to a stage whisper. "Who'd want Drew dead?" she asked. She leaned in closer and Callie took a step back. "Does it have something to do with the food contest?"

Suddenly, Max noticed the blonde and took a huge step so that he was standing between the two women. "Nice try, Marcy," he said to the woman over her protests. "I told you, no reporters!" He took her gently but firmly by the elbow and led her toward the doorway, calling over his shoulder to Callie: "No worries: Just a former Crystal Bay High classmate-turned small-town reporter. She thinks she's the new Katie Couric."

This was getting out of hand. Callie decided to address the crowd herself.

"Welcome to Callie's Kitchen, everybody. If you're here for food, we've got lots of that to choose from. If you want gossip about the tragic death of my friend, Drew Staven, sorry, but that's not something we can help you with." Callie said, raising her voice a bit so that all the customers could hear her. The din began to quiet as she spoke.

"I'm very sad about this loss. That's all I can say right now. I'm happy to serve all of my customers, but I can't talk about Drew. Thanks for your patience and understanding. Now who wants a cup of coffee ... on the house?"

That proclamation silenced the room but it was only for a moment. Almost immediately a determined few resumed the chatter, while others surged forward to accept their free dose of caffeine. A tall woman Callie had never seen before smoothed bouncy spiral curls out of her face before addressing her in a nasal tone: "I heard you found the body."

"That's enough!" This was from Max, back from his role as bouncer. "A man is dead, people!" Some of the regulars agreed vociferously while other customers made their way to the door, grumbling, but not before grabbing paper cups of steaming coffee to go. Eventually, just a few customers remained, some seated at tables and others checking the refrigerator for ready-to-eat meals. The door chimes rang again and she looked up and Callie braced herself for further interrogation, but it was only Minette and Jeff. Callie found herself smiling with gratitude at the sight of their familiar faces.

Minette's fair complexion was whiter than usual. She embraced Callie while Jeff gave a sad little wave.

"What are you two doing here? Not that I'm not happy to see you, but I saw the going out of business sign. I'm so sorry," she stammered, feeling flustered by their obvious concern for her despite their own troubles.

Jeff started to say something but Minette gave him a look and he was silent. She smoothed her disheveled pixie haircut but it didn't do much to help tame the errant blonde spikes that were sticking out every which way. "We only came to tell you we heard about Drew. It's just...I can't believe it." Minette seemed at a loss about what to say next and started twisting the bottom of her sweater, wringing the fabric over and over again as if it were a dishrag.

Jeff nodded, putting his hand on his wife's shoulder. "Truly, we are sorry. I mean, you two were an item, right?" He seemed embarrassed by his own question as Minette shot him a look and frowned.

"Yes," Callie said. "I mean, we'd been seeing each other for a couple of months." She exhaled noisily. "The whole thing seems like a nightmare, only I can't wake up." To her mortification, she felt her face starting to crumple. "But truly, it's a loss for all of us," she continued in a low voice. "His colleagues, his ... friends. The Chamber. Crystal Bay. He was a great guy," she said softly, struggling to control her emotions.

"Oh Callie," Minette said. "Was Drew really murdered? It just doesn't seem possible!" She grasped Callie's forearm tightly.

"Unfortunately, yes," Callie said. "It's true." She felt the sting of hot, unwanted tears and loosened her arm from Minette's grip to wipe her eyes.

"I'm sure it was a terrible thing for you to experience," Jeff soothed. "We don't want to make you re-live it. Do we, dear?" he asked his wife. He squeezed her shoulder.

Minette hung her head. "Forgive me. It's just that I can't believe this happened, right here, in Crystal Bay. Who would have ever thought it?" Gently she disengaged herself from her husband's grip, as even this small amount of PDA was too much of a display to a bereaved woman.

Callie couldn't pursue the topic of Drew any further without breaking down completely. She knew her friends meant well but it was time to change the subject. "Thank you both," she said. "Regarding your business please let me know how I can help. If you want to sell anything at Callie's Kitchen, I'd be happy to do that. I wouldn't charge a fee – I'd give you full profit until you get back on your feet."

The couple exchanged glances and then looked back at Callie. "You're a good friend," Minette said thickly. "We don't want to overstay our welcome. I'll call you later." The two said their goodbyes and walked out side by side, wife clinging to husband.

Callie felt bereft watching them go. If only she had someone to lean on, physically as well as mentally. Well, in a way, she did. She glanced at Max who was bustling around, pretending not to have heard the exchange. What a loyal employee he was. If her customers found out she'd been questioned at the police station, would they stay away? Not only she would suffer, but Max would, too. Shaking off that thought until later, she turned to him.

"Thank you for sticking up for me today," she said to Max as he paused to wipe a countertop. "I don't think I could have taken anymore. The good news is that we sold out of just about everything, but for all the wrong reasons. Customers clearly thought they were going to get the inside scoop on a murder along with their banana bread and *loukoumades*."

"That's why I set them straight – how can people behave that way?" Max was fuming. "Drew was murdered. And you found him! I can't imagine how bad that must have been. Oh, sorry!" he said when he saw Callie blanch. Max folded his muscled arms in front of his chest, offering a colorful view of his many tattoos.

Callie closed her eyes, trying to compose herself. It was bad all right and the ouzo hadn't helped matters. Her head throbbed. The bell over the door jingled again, but Callie couldn't field any more questions from customers, reporters or even well-wishers right now. Max would handle this particular newcomer. She turned around and busied herself by straightening the glass jars on the shelf behind the cash register, trying to breathe deeply in the hopes that additional oxygen would help get rid of her mental fog. Darn ouzo. She knew better than to drink that stuff.

"Good morning!" said a familiar voice. Callie whirled around to find Detective Sands standing before her.

"Hello?" it came out as more of a question than a statement. Max had materialized next to her as quickly as a cat. He bounced on the balls of his feet, his eyes darting from Sands to Callie and back again, like it was a tennis match and he had his money on the more inexperienced player.

"Hey buddy," Max said to Sands, looking him over from head to toe. Sands was smartly dressed today in a suit and tie with a tweed overcoat. Before Callie could speak, Max all but growled at the detective. "We're not answering any questions from reporters."

"Wise choice," Sands remarked handing Max his card and staring him in the eye. Max was tall, slightly over 6 feet, but he had to look up a little bit to meet the detective's gaze. They locked eyes and Callie could sense Max spoiling for a fight. He glanced at the card Sands had given him and looked up, shaken. "Sorry," he said gruffly, before retreating to the back of the shop where he began noisily moving large boxes of baking ingredients.

"We've been having a bit of trouble here this morning," Callie offered by way of apology. "Naturally, everybody is very concerned and looking for answers – including reporters. Apparently, Mrs. DeWitt let it slip that I found Drew. Now what can I do for you?"

Sands cleared his throat. "I'm surprised to see you here today. I stopped by your house first, but a neighbor said you'd left for work. I need you to return to the station with me. There are just a few more things I want to clear up." Sands sounded friendly, but firm.

"Didn't we cover everything last night?" Callie fretted aloud, thinking about all the baking and meal prep she'd missed yesterday. Of course, she wanted to help the police but this was a lot to ask of Max – two days in a row. And let's face it, she thought, I don't want to think about this right now. She'd just about submerged her grief in work chaos and this was going to bring the pain right back to the surface again.

"I'm afraid we didn't," Sands replied. He eyed Max, giving his eyebrow piercing, tattoos and tough-guy build a thorough once-over. "Can't your bodyguard take over for you?"

"Don't worry, I can handle it," Max said from across the room where he was avidly eavesdropping on the entire conversation.

"Max, you know how important this is. I promise this is the last time I run out on you!" Callie kept her tone genial but inside she was terrified. She wanted to call Samantha for advice.

Before she could decide what to do, the door jingled again, announcing another customer. Only it wasn't a customer. Callie's dark eyes widened in sheer horror: her father was walking purposefully toward her.

Four

"*Yassou*, Dad." Callie smiled at her father. Her facial muscles felt frozen in place and her heart was pounding – the last thing she needed was a discussion about going to the police station to report on the murder of a boyfriend her father didn't even know she had. Hoping that George was in a hurry, Callie tried to act normal. Maybe he'd leave before he figured out what Sands was doing there.

"What brings you here today?" she asked George, while shooting Sands a furtive look.

Her father wrapped Callie in one of his signature bear hugs. It seemed that he held her even more tightly than usual. "Dad," she said. "I can't breathe."

George loosened his grip. "Okay, breathe, breathe. I was in the neighborhood so I thought I'd check on your business, see if it's picked up any," George said, sitting down at the table closest to the cashier station. Leave it to her father to start right in with concerns for her business. If only he'd seen the crowds just a half an hour before, but that wouldn't have been good, come to think of it, not with all of the talk about Drew.

Callie gulped and racked her brain on how to get rid of her father without offending him. He looked so innocent sitting there, his curly grey-brown hair neatly styled, his white shirt crisp and his dark trousers well-pressed. But she knew better and his next words confirmed her fears.

"So," George began, leaning his elbows on the table and clasping his large hands. "What are you doing to bring in customers now that you've lost the contest?"

"Who told you that?" Callie said.

"I read the papers! And besides, I've heard that the young fella who won is now dead. Murdered, that's what I hear! You know this man? Yes?"

Callie looked at Sands and gulped. Please don't ask any questions, she silently begged him. Not in front of George. Don't let him find out this way.

"I knew him, Dad, yes, from the Chamber of Commerce as well as the contest."

Sands started to speak and Callie couldn't help herself. She put up a hand as if to silence him and with the other hand grabbed a tray of *loukoumades*, holding it up like a prize. "Look what I have today, Dad," she sang out cheerily. "Your favorite."

George looked at the delightful little balls of dough that Callie had artfully arranged on a plate and smiled at his daughter, the corners of his eyes crinkling up. "*Loukoumades*? Yes? Bring me a few with a cup of coffee, *hrisi mou*." My dear. George still retained a strong Greek accent and lapsed into Greek often, despite his many years in Wisconsin. He glanced at Sands quizzically, before settling back in his chair and busying himself with the paper napkin dispenser.

Sands started to speak again and Callie shot him a desperate look. "I'll be right with you sir," she said brightly. Sands narrowed his eyes at her but didn't say anything.

"Uh..." Callie faltered, glancing from Sands to George and back again. "Are you on your way to The Olympia?" Callie drizzled the *loukoumades* with warm honey and a dusting of cinnamon before handing them to her father.

"Yes, but I'm in no hurry," George answered. Drat. She poured a cup of coffee in a thick white mug and brought it to her father, kissing him on the cheek before ducking back behind the counter. Sands raised his eyebrows at Callie and motioned to her to come along with him, but she shook her head quickly before George could see her.

"One minute," she mouthed and Sands looked stern, but then looked back at George digging into his Greek doughnuts and sighed again. He looked at Callie again and shook his head at her. "Now," he mouthed, tapping his wrist watch.

"Dad, I've got to run out for a minute," Callie said, defeated. She removed her blue and white apron and hung it on a hook. "Max will be here, though, if you need anything. OK?"

"You should be here," George said. "Remember what I've always told you? The owner has to be there – or else – no good." He gave Max a dubious look and took a sip of coffee. "Aah. Hits the spot." He nodded at his plate of Greek doughnuts. "These are almost as good as my *yiayia* used to make."

Callie smiled at the backhanded compliment and thanked her father. To have her cooking even be mentioned in the same sentence with his grandmother, aka *yiayia* was massive praise in George's book.

Callie saw that Sands had walked outside and was watching her through the window while he paced back and forth. Steam appeared to be about to come from his ears. George was digging into his sweet treat and didn't appear to notice the little drama playing out in front of him. This was her chance.

"Dad, I agree. The owner should be on site as much as possible but this won't take long. I'll see you later!" Callie grabbed her purse and tried to dash out but George was out of his chair, coffee and *loukoumades* forgotten. Great. He'd noticed Sands waiting for her outside.

"Where are you going?" he demanded. "Who is that man?" George started to follow her out the door and Callie stopped short, George nearly tumbling into her.

"Dad, honestly! It's nothing. I've got to run an errand. I'll tell you all about it later." She kissed his cheek, pushed past him as gently as she could and joined Sands who placed his hand on her elbow and steered her firmly down the sidewalk.

"What was that all about?" Sands asked Callie as he led her to, thank goodness, a black unmarked police car. All she needed was for George to see her getting into a black and white cop car – *loukoumades* would be flying through the air!

"My father doesn't know I was seeing Drew," she said, feeling like a complete idiot. "He's a bit overprotective since my divorce and it's just easier sometimes not to tell him everything."

"I see," Sands said, opening the passenger door of the car for her. As she got in the car, she realized that her confession made it look like she had something to hide. Wonderful. While Sands walked around to the driver's side, she quickly texted Sam, asking her friend to meet her at the police station. Just in case, Callie told herself. Hopefully she wouldn't need Sam at all.

Callie inhaled deeply to calm herself and immediately wished she hadn't. The police car looked clean but it smelled like a combination of cigarette smoke, ammonia and air freshener. Sands looked at her green face and rolled the windows down an inch or two. "Not my usual vehicle," he said by way of explanation. "It's just a short ride."

"About not telling my dad," Callie felt like she had to explain. "He's a wonderful father but he can be old-fashioned. He would only worry, so unless things get really serious, I just prefer to keep my private life private from him."

Sands raised his eyebrows at her and didn't say anything for a minute. "My dad was strict as they come, too," he finally commented. "Still, don't you think he's going to find out now?"

"Yes," Callie agreed. "I can't believe he doesn't know, to be honest. The diner he owns, The Olympia, serves up gossip with their eggs and toast." Sands glanced at her and shook his head, a small smile forming at the corners of his mouth. Then he was stern again. Callie shifted in her seat, uncomfortable waves of anxiety flowing through her as she wondered what else the detective needed to discuss with her.

Before she knew it, Sands was pulling the car into a parking space next to the one-story brick structure that was the Crystal Bay Police Station. The detective led her into what she assumed was his office. There were framed degrees on the walls including one from University of Wisconsin and a rather untidy stack of papers on the corner of his desk.

A poster of what looked like the English countryside and a small picture of a British soccer team hung on the green painted wall. Callie squinted to get a look at the name: Leeds United. A University of Wisconsin Bucky Badger pencil cup completed the décor. No Pottery Barn evident in this place. And, Callie noted, no pictures of a wife. There was a picture of an adorable little girl with blonde pigtails and big hazel eyes like Sands. Callie opened her mouth to ask him about her when he cut her off.

"So," Sands began. "Here's the thing. We spoke to a Mrs. DeWitt yesterday evening. She had some interesting insights on the small business contest with the big cash prize. Did you know, for example, that you were next in line? In other words, if for some reason Mr. Drew couldn't claim the cash prize it would go directly to Callie's Kitchen?"

"What?" Callie was aghast. "No, I didn't know that. I had no idea!"

"Mrs. DeWitt gave me the contest rules, the fine print, you see." Sands sat back in his chair and looked through some files on his desk. "Here it is. The contest rules: 'If for any reason the primary winner cannot claim the cash prize, the secondary winner will be awarded the entirety of the prize money. Et cetera, so on."

"So," Callie struggled to come up with a coherent response. "You think I'd kill someone for prize money? Are you serious?"

"People kill for all sorts of strange reasons, Ms. Costas," Sands replied. "Unfortunately, money is a strong motive for murder."

Callie was silent while she mulled over her situation. "I truly can't believe this. I had nothing to do with Drew's death. Nothing! I would never do something like that!"

Sands ignored her statement and changed the subject. "I understand that your business is in need of funds, Ms. Costas. In fact, nearly all of the businesses on Garden Street have been struggling. Where does your business stand? When I arrived today, it seemed fairly empty."

"You should have seen it thirty minutes before you arrived. It was packed with a line outside the door!" Little did he know the real reason for the throng on her doorstep – it was the same reason that motorists slowed down to look at a car crash.

"But you could always use the money, couldn't you? As a small business owner and single mother raising a daughter," Sands prompted. So they'd been digging into her private life. Callie had had enough.

"Listen," she said, feeling her color rise along with her anger. "Leave my daughter out of this. I've done nothing wrong and I don't like what you're trying to imply. I would like to speak to my attorney if you have any other questions for me." Where was Samantha? Hopefully not in court that morning, but she needn't have worried. At that moment Sam sailed through the door looking like a million bucks in a clingy plum suit with a cinched-in waist. A colorful scarf completed the outfit.

"Samantha Madine. You might remember me from last night when I accompanied Callie for her statement." Sands gave Samantha a grudging nod. "May I speak to my client a few moments in the hallway?" Sands sighed extravagantly and finally, gestured to the door. Samantha hustled Callie out.

"You were lucky today, friend. I almost missed you. Now Callie, listen up. We're going back in but I don't want you to say anything until I tell you to. Nothing. Don't even breathe unless I say you can. Are you with me?"

Callie nodded. "Yes, I've got it." Samantha grabbed her by the arm and led her back inside Sand's office.

"Detective Sands," Samantha began once they were all seated. "I'm not certain as to your line of questioning. I was here with Ms. Costas last night – she has already made her official statement."

"True." He pushed a piece of paper toward them – it appeared to be a typed document detailing the basics of her discovery of Drew's body. He sat back and exhaled impatiently. "In addition, we have some new developments that I find interesting." He smiled pleasantly enough but his words chilled Callie to the bone.

"Such as?" Samantha raised a beautifully arched eyebrow.

"Such as the fact that Ms. Costas was next in line for the prize money to help her business. A substantial prize of $10,000 donated by Mrs. DeWitt of Crystal Bay and some Crystal Bay College alumni. We spoke to Ms. DeWitt this morning."

"I know about the contest. And that's it?" Samantha appeared to take this news in stride.

"She was first on the scene," Sands said. "She broke a window." He glanced at her sharply with his sad hazel eyes.

"Do you have physical evidence or any proof that Ms. Costas had anything to do with Drew's death?" Samantha asked.

All were silent for a minute. Then Detective Sands leaned forward in his chair. "You must understand how this looks. You're first on the scene, you break a window and then it turns out you may have monetary gain from Mr. Staven's death. A person is innocent until proven guilty, of course. But there are a few odd things here that I don't like. Not at all."

Callie eyed Samantha, who slightly shook her head. "Ms. Costas has nothing more to say at this time. If that's all," Samantha said, standing up and motioning for Callie to stand up with her. "If you are not prepared to bring formal charges, then I'm going to have to demand that you release her." Sands looked at them both for a minute before speaking.

"Ms. Costas, as part of the investigation, we are going to have to fingerprint you. I would also like you to turn over your cell phone to us. I can get a warrant if you refuse to do so, but it would be easier for you all around if you relinquished it voluntarily. I'll leave that to the discretion of your attorney. And, should you have new information, please let us know immediately. You have my number and remember, we may need to speak to you again."

Feeling numb, Callie nodded and followed Samantha out the door.

Five

Callie was led out to the main office where a young officer placed each one of her fingers in a sticky black substance and then onto a sheet. This wasn't like visiting the local police station with the Girl Scouts as she'd done with her daughter in recent years. This was pure humiliation. The young officer who took her prints apologized for the mess, saying that they were still hoping funds would come through for a digital fingerprinting system.

Callie's hands shook as she cleaned them with a pack of wet wipes that Samantha offered to her. She really needed to get to a drugstore to restock, she thought. *As if that were her most pressing problem right now.* She threw the wipes in a trash can.

Sam took her firmly by the arm, steered out the door and finally spoke once they were outside the Crystal Bay police station. "I'm so, so sorry that you're going through this," Samantha said, drawing her friend into a warm, Chanel-scented embrace. "And this isn't helping things, I know."

The adrenaline rush that had been sustaining Callie for the last few hours was leaving her. She felt her shoulders slump. And she'd naively thought she'd already experienced her worst moment when she'd found Drew dead. It appeared that things were going downhill from there.

"As far as the cell phone, I didn't think it would look well for you to refuse to hand it over," Sam said, holding Callie by the shoulders. She faced her friend, her expression as serious as she'd ever seen it. "This was the right thing to do. You have nothing to hide. And you called Drew and the police on that phone? At least that's what you told me last night?" Callie nodded.

"OK, then. This is all going to work out." Sam shook Callie a little bit for emphasis. "I'm going to help you. Now, what is this about you being a runner up?"

"I didn't even know about that. I guess I didn't read 'the fine print' of the contest when I filled out my registration. I was too excited about the prospect of winning the cash prize." Callie closed her eyes as a wave of fatigue washed over her.

"Right," said Samantha. "The winner would either have to reject the prize — and why would they? Or they would have to die. Sorry," she said when she saw the look on Callie's face. "I'll see if I can find out whom, if anyone else, they're questioning. In the meantime, stay out of trouble. Manage your shop, take care of Olivia and talk to George about this if you absolutely must, but no one else."

"Thanks for everything, Samantha. I never thought I would need your services."

Her friend smiled at her and gave her a quick hug. "Wait until you see my bill. I've got to run but I'll call you later and we'll catch up with everything. Are you sure you're all right? What are you doing out and about anyway? You've got to be in shock – home is the best place for you."

Callie bristled a bit even though she knew Sam meant well. Staying home would have been heavenly but it wasn't going to help anything. And she had to work – didn't she? Callie's shoulders sagged with exhaustion. She wasn't irritated with her friend who was being incredibly helpful. It was the entire situation that had her frightened and on edge. "I know," she finally managed. "But I just couldn't bring myself to stay home today – I needed to be at work and feel like I'm in control of something."

Sam gave her a look full of sympathy and understanding. "I know. Well, in the meantime, I don't want you wandering around without a phone. You've just been way too close to a murderer." Samantha handed Callie her own cell phone. "I'll pick it up later. Just keep it for now." Sam patted her on the shoulder and headed for the parking lot. Callie waved at her as she drove off before remembering that she had been driven to the station by Sands, nearly two miles from Garden Street and her shop.

Even though Samantha had said not to do anything on her own behalf, how could she listen to that advice? She felt like a wooden target at hunting season. It seemed that at any minute, Sands would arrive with some form of "evidence" to arrest her and then what about Olivia? Her family? Her business? No, she had to figure out who the true culprit was. All signs pointed to the killer being some-one Drew knew —no sign of a struggle, no robbery, except for the computer, which was a negligible cost, and no forced entry into his home. Besides, if Drew knew his killer, maybe she knew him – or her – as well.

As Callie walked slowly down the street, her weariness overtook her and she sank down on a nearby bench. Might as well seize the day and call Mrs. DeWitt, she thought as she pulled Sam's cell phone from her purse. Surprisingly, Mrs. DeWitt said yes when Callie asked if she could stop by and chat. Then she called Grandma Viv, who an-swered on the second ring.

"Callie, darling!" Grandma Viv sounded surprised to hear from her granddaughter. "This isn't your cell phone number. Did you get a new phone?"

"No, I'm borrowing Sam's phone," Callie explained. "It's a long story. I've had a bit of an unusual morning. I wondered if you'd drive with me to Mrs. DeWitt's house. I can explain when you get here." If Viv was there, Mrs. DeWitt would be more assured that no Wusthof knives would find their way into her back, Callie thought.

"Why of course I'll go. But what is it? Are you in some kind of trouble?"

"You could say that," Callie said but immediately regretted it as Viv started a rapid-fire string of questions. After assuring her that she was not in physical danger and that Olivia was alive and well, Viv calmed down a bit.

"Honey, I'll be there in two shakes of a lamb's tail."

Viv was as good as her word, showing up in her new champagne-colored SUV and talking a mile a minute as she and Callie made their way along the lakefront to Mrs. DeWitt's stately home. Driving with Viv was always an invigorating experience. She had come to driving relatively late in life and she claimed that she didn't enjoy it much. However, when she did drive, she favored speed.

Callie cringed as Grandma Viv swerved around a pedestrian who was crossing against the traffic light. "What do they want, a fanny full of headlights?" Viv exclaimed as she narrowly missed the jay-walking pedestrian and then proceeded to tailgate a slow-moving truck full of livestock that was headed toward the highway. Other than a "Grandma, slow down!" that slipped out before she could catch herself, Callie gritted her teeth and kept her peace. Who was she to question crazy driving at this point – it wasn't like she had her own life in order.

Finally, the street opened up and the two women found them-selves on the peaceful road that ran alongside the lake. Now that they were out of the heavier traffic, Callie felt safe to share her dis-turbing news with her grandmother. As concisely as possible, she filled Viv in on the current situation and her role in it. Viv was stunned into silence for several seconds – a feat unto itself. Still, it wasn't long before the deluge began.

"Why didn't you tell us you were dating someone? And he was murdered? This is horrible, absolutely horrible. If anything had hap-pened to you..." Viv trailed off miserably. "I can't lose you, not like I lost your mother!" Viv sniffled and Callie was mortified to see her grandmother tearing up.

"Please, don't cry," she begged, touching Viv's arm. She started to get choked up herself, thinking of her mother who passed away when Callie was only 12 years old. "I'm sorry I didn't tell you – or Dad. You know how he worries. I figured if it got serious enough, I'd tell everyone. Olivia didn't know either." Callie gulped and continued. "I know the whole thing is terrible but I'm safe. I'll be OK but right now I just feel heartbroken. I was really starting to care for Drew."

Viv made sympathetic noises and Callie was emboldened to tell the rest of her tale. "I'm being questioned about this by the police and they even took my cell phone, since I found him and we were competitors in the business contest. That's why I need to see Mrs. DeWitt. I'm hoping she can shed some light on this contest."

"Well, darling, then I'm your partner in crime." Viv winced. "Sorry, poor choice of words. You know what I mean." Her grandmother took a deep breath. "One thing I've learned in all my many years. You can always catch more flies with honey than vinegar. Let's be as sweet as we can to Gertrude and see what she knows."

Callie felt a little apprehensive as the car made its way up the winding path to Mrs. DeWitt's house. Situated on a hilltop with a long and winding driveway, the large home boasted Colonial-style grandeur, complete with a beautiful gazebo and an abundant garden. With fall well underway, the garden now boasted a symphony of color in the form of mums and other seasonal flowers. Maple trees in full autumn color lined the driveway and grounds.

The property had a beautiful view of the bay, too. A double-decker back porch boasted two screened-in seating areas so that visitors could enjoy the scenic vista of both the water and Mrs. DeWitt's personal pier. On a more cheerful occasion, Callie would have enjoyed taking a walk in the garden and then lounging in the gazebo before strolling over to the pier to sunbathe and watch the water, which sparkled in the late September sunlight and appeared as calm as a mirror.

The door was answered by Mrs. DeWitt's longtime house assistant, Ava. In her late fifties, petite and bubbly with bright blue eyes and an energetic approach to everything she did, Ava greeted Viv and Callie like old friends. "Ladies. Mrs. DeWitt is expecting you. I made scones today so I'll bring some in after you get settled."

Callie nodded and Viv smiled delightedly at the prospect of scones. Walking briskly, Ava led them into a spacious sitting room on the first floor with full length windows offering a peaceful view of the water that temporarily soothed Callie's frayed nerves. After both ladies were seated comfortably, Ava went to retrieve Mrs. DeWitt.

"Callie, Viv," Mrs. DeWitt strode into the room in leggings, a loose-fitting grey shirt and designer athletic shoes. "Don't mind me. I was just doing my walking workout routine. I never miss it." Mrs. DeWitt held out her hand to Callie, but accepted an embrace from Viv who was, as she put it, a "hugger."

"Gertrude, you look wonderful! Of course we don't mind your attire. We young girls need to stay active," Viv gushed. Callie grimaced. She hoped Viv wasn't laying it on too thick. Mrs. DeWitt looked bashful at this comment as she ran both hands through her short gray hair and gazed down at her figure. She had a few too many pounds around the waist but overall, she appeared to be strong and healthy.

"I could say the same to you," Mrs. DeWitt responded, not the least bit rattled. "Viv, when are you going to age like the rest of us?" Callie had to admit that Grandma Viv did look fantastic. Dressed in a tailored burgundy pantsuit, she looked put together and much younger than her 85 years. Viv credited good genes, sweets in moderation and a busy social life with staying fit. Callie hoped she would be the same someday.

"Thanks for meeting us, Mrs. DeWitt. We won't keep you for long." Callie fidgeted and felt as wired as if she'd been drinking coffee all morning. She wished.

"Not to worry, of course I have time this morning, especially after what happened to Drew," Mrs. DeWitt said gesturing at the chairs and sofas in the room. "Sit down, please." Viv and Callie did as they were told. "Ava, can you bring the refreshments? I'm starved and these two ladies look famished." The housekeeper nodded, smiled and bounced out of the room, giving them the privacy Callie craved.

"Now girls," Mrs. DeWitt said, settling on a chenille-covered chaise lounge with a sigh. "I know you didn't come here to talk about how wonderful we all look." Mrs. DeWitt turned her gaze to Callie. "Last night was just dreadful. I'm sorry that I spoke too freely to that reporter, by the way, letting them know you were the one who found Drew. It just slipped out. That police detective wasn't too happy, let me tell you. He called and told me not to mention anything else to the media – or else."

Callie took in this apology with a nod. "It's okay," she said. What good would getting angry do? "The world seems turned upside down right now."

"You said you had some questions about the contest and I'm happy to help," Mrs. DeWitt briskly changed the subject. "In fact, this whole thing has me devastated," she said. "I can't believe it turned out like this. Drew Staven, dead?" Mrs. DeWitt shuddered and continued.

"I'm horrified that our contest is thought to be involved in any way. We were only trying to help the small business scene. And just look...." The last part of her speech came out in a near sob. Mrs. DeWitt's brisk demeanor was quickly fading into despair. She'd lost much of the bravado she'd displayed when she sparred with Detective Sands the previous evening.

"We know you meant to help, Mrs. DeWitt. And you did, at least, I can speak for my own business. The contest has already inspired some positive changes in my shop. In fact, I just hosted my first cooking class." No need to mention the oven fire and faulty kitchen equipment that drove the students right out of her kitchen.

Callie continued. "The police may view me as suspicious because apparently, I was next in line for the prize. I was told that there was some 'fine print' in the rules regarding a second place winner and so on. I'll admit I didn't read every word of my registration for the contest but this is the first I've heard of it and I can assure you that at least one of my fellow contestants would have mentioned it. Can you tell me more about the contest rules?"

"I know my granddaughter," Viv chimed in. "And she's not a murderer! If she says she had nothing to do with this, then she didn't." Viv turned to Mrs. DeWitt. "Gert, you know this isn't right. What can we do?"

"Well, unfortunately for the detective and fortunately for you, he got it a little bit wrong," said Mrs. DeWitt. "But one thing I've found in my life is that men rarely listen when women speak. Something about women's vocal tones being on a frequency that men tune out. I heard about it on the news. Convenient for them, isn't it? The world would be a much better place if they did listen to us, at least once in a while."

Callie suppressed a grin. Mrs. DeWitt's late husband had frequently "forgotten" his hearing aids, according to local lore. She wouldn't make the same mistake Sands had made, though. Callie leaned forward slightly and she gave Mrs. DeWitt her full attention, ears wide open.

"I'm sorry to say that I made a mistake." Mrs. DeWitt shrugged nonchalantly. Well, her life wasn't on the line. "The documents that I gave to Detective Sands weren't the actual contest rules that went out to all of the contestants. There was no reason to include that information because we didn't intend to have a second place winner. We wanted one winner – that is the Crystal Bay Chamber, me and the business school alumni – wanted one winner and one winner on-ly."

Mrs. DeWitt turned slightly in her chair to face Callie. "What the detective saw was an earlier version of the contest rules that we decided not to use. I must have given him those by accident. When he mentioned to me that you, Callie, must be the recipient of the prize in Drew's, uh, absence, I told him of my mistake. Apparently, he didn't quite follow what I was telling him." Mrs. DeWitt sat back and crossed her ankles.

"An earlier version of the rules? So the only people who would have a clue that there had been different rules tossed around for discussion were just a few people." Callie sat back limply as the light dawned. That was the reason that the second and third place winners hadn't made it through the active Garden Street grapevine.

"That's right." Mrs. DeWitt gave Callie a small smile. "There is no way you could have known that you were next in line. Unless someone had told you about the previous rules and why would anyone have cared about those? They weren't going to be enforced. Our ultimate goal was to encourage all of Crystal Bay's small business owners and prompt our Garden Street businesses to succeed. We felt that if we had second and third place it didn't give the contest the same edge."

It gave it an edge all right, Callie thought. A Wusthof knife edge.

"Well, that helps to clear Callie, doesn't it?" Viv asked with triumph in her voice.

Just then, Ava returned with a tea tray and the three women were busy as they helped themselves to steaming tea and a variety of warm, flaky scones – blueberry, lemon and chocolate chip. Callie wolfed down a blueberry scone in record time and hoping that no one noticed her greediness she placed another scone, chocolate chip this time, on her plate. She was amazed that her appetite had returned. But what was George always saying? "No matter what, people need to eat."

"I don't know if that clears me or not," she admitted. "How do I prove that no one told me? And everyone knows that you and Gert are friendly," she said addressing Viv. "Plus, Gert is a regular customer of Callie's Kitchen. We all know she wouldn't tell contestants about rules that weren't even put into place, but what about the police? I need more than this. Still, it's a good start."

Let's see what Sands would do with that information, Callie thought. "So I'm supposed to be the second place winner? Which means, what?"

"Well, dear, with poor Drew gone I suppose, based on our point system, that you are the runner-up and would be the winner. I don't think we should announce it just yet, though. I would like to have a long talk with the Chamber heads, including Jane Willoughby. I'll be honest with you: I'm not sure how to proceed. It's just all so unprecedented! And Callie, even though I believe in your innocence as strongly as Viv, while you're under investigation, I don't know that we should award anyone anything right now."

Callie agreed. Money was nice but ethics came first. Her joy at the prospect of prize money was greatly dampened by thoughts of how she might be potentially winning the money. "I won't say a word. I'm grateful to you and the Chamber but..."

"Of course you are!" Viv was vehement. "Mrs. DeWitt will come to the right decision, don't you worry. Right, Gert?"

The philanthropist nodded solemnly and smiled at Callie. "It will all work out. I've been involved with the business school for a long time. Even though we've never been faced with a situation quite like this, a little space and discussion is all we need. I know we'll figure out the best course of action." And, Callie thought, you need to be sure that I'm not the killer. Suddenly Ava's delicious scones felt like lead in her stomach.

"What about the police?" Viv asked before Callie could pose that very question. "Will you straighten them out if they come to you with any more foolishness about Callie being involved in a murder?"

Mrs. DeWitt assured the ladies that she would speak to the police if they needed further clarification and seemed to consider the matter settled. If only, Callie thought.

The conversation turned to what would become of Drew's bistro and other practical matters related to his death that Callie tried to tune out – it was too painful to hear. The two old friends chatted together amiably, with Callie nodding in the right places.

As she sat there gazing at the breathtaking views from Mrs. DeWitt's full-length windows, she realized that Drew's home wasn't that far away from the home she sat in now. The disturbing proximity to the death scene motivated Callie to get moving. But first, she would return to her shop to relieve Max for a while. In any case, it was time to go.

Shooting Grandma Viv a meaningful glance, Callie slowly arose from her chair and stretched her hand out to Mrs. DeWitt. "Thank you so much for seeing me today, but I have to be getting back to work. I hope we haven't bothered you."

"Of course not. I'm always glad to see you." Mrs. DeWitt seemed to have regained her usual composure. "I'm happy to clear the business contest's role in it any way I can. It's a shame about Mr. Staven. It's a tragedy, in fact. But what about Crystal Bay's small businesses? Something like this could set us back for years!"

With a twinge, Callie wondered how Mrs. DeWitt could even think of such a thing. But then she remembered the hordes in her shop that morning and realized that Mrs. DeWitt was right. Once the novelty wore off, a murder lent a ghoulish taint to the Garden Street business district. Customers had to walk by Drew's bistro on their way to Callie's Kitchen – not a very appetizing prospect if an unsolved murder was associated even tangentially with both establishments.

Still, it wasn't Drew's fault that he was murdered! Mrs. DeWitt must be really upset to make such an insensitive comment. Callie gritted her teeth and tried to think of a topic that didn't involve Drew.

"Speaking of business setbacks, did you know that Minette's Chocolates closed down?" Callie asked.

Mrs. DeWitt looked pained. "I just ran into Jeff the other day. The chocolate shop just closed this week and apparently Minette is taking the loss of her business very hard. Jeff was vague on the details of the closure," Mrs. DeWitt said with obvious regret as she loved to be in the know regarding local news. "I don't expect he wanted to discuss specifics with me."

After she and Viv had said their goodbyes to Mrs. DeWitt and Ava, Callie debated what to do first. She wanted to speak to Jane Willoughby for starters. Jane must have known about the discussions surrounding the cash prize and was no doubt part of them. Would she have told someone, even in passing? Jane might not even know that she had information that pointed to Drew's killer. In fact, she might be in danger. Callie rationalized that was as good an excuse as any for why she had to get in touch with Jane.

Second, who had taken Drew's computer and electronics? It could have been a burglary gone wrong, but Callie didn't think so. His computer must have some clues about his business dealings at the very least.

Grandma Viv cut into Callie's swirling thoughts as they returned to her car. "Gert is one heck of a gal, isn't she? I just love her. Though, it is odd that she was so careless as to give someone the wrong information in a murder investigation. If Gertrude is one thing, she's detail-oriented." Viv shook her head.

"I know. It is strange," Callie agreed. "She's a busy lady, though. Maybe her papers just got mixed up. She is obviously pretty distraught about Drew's death and anyone can make a mistake." Or could Mrs. DeWitt have another reason for misleading Detective Sands? Callie decided to keep that thought to herself for the time being.

"Oh, you're probably right," Viv shrugged. "Though she has a housekeeper, so you'd think she'd be better organized." She sighed and then brightened a bit. "How about those scones? Ava is a keeper. Now, where to next? Should I take you home? After what you've been through, you should be somewhere quiet with your feet up. I could stay with you, if you like, and cancel my volunteer spot at the library. It's no trouble, dear."

With Viv as a guest reader, Story Time was a big hit with kids and parents alike. If she missed, the kids would be disappointed and anyway, Callie had to get back to work.

"No, you go ahead. I feel awful but I feel like I need to go to work. I can't leave Max to handle everything, especially because we've had a huge crowd this morning. Max thinks it's because Mrs. DeWitt let it slip that I found Drew."

Thankful that Viv was keeping her eyes on the road, Callie shifted in her seat and spotted a book on the backseat of the car that she hadn't noticed before. She reached back and grabbed it, glancing at the title: *My Life in France* by Julia Child. "Great book," she said to her grandmother.

"Why don't you borrow it, Callie? It's got a week to go on my card since I finished it so quickly. Maybe it will help you to relax."

"I love this book but it's been ages since I read it. Thanks. Any distraction would be good." Maybe reading about Julia's trials and tribulations as she found her footing and started a new life in 1950s France would take her mind off of her own troubles. Callie remembered that Julia's stories about cooking, life, even her charmingly squalid Paris apartment were inspiring as well as entertaining.

"I'm glad." Viv beamed at her granddaughter. "Sometimes reading a book you've read before and enjoyed is like visiting an old friend." Viv swerved around a squirrel that darted across her path and Callie watched the creature scamper up a tree before exhaling with relief. Viv didn't seem to notice and was looking at Callie again instead at the street before her.

"Please, Grandma, eyes on the road!" Callie couldn't help but exclaim.

"Sorry, darling!" She turned her gaze back to the winding road that led them back to the Garden Street business district. "I'm just so worried. Please keep me posted. I've got my cell."

"Thanks, you know I will. If you'd just drop me off at my shop, I'll be out of your hair. For now, anyway." The women exchanged smiles. Callie was relieved when Viv appeared to make a conscious effort to study the road once again.

The duo grew thoughtful as they made their way back to Crystal Bay's downtown. The events of the past day and a half were starting to catch up with Callie, but there was no time for fatigue. Thinking of one of her favorite poems, she realized that she had "miles to go before she slept." Today, Frost's double meaning of the word "sleep" seemed to crackle with sinister symbolism. Drew had been someone with "miles to go" before he slept, too, someone who appeared to have everything to live for. His killer had clearly disagreed.

Six

When Callie arrived at work the next morning she waved at Max who stood behind the counter and then did a double-take. Usually, her display cases would be well picked over by now as customers snapped up their early morning baked goods and lunchtime items. Instead, they were full. Since Callie and Max baked a set amount of fresh goods each day, she knew he hadn't simply replenished the stock.

Max followed her gaze to the display cases and gave a shoulder shrug. "I guess you haven't seen the newspaper article yet."

"What newspaper?" Callie said, on her guard.

Max held up a copy of the local *Crystal Bay Courier*. The cover story featured Drew's picture and she blinked back a few tears when she saw his handsome visage staring out at her. But then her eyes narrowed at the headline and subhead: "*Bistro Owner Slain*: Rival Food Business Owner Questioned by Police."

"Oh no!" Callie cried, as she saw the future of Callie's Kitchen melt away in front of her eyes. "No!"

"I'm sorry. I guess that reporter in here yesterday decided to write a story. She's probably sold a lot of papers. It's online too, where nothing ever dies. Unfortunately, we're not selling much food now as a result."

"I just saw Mrs. DeWitt yesterday," Callie said slowly. "I never did ask her why she talked to reporters. I was preoccupied, I guess."

"I'm sure you were," Max said. "You've had enough stress the last couple of days. Callie, don't worry about it. Our clients are probably just freaking out. They'll come back. You're innocent."

"I know that and you know that, but I don't think that the detective in charge of the case knows that," Callie said, still staring at the Courier article. A big story like that certainly wasn't going to do her any favors with the police, either.

The phone trilled and Max picked it up. "Yep. Uh-huh. We can do that. Wait. You need it when? Just a minute, please."

"Callie," Max said breathlessly. "We've got Lucille on the line and she wants 100 mini coffee cakes for tomorrow morning. It's a breakfast at the bank. What do you think? We've got no customers right now, anyway."

Callie nodded and grabbed the phone. "Lucille? I understand you need some coffee cakes for tomorrow?"

"You've got to help me," pleaded Lucille Reynolds, assistant to the vice president of the First Bank of Crystal Bay. "We have a big breakfast meeting tomorrow – very last-minute and now they want me to provide a feast fit for a king. You know I always give you advance notice but this time I promise, I had no idea. Corporate is coming down and Dave" – Lucille's boss – "has been bragging about your coffee cakes. Please say you can get these to me. We'll pay extra for the short notice, of course." The panic in her tone was unmistakable.

Despite all of her troubles, a glow of gratitude warmed Callie's heart. At least someone still trusted her to provide food. Or maybe it was just that she hadn't seen the newspaper story yet. Never mind, a customer was a customer.

Callie calculated how many cakes she already had in her freezer: probably about two dozen. She'd have quite a few more to bake, but she would be able to charge her rush delivery price. That settled it. Talking to Jane Willoughby would have to wait.

"I'll do it, Lucille. I'm happy to help."

"Thank you, you're a Greek goddess!" Lucille's enthusiasm was contagious and once again, Callie felt grateful for her vote of confidence.

"Only half Greek," Callie reminded her, with a smile. "As my dad says, the better half." Lucille laughed at the quip and said something that Callie couldn't hear. She strained to listen to Lucille who had dropped her voice to a near whisper.

"Listen. I'm sorry about Drew. It was terrible what happened to him and everything and I know you were going out, but that guy was weird." Lucille kept her voice low.

"What do you mean?" Callie said, startled by this abrupt change in the conversation.

"I can't talk about it right now," Lucille hedged. Callie heard voices and assumed someone was coming into her office space. "I'll tell you about it tomorrow when you deliver the cakes. Thanks again!" Lucille hung up abruptly.

Strange. But Callie had little time to decipher Lucille's words, at least at the moment. She had cakes to bake, a daughter to care for and a dog that needed walking, feeding and grooming, in that order. She had to get going if she didn't plan to be home by midnight. Maybe she'd finish in time to head over to the fitness center and ask Jane Willoughby some questions.

After filling Max in on the news that they needed about seventy-five more miniature coffee cakes by tomorrow morning, Callie left him at the register and got to work. With their delicious brown sugar and cinnamon streusel topping and rich, velvety crumb, Callie's coffee cakes were a customer favorite. She'd gotten the idea to bake minis because so many customers were reluctant to purchase an entire coffee cake.

Callie's Kitchen cakes used low-fat Greek yogurt in place of the more traditional sour cream so they were healthier than most, but the miniature version of the cakes made her customers feel less guilty. As a result, the minis were even more popular than the original sized cakes that baked up rich and gorgeous in a 10-inch tube pan.

Never underestimate the power of adorable, individually-sized food portions was a rule that Callie had learned to obey.

Callie began gathering some of the cake's decadent ingredients: lots of unsalted butter, thick and creamy Greek yogurt, large organic eggs, spicy cinnamon, dark brown sugar and aromatic pure vanilla extract. As she measured out flour and greased her extra-large cupcake pans, her thoughts returned to Drew and his mysterious death. If only she could have had a chance to speak to Jane Willoughby in person.

Callie was just sprinkling streusel topping on a divine-smelling batch of batter when the bell over the door gave its cheerful jingle. She looked up, hoping to see her usual lunchtime crowd of hungry locals and tourists. Instead, she was surprised to see that it was only one lone client, Steve Willoughby, approaching the counter where Max was placing cookies in an artful array.

Jane Willoughby's handsome husband jingled his car keys and didn't say anything. He wasn't a frequent customer and Callie found it odd that he would stop in now, when so many regulars were avoiding her business.

Max said hello and stood waiting for Steve's order, while Callie kept sprinkling streusel topping on her cake batter, wondering if she could ask Steve to tell her about Jane's schedule. As she worked, Callie realized that Max was trying to engage Steve in conversation and appeared to be receiving one-word answers. She decided to offer him a fresh-baked cookie on the house in an effort to break the ice. A food bribe was never a bad idea.

"Steve, won't you try one of these butter cookies?" Callie asked in as chipper a tone as she could muster. Her lips felt dry and chapped, devoid of her usual colorful lipstick. She'd been too tired and upset to put on any makeup.

Max, who had clearly worn out his conversational topics, looked relieved to see Callie take over. Quickly, he returned to his cookie display.

"Uh, sure," was Steve's lukewarm response. "I guess so."

He took the proffered cookie and destroyed it in one huge bite. Chewing, Steve seemed to relax a little bit. His usually slicked back blonde hair was mussed up and his clothing – a blue button-down shirt and khaki pants – were rumpled. Callie noticed that his normally lively turquoise eyes were puffy and tired-looking and a day's worth of stubble coated his cheeks and chin. Steve was not his usual dapper self.

"I was hoping to pick up some dinner for tonight," he said, wiping his mouth. "I don't want Jane to have to cook." He looked down, appearing to consider his next words. "I suppose Jane wouldn't mind if I told you about her recent problems, seeing as you're friends."

Callie nodded at him encouragingly.

"Jane lost a pregnancy," he confessed, his voice cracking.

Callie felt helpless at this show of emotion. Was he going to break down right here? She tried to look around for Max without Steve noticing but before she could, he plowed ahead with the rest of his sad story.

"She's – that is, we're both – hurting. It's been really hard. I'm sure it's harder on her, though, physically as well as mentally. So I'm trying to treat her extra well and I figured having some prepared meals on hand would be a nice touch."

"Oh, Steve," Callie said. "I am so sorry. Of course we'll find some delicious and healthy meals for you and Jane." Emerging from behind the counter she took his arm and led him over to her refrigerated case with clear glass walls and shelving. "Would you like some of my Greek chicken stew? And let's see, I've got salad and pita bread, too. Plus, cucumber yogurt sauce for the bread. Healthy and comforting."

"Yeah," Steve said, brightening a little bit. "That sounds good."

Callie began gathering up the items and placing them in one of her signature blue and white shopping bags.

"Things haven't been so great for several people in Crystal Bay lately," Steve observed as Callie brought the bags to the cash register. She slipped some more cookies into a paper bag and placed them with the other items.

"My treat," she explained. "These butter cookies, or *koulourakia*, are my grandmother's recipe, George's mother, that is." "*Yiayia*, we called her, which is Greek for 'grandmother'." She realized she was babbling but Steve didn't seem to mind.

"Thanks," Steve said wryly. "What I meant to say is that it was terrible what happened to Drew. And then, that newspaper article." He looked Callie in the eye. "That had to be a surprise."

Callie felt her face redden and she tried to keep her customer-friendly smile on her face but it froze before it reached the corners of her mouth. "It was a blow," she said, trying to control her voice and forbidding herself to cry. She pulled herself together and forced a tepid smile.

However, Steve was looking around the shop; he didn't seem to have noticed Callie's emotional turmoil. "So," he said suddenly brisk. "How is this place doing anyway?"

"Oh, you know," Callie said with a shrug, a little surprised at the sudden change in topic. "As well as can be expected, I guess. We're struggling like everyone else."

"No kidding. At least you're still in business. I couldn't believe it when I saw that Minette's Chocolates had shut down." He shook his head.

"Yes, I was shocked about that, too," Callie remarked. "Steve," she said, deciding to take advantage of this chance meeting. "I need to talk to Jane. Do you know if she'll be at the fitness center tomorrow?"

Steve handed Callie some cash and started gathering his bags as she rang up the sale. "She should be. In fact, work seems to be the only place she can stand to be right now." He seemed to be about to say something and then stopped. "She's there most mornings, evenings and everything in between." He frowned and busied himself with his wallet. "Thanks for the meal and the cookies," he said. He waved at her and hustled out the door.

Why was chatty Steve in such a hurry after sharing so much personal information? Probably he was embarrassed to have shared quite so much, Callie thought as she wiped the counter with a clean cloth.

"What's up with Willoughby?" Max said sidling up from cleaning tables in the front of the shop. "Dude looked like he was upset about something."

"I know. I feel terrible for him." Callie said. "His wife had a miscarriage."

"Yeah, I heard." At least Max had the good grace to blush at his obvious eavesdropping.

Callie just shook her head at her inquisitive protégé. "Let's get baking, buster," she said. "Mini coffee cakes are calling."

While they worked, Max seemed to have experienced a burst of energy. Callie watched, impressed, as he expertly but speedily scooped batter into the large muffin cups and sprinkled the luscious streusel combination over all.

"Max, you're a hero. As soon as things get back to normal, let's see about getting you some time off. In fact, I had been hoping that I could win the business contest so that I would get some additional employees to help you. Provided business picks up again, that is. I also need a social media expert but that looks like it's going to have to be me, for now. And I'm no expert."

"Social networking? I have a friend who's a pro at all of that stuff," Max enthused. "She's still in school at Crystal Bay College but she studies online marketing, web design, social media, all of that. Maybe we could ask her for some pointers. You might even want to hire her part-time. You know, provided things are going well."

"Who is this friend? Have you mentioned her before?" Callie's voice was gently teasing but she saw that she'd hit a nerve when Max blushed to the roots of his artfully spiked hair.

"No, it's someone I've just gotten to know recently. Her name is Piper and she's really smart. I mean, she's a computer nerd and all that but in a good way and really artistic. I met her when I was visiting my friend Jack a couple of weeks ago in Madison. She happened to be visiting a friend, too. Piper just moved to Crystal Bay. I knew there was a reason I hadn't noticed her before." Max shifted from foot to foot, trying to look casual.

"I'd love her input. I wish I could hire her! She sounds like just the person I need."

Max smiled as he finished sprinkling streusel on top of the last of the coffee cakes. "I could call her and ask her to take a look at our web site. What else do you want to do?"

"We need to be on Facebook and Twitter. Instagram and Pinterest are probably a good idea, too, since it's a great way to advertise food using enticing photos of Callie's Kitchen creations. But I just don't have the time to manage all of those sites on my own. You really think she'd be interested in helping out?"

"I think so." Max looked thrilled. "Maybe she could even get college credit, you know, like an internship?"

"That would be great." Doubly great, thought Callie, since an internship didn't pay in dollars, just in experience and like Max said, college credit. A real part-time employee would be nice but maybe this Piper could offer a stopgap until Callie laid her hands on some additional funds.

"I'd love to chat with her. Tell her to stop into the shop sometime."

"Will do!" Max beamed. Piper must be pretty special after all. Max wasn't exactly unpopular.

"One task I will take off your hands tomorrow is delivering these cakes to the bank," Callie informed Max as they carefully boxed the cakes. "Lucille made a personal request for my presence. No offense, I hope."

"No problem," said Max as he flexed his muscles stacking cakes on the shelving unit in the back of the shop. "I'm coming in early to bake and I'll be back at the shop until about two."

"Right," said Callie. "Hopefully tomorrow we'll have some more customers to feed." In the meantime, how was she going to find time to see Jane Willoughby? She also needed to stop in Drew's restaurant and check to see if she could find anything that might help offer a clue to his murderer.

Callie stepped outside to get some air. The last warm days of Indian summer had come to a close and she could feel the familiar chill of a Wisconsin autumn in the darkening evening. Usually a brisk change in weather meant customers seeking out her heartier dishes, like soups and stews. Tonight, one or two tourists straggled in but everyone else stayed away. It was terrible to know that the customer base she'd worked so hard to fill had been lost, perhaps forever.

It wasn't only the fear of not earning enough money that caused her despair. She missed the banter and conversation of her customers, the compliments to her cooking, even the customers who flirted with Max while she smiled tolerantly.

As she locked up Callie's Kitchen for the evening, Callie felt afraid again, almost like someone was watching her. She asked Max to walk her to her car, but as the darkness settled in, she did not feel safe.

* * *

The morning dawned sunny but cold as Callie got up early and prepared to deliver the cakes to the breakfast meeting at the bank. Olivia was sleepy at breakfast and a little wheezy, so Callie insisted that she do a breathing treatment and made her promise to go to the nurse if necessary. She hated to sound like such a worry wart but she couldn't help wondering if her daughter's asthma was getting worse.

After handing her daughter an overflowing backpack to shoulder, Callie had Olivia out the door early. She quickly walked Koukla and then set off for work, where she had to load the cakes for the First Bank of Crystal Bay and Lucille's breakfast meeting.

The First Bank of Crystal Bay was a small building with a quaintly majestic air. Built in the town's early days, the building's red brick facade featured white scrolls and columns as extra flourishes to enhance its stately appearance. Originally part of the town center, most of the small businesses had left for the Garden Street Business District, and the bank now shared the block with a small dry cleaning service, shoe repair, dentist and small drugstore that was housed in one of the town's earliest building structures.

Lucille was sitting at her corner desk in front of a conference room that was set up for a meeting but was currently empty of people. Callie could see fruit, napkins and coffee urns in the center of the table, along with bottles of water in a bowl full of ice.

"Hi!" Lucille greeted Callie in an exaggerated stage whisper so as not to disturb the other customers. "Thanks again. You're an angel to deliver these cakes on such short notice."

"No problem," Callie stage-whispered back. "I just hope they're a hit. It sounds like they've got a lot to live up to, since Dave was talking them up." And wait until you get my bill, Callie thought, echoing Samantha's words to her outside the police station.

"Unfortunately for my personal trainer, your mini coffee cakes are my favorite," Lucille enthused. "The only thing that tempts me more is Minette's Chocolate Shop. I suppose closing it is a good thing for all of our figures, but the owner was in here today looking for a loan. Maybe they'll get one." Lucille tugged at the pencil skirt that hugged her slender waist as if it were too tight, then rose from her seat. "Can you help me set up?"

"Sure thing," said Callie, unpacking the first box. "Minette was here this morning?"

"No, not her. It was her husband, Jeff. He really wants that business to reopen – it's so romantic the way he talked about his wife! He said their chocolate shop was like their baby and he had to try and save it because they both loved it so much." Lucille fanned herself with a brochure for home loans. "Working at a bank these days is no fun. They say the economy is slowly getting better, but tell that to people dealing with home foreclosures and failing businesses." No kidding. If she didn't start serving more than one or two customers a day at Callie's Kitchen – and soon – she'd be another one of those statistics.

Callie finished setting the breakfast treats on the cake stands. The cakes did look scrumptious and she was glad she had a few extra in the delivery truck. Lucille was sipping a bottle of water, quiet for the first time in several minutes, so Callie decided to pounce.

"You had something to tell me. About Drew? What was it?"

"Oh, that," Lucille hedged. "Just something that seemed strange to me. But you can't tell anyone I told you this or I could get into trouble." Twenty-something Lucille fidgeted a bit on her high heels and chewed on a pen cap. She looked like a worried six-year-old who doesn't want to tattle to the teacher.

"I understand," Callie said, smoothing a crumb off of the cake stand and into her waiting hand.

"Drew recently came in about two weeks ago and applied for a huge loan. Somewhere in the arena of $100,000. I know I shouldn't have, but I peeked at his loan application materials." Lucille waited for criticism and when none came, she shrugged and kept on with her tale. "He was in debt, both his business and his home. He really needed money. I thought his business was in the black. He had one of the nicest homes and nicest cars in Crystal Bay! It just doesn't make sense."

"No, it doesn't make sense at all," Callie said. Why would prosperous Drew need such a large bank loan? "Thanks for telling me. The police will probably be investigating Drew's finances, too, so please, tell them everything you know. They have been investigating me, too, since I'm the one who found him." Callie stopped gathering her empty cake boxes and leaned against the table.

"I know, I heard. I read the newspaper article in the Courier. That journalist really made me mad. You don't seem like the murdering type to me, whatever that is. Besides, anyone who bakes as well as you just can't have done something so awful!"

Callie smiled. Lucille was a little bit ditzy, but she was loyal. Callie gave the younger woman a quick hug. "Thanks. I really appreciate your support. It's been a difficult time."

"I bet!" Lucille rolled her eyes. "If I found a dead body, I'd hide under my covers and refuse to come out."

The two women cleaned up the rest of the boxes and said their goodbyes, with Lucille calling to Callie on her way out the door to send her the bill for the rush delivery on the cakes. A couple of bank patrons exchanged glances when they heard her name.

The Crystal Bay gossip network was working overtime on Drew's murder, especially with the release of the news story, but Callie couldn't be bothered with that right now. She had bigger fish to fry. Such as: why in the world did Drew need a loan?

Seven

When she returned to work, a customer – not one that Callie recognized – was leaving with a small container of what appeared to be Greek chicken stew. Other than that, the shop was empty except for Max, who gave her a wave as she joined him in the cooking area.

Delicious smells wafted from the ovens and Callie inhaled deeply. Lemon, butter, sugar: Max must be making cookies. However, that delicate scent was nearly overpowered by the fragrant odors of tomato sauce, chicken, cinnamon and above it all, the sharper scent of cucumbers and yogurt that would make a sauce for the pita bread to go along with it.

The food smelled great, but where was the usual flow of customers to appreciate it? If business didn't pick up, she was regretfully going to have to tell Max not to make so much food. It would only go to waste, along with the little money she had left.

The phone rang and Callie picked it up, tucking the receiver under her ear while she stirred the contents of a massive stockpot.

"When were you planning on telling me about your boyfriend's murder? And what about Olivia? Are you two safe? I don't like this. I don't like it at all." Hugh, Callie's ex-husband, sounded more than a little agitated.

Deep breath, count to 10, Callie recited to herself. Reminding herself that Hugh was simply a concerned father, she kept her frustration in check.

"Hugh, hello! Nice to hear from you, too. Can I ask who told you about this?"

"Some detective named Sands. He came to interview Raine and me. He found our phone numbers on a cell phone that they confiscated from you."

At this news, Callie silently ran through a string of Greek curse words she'd learned from a cousin long ago. Now Sands was talking to Hugh. Things must be worse for her than she thought. Or maybe – could they possibly suspect her ex-husband? What a joke. He was thrilled with his new wife and appeared to have no interest whatsoever in her dating life, other than how it might affect their daughter.

"Hugh, we're fine. I'm being careful. And I'm innocent by the way. I'm cooperating with the police so that I can prove that. Dad watches Olivia after school most days or she goes to a friend's house when I'm stuck at work. She never walks by herself. Plus, I've even got a few karate moves I picked up from Samantha when she forced me to take that self-defense course. I know you're worried, but I promise we're okay." Callie stirred the tomato sauce slowly, wishing she could dive into the warm chicken stew and sail away from her troubles.

"I knew you would say that." Hugh appeared to be relaxing, as was his way. Get angry first, ask questions later. "Does George know about this guy?"

"No. And don't tell him. I haven't yet."

Hugh chuckled. "Still the same strict old George, I see. Well, you're all grown up now. You can go out with who you want, right? Anyway, I'm sorry to hear about your loss. Let me know if you need anything." Hugh cleared his throat. "Look, why don't I take Olivia for a couple of days?"

"What about school?" Callie countered. Hugh lived two towns over, closer to Madison. It would not be impossible to drive Olivia to school from there, but not exactly convenient, either.

Hugh persisted. "How about I pick her up after school on Thursday and she can only miss one day? I can take her out on my boat with Raine." The new wife. Loyal Samantha had given Hugh's new wife the nickname "Raine on My Parade."

A boat ride. How cozy that sounded for the three of them! Callie would no doubt be eating cookies and sitting at home with Koukla – if she were lucky and not in jail.

"I guess so," Callie agreed with a sigh. "But she'll want to ask her teachers for work in advance and then she might have to do some over the weekend. She doesn't like to get behind." Olivia could be a little rigid about having to make up school work. Another Type A personality in the making?

"Yeah, sure, I'll help her figure out her homework situation. This is great. I can't wait to tell Raine. She'll be so thrilled, she just loves Livvie." Well, it was better than not loving her, but it still hurt to see her child go off with another woman. Thank goodness for Koukla – she had made it clear a long time ago that she preferred Callie to any other human on earth. That was probably due to Callie's generosity with chicken, her warm lap and her habit of bringing home new dog treats, but it was true love just the same.

"You do that, Hugh. Listen, I'm up to my eyeballs in Greek chicken, so I'll work out the details with you later." Callie wanted to get back to cooking, but Hugh wanted to stay on the line, another thing he never did when they were married.

"I always did love that stew. And that Greek soup you make with lemon, rice and egg." Hugh sounded wistful. Maybe Raine wasn't such a great cook.

"Hugh, I've got to run, but thanks for your concern. I'll even save you some food. Bye!" How would Raine like to sit down to a dinner cooked by Hugh's ex-wife? She probably wouldn't mind all that much. Like most of Callie's customers, she would probably just be happy she didn't have to do the cooking.

After she hung up, Callie felt her blood continued to boil at a low simmer, just like the stew on the stove. Hugh could still get her angry, much to her chagrin. But darn him, he always felt like he knew better than she did – in everything.

Early in their relationship, when she was younger and unsure of herself, Callie had appreciated Hugh's take-charge attitude. The more independent she grew, the more she and Hugh had grown apart. Anyway, she'd had enough of a "take-charge" attitude from George to last her a lifetime.

It was as if her thinking of George conjured him up. When Callie took her stew off the stove, the doorbells chimed and there stood her father. This time, he didn't look like he was seeking doughnuts or small talk. His bushy black and grey eyebrows were drawn close together over his nose and his brown eyes snapped with fire.

"Hi, Dad," Callie tried the lighthearted approach. "No *loukoumades* today but I've got Greek yogurt coffee cake."

Without a word, George walked behind the counter and enveloped Callie in a bear hug. His actions were tender, but his words were anything but. "How can a daughter of mine be mixed up in a murder?" He pulled back and stared at his daughter. "This is how I raised you? And when were you going to tell me about this Drew? I knew about him, don't think I didn't. I was waiting for you to come to me and tell me you had someone new in your life. But no, you didn't trust me. Your own father."

"Dad," Callie began, but he kept on speaking, his words tumbling over themselves, his Greek accent becoming more pronounced. "This is scandal! A man is murdered – a man you are seeing – and you don't tell me. I had to find out at The Olympia from an employee who was only too happy to show me a newspaper article, stating that a female Greek food business owner had been questioned – obviously, you! I pretended to know what he was talking about but I would have expected you to tell me yourself!" George was growling now and didn't resemble a cuddly bear any longer. He was more like a bear who had stumbled into a wasp nest.

His angry outburst riled her, along with a burning sense of shame and embarrassment that her father had known about Drew but had kept her in the dark about this knowledge. Apparently, the two were more alike than Callie wanted to admit.

"You can't blame me for not telling you I was dating someone! You wouldn't have approved. You don't think I can handle my own affairs!" Bad choice of words, Callie realized, but George didn't appear to notice the double entendre.

"A father should be there to protect his daughter. You don't allow me to be a true father when you shut me out." George was losing steam; now he just looked sad. His craggy face sagged.

Callie bit back another angry response. Her father was only concerned about her, just like Hugh was concerned with Olivia.

"Dad," she said again, and this time he was quiet. "I'm sorry. I should have told you about the murder right away. I planned to do it today, I swear." She hugged her father and he squeezed her back in one of his infamous rib-cracking embraces. The two stepped back and stood looking at each other.

Callie was ashamed. How often George must have wanted to question her or, God forbid, to say something critical of Drew, as was his habit with any man who'd ever been in her life, but he'd never said a word.

"I should have come to you," she repeated, "but I didn't really know how things would turn out, so I just didn't mention it." *And of course, I certainly didn't know it would end in a murder!* Callie thought.

"You're embarrassed that your marriage failed," George said and Callie winced at his words. "But you have no cause to be. It's my fault that you feel this way about yourself. I made you feel like you failed. But this is only because I felt like I'd failed you, that I hadn't been a good enough father AND mother to you." Callie looked at him in surprise. He continued, tears starting in the corners of his faded brown eyes.

"You've been a wonderful father," Callie said, shocked at his words. She'd always felt like he blamed her for the divorce.

"But," George said, his sharp tone returning. "Who is this Drew that he winds up murdered in his own home? Mark my words, he's done something wrong. These things don't just happen."

Callie felt her own brows knit together as she started to assemble a smart comeback, but then thought the better of it. George was being as magnanimous as he knew how and she shouldn't waste the moment.

"You might be right, Dad," she said, thinking of what Lucille at the bank had told her about Drew's mysterious loan.

The two were silent a minute. "Well, now what do we do?" Callie asked her father.

George appeared to be thinking carefully about his response. "You said you have coffee cake?" he finally asked.

"Yep." Callie smiled at her father.

"Well, am I going to go and get it, or are you?"

Eight

The next morning, Callie's Kitchen was once again nearly devoid of customers. A few brave regulars came in for coffee and their usual meals to go, but nothing like her usual happy, hungry crowd.

Callie mulled over the ingredients in her refrigerator. She should probably try to make some dishes and freeze them so that she didn't waste food, but instead of menus, her mind kept replaying her short but intense visit with Samantha the previous evening. They'd caught up on a few things, but only briefly, as Sam was in the middle of a big case.

According to Sam, Detective Sands was questioning all of Drew's friends and colleagues. No funeral was planned yet as Drew's body had not yet been released. With apologies, Sam had also taken back her cell phone, so Callie was left without that familiar tether to the outside world. She wanted to get a new phone but would the police take that away, too?

After the morbid news about Drew, and her worries about the police investigation, Callie had slept fitfully and was now more tired than ever. She decided to take a break from menu planning and depressing thoughts of spoiled food and wasted money, and switch gears to her social media plans. It seemed as if every time she figured out how a social network operated, the company changed it. This Piper friend of Max's sounded like the answer to her prayers. If only she could convince her to work for college credit — or at least for food.

Closing her laptop, Callie was surprised to see Minette walk through the door, this time without her husband. Callie waved and came out from behind the counter to greet her friend.

"How are you?" Minette said. Her hair was pushed back in a headband and she looked tired, with greyish circles under her usually bright eyes. "Back at work, I see."

"Somebody's got to do it," Callie said. "Anyway, it's not like I have customers beating down the door, which is starting to become an issue. Still, I'd rather be here. At home all I have is time to think about everything – and that's not good."

"Yeah, I know what you mean," Minette said, slumping into a table in front of the bakery cases. "I saw the news article. Sorry about that." She waved away Callie's offer of coffee and rested her chin on her folded hands.

"This whole going out of business thing is too much for me. I left Jeff at the chocolate shop – he's buzzing around the place, still trying to charm customers. I don't think he gets it. The shop is closing. I don't even think winning the Taste of Crystal Bay money could have saved us." Minette sighed gustily.

"I had no idea things were going so poorly for you. I wish you'd told me." Callie patted her friend's hand.

Minette let out a strangled laugh. "You couldn't have helped. We need big money to get out of trouble and we decided the best thing to do would be to close. At least I thought that was our plan. Jeff seems to have other ideas." Minette sat up and ran her fingers through her blonde pixie cut. "Anyway, that's life, right?"

"Come on," Callie protested. "Maybe there's a way. I remember how excited you were when you opened Minette's Chocolates." She sat down next to her friend and nudged her shoulder affectionately. "Remember what you said?"

Minette blinked and a shadow of a smile flickered across her lips. "I do. I said I had the perfect name to be the owner of a French-themed chocolate shop so it was destined to be a success! Do you remember how I told you that my mother was a Julia Child fan, from way back?" Minette had a starry look in her eyes and Callie decided it was good for her to vent a bit even though she had heard the story before. She nodded encouragingly at her friend.

"Mom said that Julia loved cats and sometimes, on her TV show, she talked about the cats she had in Paris. So Mom looked it up and it turns out that 'Minette' is an endearment for felines in French. She thought it had a beautiful sound to it and the rest is history. So much for my name. In the end, it didn't make much difference."

Callie was dismayed to see her friend so low. "Everybody is struggling right now," she said gently. "Maybe you can find a way to stay open. If Jeff hasn't given up, maybe you shouldn't either."

"Calliope Costas, The Eternal Optimist," Minette said. "I wish things would work out but I don't know." She pushed back from the table and stood up. "Thanks for listening. I know you have your own problems. I'm really sorry about Drew. You know you can talk to me any time." She gave Callie a rueful smile. "I'd better get back to work and see this thing through."

"That's the spirit. And I'm not always such an optimist – I just know that you and Jeff are chocolate artists. Or should I say artistes."

"Thanks, Callie," Minette's chin wobbled and she appeared to be struggling to contain strong emotions. "I've got to go." She was out the door before Callie could formulate the word "Goodbye."

Poor Minette. The door jingled again and Callie's heart gave a little leap. Could it be customers at last? No such luck. It was Detective Sands, accompanied by the officer who had been on the scene the night of Drew's murder.

"Hello," he said, looking around her shop. "It certainly smells good in here." Callie smiled uncertainly at him – maybe he was only here on a casual visit.

"Thanks. What I can I do for you? Would you like some meals-from-scratch to heat up at home or the office? Lots of good stuff available today."

"Not exactly," Sands said. Callie took in his sad hazel eyes and unruly hair. He really was a rather attractive man when he wasn't interrogating her, she thought, then blushed deep red, feeling both ridiculous and disloyal to Drew's memory.

"Well?" Callie asked, hoping the detective didn't notice her beet-red face.

"Ms. Costas, I have a warrant. You're going to have to turn your knives over to me as part of our investigation."

"My knives? Well, what am I supposed to work with? Why do you need my knives?" Callie heard her voice shoot up several octaves and willed herself to calm down.

"All part of our investigation. Shall we?" Sands asked, motioning for Callie to lead him into the kitchen.

Numbly, Callie led the two men to the cooking area. Sands gave a nod to his partner, and the officer started rummaging through kitchen drawers and cabinets. Each knife that he found was placed in a clear cylindrical tube. He then took each knife from the wooden knife block on her countertop and performed the same careful storage process.

Callie found herself wanting to cry out and stop him, but she knew that she couldn't. Sands looked at her, almost with sympathy, she thought, but that look was quickly replaced by an expression of resolve. With gloved hands, he placed the empty wooden knife block into a clear plastic bag.

Callie found her voice again. "Wait. This proves nothing. I have several kinds of knives and anyway, the murder weapon was there, when I found Drew. This makes no sense!" She started to tremble but refused to let them see her cry. Damn them. How was she going to cook without knives, an expensive kitchen tool? An even worse – they obviously suspected her of the murder!

"I am truly sorry, but I can't discuss this with you. I suggest you speak to your friend, the lawyer. In the meantime, I appreciate your cooperation. If you have nothing to hide, you should have nothing to worry about," Sands said. She felt him giving her one of his penetrating looks but she couldn't look him in the eye. She was terrified and angry beyond belief all at the same time.

"Right." Callie bit off the word. "Just tell me when I can have them back."

"There is no telling," Sands said. "I wish I could give you details, but I can't. Thank you. We'll just be leaving now." If he thought Callie was going to wish him a fond goodbye, he had another think coming, as Viv would say.

Once she was alone again, Callie shed hot tears. She was in real trouble, there was no denying it. No customers. A confiscated cell-phone. Now, no knives. Would they assign her to kitchen duty in prison?

With trembling fingers she dialed Samantha's cell phone. Sam didn't answer and Callie left a terse and hopefully – coherent – message.

There was nothing to do but to close up shop for the day, get a new phone and replace at least some of the knives. Callie had one emergency credit card and this situation definitely qualified. Plus, she had to confront Jane Willoughby. She didn't have any more time to waste.

Callie stored food, wiped down surfaces, and as an afterthought, she boxed up some cookies and pastries to give to Jane. Sweets for the sweet? Hardly, but she felt like bringing a gift might at least break the ice.

Deciding that she couldn't spare the 30 minutes it would take to drive to the shopping mall, Callie visited a touristy kitchen store.

There, she secured professional-grade knives for a small fortune, ignoring the inquisitive look of the cashier. Next stop was her cell phone provider where she got a new phone, telling them it was for her daughter. She imagined her emergency credit card buckling and straining under its unaccustomed use.

Impatient at still having no word from Sam, Callie sent her a text, giving her friend her new cell phone number and briefly explaining her situation. Finally, she was ready to confront Jane.

On Tuesdays, Jane was usually at Bodies by the Bay, something that Callie remembered from dealing with the Chamber. She decided to dress in workout gear as a pretense for being there. Callie went home where she changed clothes, fed and watered Koukla and packed a gym bag to complete her ruse.

The low-slung modern building housing Bodies by the Bay had stellar lake views to match its state-of-the-art equipment. Today the expensive concrete work sparkled like diamonds in the sun. Colorful mums flourished in solid-looking ceramic pots that flanked the front doorway. Callie saw a price tag on the back of the pot and leaned down to look more closely — and the price astounded her. True, the arrangement was large and perfectly gorgeous, but that was a lot of cash for two containers of flowers.

Jane was one of the few business owners in Crystal Bay with money to burn these days. In some ways, it was surprising that her business had done so well, considering that Crystal Bay residents were usually so bundled up in their cold-weather clothing there wasn't much chance to flaunt a toned physique.

It didn't hurt that Jane Willoughby came from a wealthy family and was able to funnel a lot of her own money into making it great, offering clients a wide range of classes and activities. In addition to cardio-training and spinning classes, Bodies by the Bay even offered rehab services for people recuperating from injury. Besides all of that, there were few places in town for singles to meet and the fitness center tended to be the singles meeting place for everyone aged 25 and over.

For the middle of a weekday, the place was buzzing with clientele – lots of young mothers, clients of all ages undergoing physical therapy, some college-aged boys playing basketball in the center of the facility. Callie wasn't used to doing anything leisurely at this time of day; it was interesting to see how the other half lived.

The sharp smell of chlorine stung Callie's nostrils as she handed her infrequently-used club membership card to the receptionist, then passed the indoor pool area, complete with a warm physical therapy pool and superhot Jacuzzi. Callie could never stand that Jacuzzi more than a few minutes. The temp was borderline scalding.

Near the back of the fitness center, past the indoor track, basketball court and machines was the locker room. As Callie stored her gym bag in one of the slender gray lockers and picked up a fresh towel from an artfully rolled pile on a bench, she noticed a woman in a green polo and khaki pants. The fitness center logo – the silhouette of a thin woman running – was emblazoned on the left shoulder of her shirt. "Excuse me, where can I find Jane Willoughby?" she asked as the young woman rushed by her.

"Ms. Willoughby is very busy today. Do you have an appointment?" the young woman responded curtly with a flick of her brunette ponytail. She wore blunt-cut bangs, bright red lipstick and dramatically arched penciled eyebrows, a stark contrast to her preppy-looking uniform. With her hairstyle and makeup, Callie had an easier time picturing her in a vintage 1950s dress.

"No," Callie said, thinking quickly. "I'm dropping off some treats today after my workout. I'm the owner of Callie's Kitchen on Garden Street."

"Oooh, what kind of treats?" Suddenly, Ms. Ponytail with an Attitude was all smiles. Callie gave her a big smile in return. "Oh, a little of this, a little of that. Mini coffee cakes. Some Greek cookies. A few brownies."

"Yum! Well, you come with me. Jane hasn't been eating much lately, I'm sure this will cheer her up! And she works out almost constantly, so she'll burn it off in no time."

"She works out almost constantly," Callie echoed, thinking of Jane's recent miscarriage. Surely the doctor would have her modifying her exercise activity, at least for a while.

"Of course," the young woman said, leading Callie past the pool again and to offices behind the reception area. She waved at a few workers sitting at their desks, then led Callie down a long hallway to an office with Jane's nameplate on the door and gestured to it.

"In fact, she was just on the elliptical machine for at least an hour when I got here today. Well, here you are. You be sure and save me some of those brownies!" Ms. Ponytail winked and jogged off down the hall.

Here goes nothing, Callie thought, knocking on the door.

"Come in," called a familiar voice. Callie slowly opened the door and stepped inside. Jane's mouth gave her signature cheery smile but it seemed to fade before it reached her eyes. Callie swallowed and offered her friend an upbeat "hello."

Jane nodded at Callie. "Steve said he stopped at your shop last night. Your dinner was really good. Of course, I couldn't eat much, since I'm watching my weight."

Callie couldn't resist a plug for her healthy if comforting cuisine. "Well, you can eat my food – at least the entrees—mostly without guilt. I pride myself on healthful food."

Jane didn't respond to this mini advertisement for Callie's Kitchen. "What can I do for you today? Is this about your membership? Don't worry if you let it slide. We can re-sign you in no time." Jane's eyes raked Callie's figure. "Too many cakes and hearty soups and such plus too little exercise can be a deadly combination."

Callie's face felt like it was on fire after that unexpected insult. She was no exercise fanatic and working in the food industry, she was sure she could shed a few pounds, but she didn't think she looked so bad. It could be the exercise clothes; they tended to hug her figure in all the wrong places, like her lower belly, still slightly distended after her Caesarean section ten years prior. Unconsciously she sucked in her abdomen and stood up straighter. She decided to ignore Jane's dig.

"My membership is still good. I had a quick question for you if you don't mind." Suddenly, it seemed far too awkward to stand. "Do you mind if I sit for a minute? It won't take long."

Jane waved a hand toward the chair in front of her desk. "Fine, but I don't have a lot of time. Busy day and all of that. What's the problem?"

Callie waited until she had seated herself and took a closer look at her Chamber of Commerce colleague. Face to face, Jane's normally-sparkling green eyes looked fatigued, which was understandable since she must be depressed and still mourning the loss of her pregnancy. The excessive working out didn't fit that profile, though.

"I know you've heard of Drew's death by now," Callie began.

Jane had been studying some papers on her desk but at this her head snapped up so quickly on her graceful, flower stalk neck that Callie half-expected it to snap right off of her body like a Barbie doll. "Yes, I'm...sorry. I should have said so when you came in. You and Drew were seeing each other." Jane smoothed her hair back from her forehead and sat up, her hands folded in front of her. "Well? Is this about the Chamber?"

"No, my question is about the business contest. I spoke to Mrs. DeWitt today and she said..."

Jane put up a hand. "Callie, I don't mean to be rude." She shifted in her seat a bit and seemed unsure how to continue. "I just can't talk about that right now. We are very behind in work over here and to tell you the truth, I'm really not sure how we're going to handle the contest. I don't know how I'm going to get everything done!" She bent her head before Callie could see the tears fall. Jane's long, graceful arm shot out and discreetly reached for a tissue at the corner of her desk.

Callie was a little taken aback. She'd never seen Jane's businesslike composure crack and her heart warmed to her. So this can-do woman with the amazing figure was human after all. But if she didn't get to the point with Jane soon, she wasn't sure how she was going to get everything done, either.

"I had nothing to do with his death but I'm under suspicion. And that's why I'm here. I'm trying to get out of trouble, not cause it for anyone else," she spoke softly and Jane sniffed, looking at her wedding ring as she twisted it around her finger. The enormous diamond glowed under the bright office lights.

Finally, Jane decided to respond. "I saw the newspaper article. It looks like you've been the target of a journalist. Sorry."

"I wanted to say I'm sorry to you, too," Callie continued. "I heard about your miscarriage." Jane nodded and whispered "Thank you."

Callie sighed. She decided to share her concerns quickly and leave Jane in peace.

"I know this is an awkward time for everyone but I need your help. The police think that Drew's murder might have something to do with his winning the Taste of Crystal Bay. All I want to know is a couple of details about the contest rules. It seems that Mrs. DeWitt may have misled the head detective working Drew's case. She told him that the original rules outlined a second and third place winner, but you all decided as a group to nix that to give the contest some extra competitive edge."

Jane shrugged. "So? Seriously, I've got to get to work."

"So my question is—who knew about those original rules? And did you personally tell anyone about it? Because apparently I was second in line, and it's causing the police some suspicion." This admission hurt Callie's pride, but she had to be honest if she was going to get anywhere.

Jane sighed. "I don't know what you're getting at, Callie."

Callie felt the blood rush to her face in exasperation. "Mrs. DeWitt said that you kept the section about giving the winnings to the runner-up if for some reason the first place winner couldn't accept it and that those rules were just there for clerical purposes. I'm sure you never thought they'd come into play. However, law enforcement has the idea that maybe someone killed Drew because they knew about the pecking order for the prize." She didn't mention that the police were zeroing in on her. Likely, Jane knew that already, or had guessed, if she'd read that blasted news article.

Jane gave Callie an impatient glance. "All of that may be true but what can I do about it now?" She looked at her watch.

"Don't you see — even if you mentioned something about the contest in passing they could have told someone? And that person could be the killer, or could lead us to the killer. Or maybe the third place winner found out somehow, and they're the killer! Please, you have to tell me what you know, for both of our sakes."

Jane rolled her eyes. "Just tell the detective – or I will – that only Mrs. DeWitt and I were in that meeting for the contest rules. We scratched the original premise of a first, second and third place winner, so it doesn't really matter." She sounded more exhausted than angry and Callie was beginning to regret that she'd ever begun this conversation. What kind of a monster bothers a woman mourning a pregnancy loss? She was as bad as the information-seekers at Callie's Kitchen the morning after Drew's murder.

Jane looked Callie dead in the eye and held up her hand in a Girl Scout salute: "I never told anyone about the original rules and I'd have to go back and tally it up to find out who won third. It just doesn't matter at this point. Okay, Callie – is that all? As I said, I really need to tend to my work today."

Desperate to get some helpful information of out of Jane, Callie gritted her teeth and braved one more topic. "I hear that Drew took out a large loan. It looked like he was in debt. I thought he was doing great. It just seems odd that he would need so much money when he appeared to be doing so well."

"Is this just going to be a gossip session? Who told you that? Wait, I know. I'll bet it was Lucille. She is such a blabbermouth. That's it, I'm switching banks. She ought to be reported. I wouldn't tolerate that from one of *my* employees."

Callie realized she'd said more than she should have. Lucille had sworn her to confidence. Rapidly, she tried to backpedal.

"You have nothing to fear from Lucille. You know how people love to talk. Just about everybody comes through my shop at one time or another. People talk about anything except anything that's their own business, especially now, with Drew's murder the talk of the town."

"Oh, come on. We all know Lucille means well, but she doesn't know how to keep her mouth shut and her busy little body out of other people's business. I'd be careful around her if I were you." Jane's cheeks were growing pale and there were dark circles and lines under her eyes that makeup couldn't hide.

Callie stood up, defeated. This interview was clearly over. Despite Jane's impatience, Callie did feel badly for her and was worried about her health. "I'm sorry I bothered you today. Please take care of yourself. Working out infrequently may pile on the pounds, but working out too hard following a miscarriage could cause serious health problems."

"So now you're an OB-GYN in addition to a cook?" Jane said, but wearily. She sighed again and her voice softened. "Callie, I'm sorry. I promise I'll get in touch if I learn any new details. And don't worry about my working out. It makes me feel better. Exercise is going get rid of the belly I started to grow when I was pregnant so that every time I look at my body, I'm not thinking about what I've..." She gulped and finished her thought. "It helps me forget what I've lost."

Callie felt tears of sympathy spring into her eyes. She'd never thought about her belly flab that way, only been embarrassed by it. She reached across the desk and grabbed Jane's hand. "It's okay," she said. "I know you're upset. Listen, if you find out anything, will you please tell me? It would mean a lot."

Jane nodded and blew her nose in a fresh tissue. "I will."

"Oh, and I almost forgot. These are for you and your staff." She handed Jane the baked goods assortment, squeezed Jane's hand and walked out, closing the door behind her. She leaned against it for a minute, collecting her thoughts. Callie was already as tired as if she'd had a workout and she hadn't even broken a sweat yet!

Nine

Callie debated going straight back to her kitchen to drown her sorrows in cookies and pita bread. Instead, she checked her new phone. Thank goodness! Samantha had returned her text: "In a meeting but I will get back to you ASAP!"

Now what? Callie wanted to stick around and see how busy Jane really was. Since Sam couldn't talk to her yet, she decided to stay and walk the treadmill. She was dressed for it, at least. Maybe walking would help her to think – and maybe she'd be able to watch Jane's activities unobserved. Something was off. Jane was brisk by nature but usually eager to help others.

Plus, Drew's death was haunting Callie. She could barely close her eyes without seeing the knife in his chest. Add to that her emerging status as prime suspect and she wondered if she'd ever be able to relax again. Maybe the exercise would tire her out enough that she would get some real sleep for one night.

Scanning the machines, most of which were filled with sweating, grunting exercisers of all shapes, ages and sizes, she finally settled on the treadmill as it seemed the simplest to operate and use. However, it had been a long time since she'd used fitness equipment. Pushing one button that made the incline too steep, then another button that made the treadmill go too fast, Callie saw Ms. Ponytail walking by and out of desperation, she called to her.

"Can you help me program this thing? Sorry, it's been awhile and I don't want to go flying off into oblivion."

"No problem! Here's what you do." The girl punched a few buttons and the treadmill began moving at a reasonable pace. "Thanks,"

Callie said, trying not to huff and puff. She took a closer look at the girl's badge. It read "Piper Anderson." Piper! This had to be "the" Piper. It wasn't a name you heard all that frequently.

"I'm Callie Costas of Callie's Kitchen. My assistant, Max, said you're a computer whiz and that you're really good at social media, in addition to adjusting athletic equipment like a pro."

Piper's rouged cheeks turned an even darker shade of pink. "Nice to meet you! Yes, I know Max." She smiled brightly and Callie noticed perfect white teeth and how blue Piper's eyes were. Yep, Max didn't stand a chance. "How sweet of him to brag about me like that." Piper lowered her thick eyelashes demurely.

Callie's breathing grew more labored as the treadmill increased speed. "I need someone to help me with my social media at my food business. Max said you might be interested in doing it for college credit. Can I leave you my card after I'm finished here?"

"Absolutely! I work here part-time but I'd love something that tied into my marketing degree. I can talk to my college advisor about it."

Callie was beginning to perspire: Time to focus on exercise. "Where can I find you in about 45 minutes?"

"I should be in the main office, right inside the locker room. That's my usual station and I also monitor the equipment. Well, have a good workout!" As Piper walked away, she had a spring in her step, no question about it. That Max.

The prospect of her social media problems being solved gave Callie a faint feeling of hope. If she was able to hang onto Callie's Kitchen, that is. She watched Jane's office out of one eye, but Jane did not emerge.

Dashing self-pitying thoughts from her mind, Callie finished her exercise, followed by a walk around the track to cool down. Toweling off her sweaty face and neck, she headed to the locker room in search of her would-be social media savior.

No one was in the office when Callie returned, so she waited a few minutes, scanning the walls featuring ads for exercise classes: spinning, Zumba and Body Pump all sounded good, if strenuous. When Piper didn't return after a 10-minute wait, Callie decided to go to the desk and leave a note along with her business card. Since she didn't have her purse with her, she started searching the drawers for pencils and notepads. The top drawer was open and right on top was a notepad with the Bodies by the Bay logo.

Callie was just finishing her note to Piper when the young woman breezed in. "I was just writing you a note. Here's my card," Callie handed the notepaper and her business card across the desk to the young woman.

"Thanks!" Piper beamed. "You can reach me here on Mondays and Wednesdays from 1-5, or Max can reach me too."

"Wonderful." Callie discarded her towel in the bin outside the office as Piper followed her out. "While I was looking for something to write on, I noticed a few drawers were locked. I'm sorry if I disturbed anything private."

Piper glanced around her and noticing a group of women trooping toward the showers, she ushered Callie back into her office and closed the door. "It's not what you're thinking. We don't have cash or anything in the drawers. But we've had an epidemic of another kind of theft."

"Theft? If you don't have cash, what are they taking?"

"Syrup of ipecac." Piper opened the first locked drawer and removed a small bottle. Callie recognized it immediately; she remembered when the pediatrician had suggested she have it in the house for accidental poisonings. She'd had a bottle when Olivia was very small, hadn't bought any for years. In fact, she didn't think you could get it over the counter anymore.

"You know what this stuff does?" Piper made a face. "It makes people throw up. It's supposed to be used in case of an accidental poison ingestion and we had it as part of our first aid kit – you know, just in case somebody mistook cleaning fluid for their sports drink or something. Teenagers and older women have been stealing it."

"What for?" Callie believed throwing up to be one of life's worst experiences. "They are purposefully drinking it so that they toss their cookies?"

"Yes," Piper looked grim. "So many people who come here do so for the right reasons — to be healthy – but a surprising number of people want to binge and purge. Ipecac helps them to purge and they work out trying to lose even more weight. So we've started locking it up. I wanted to get rid of it altogether but Jane said no." Piper shrugged.

"It used to be recommended that all parents and food service people have it, but I'm pretty sure that my doctor said it's not even available over the counter any more, just by prescription." Callie shook her head. "It must be hard to get these days. If your doctor suspects you of an eating disorder, you definitely won't get a script for ipecac." She was thankful that she viewed food as something positive, but so many women did not.

"I know. It's weird," said Piper. "Not to change the subject and I hope you don't mind my asking, but how did it go with Jane? She seems really down."

No kidding. "It went fine?" Callie realized she had made her statement sound more like a question. "Yes, well, Jane seems exhausted more than anything. I told her to take care of herself."

"I know. I heard she had a miscarriage," Piper whispered. "It's doubly sad because she's been struggling with infertility. The pregnancy was a really nice surprise." Piper blushed deeply. "I'm not supposed to know that, but working here, you hear things."

When Callie didn't respond right away, Piper seemed to realize that she'd been indiscreet. "Please know that I wouldn't tell just anyone about Jane, but you're one of the only people who seem to have reached out to her, bringing her treats and everything. Even with all of the people Jane knows, I don't think she opens up to most people."

Was Piper this insightful about everyone she worked for? Maybe she wouldn't be an asset to the shop. The last thing Callie needed was a mind reading co-worker analyzing her behavior and relationships! Then again, it could be that Piper was simply thoughtful and cared about others. Desperate to find cheap labor for her Internet needs, Callie decided to believe the latter, for now. She thanked Piper again and headed out of the office to freshen up before heading back to work.

After a brief shower, Callie slipped on a scoop neck T-shirt with the Callie's Kitchen blue-and-white logo and some jean capris before sliding her feet into ballet flats. In all of her preoccupation with Jane Willoughby and Piper's revelations, she realized that Sam might be trying to reach her. She checked her phone, but Sam still hadn't followed up on her original text. She must still be busy.

Debating whether or not she should hunt Sam down at her office, Callie made a beeline for the exit, head down. Suddenly, she walked straight into what felt like a brick wall.

"Jeff, are you OK?" Callie rubbed the spot on her shoulder that took the brunt of the direct hit. Her old college friend didn't appear hurt but he did appear embarrassed. Once they had both apologized to each other several times and ascertained they had no injuries, Jeff laughed.

"What are you doing here? I never see you at this time of day!" He was kind enough not to mention that no one usually saw her at the fitness center, no matter what time of day.

"I just stopped by to see Jane and decided a workout might do me good," Callie offered by way of explanation. There was no reason he would need to know about her private attempts at sleuthing.

Jeff nodded slowly. "Great idea. That's why I'm here, too. It sometimes helps to get moving. Figured I'd use my gym membership while I can still afford it." He gave another mirthless laugh.

Callie hugged her old friend spontaneously, grateful for his kindness after the last stressful, strange and tragic few days. "Thanks again for stopping by the other day." She hesitated. "Can you tell me what happened to your shop? I'm really sorry to hear about it." Minette had vented about her troubles, but Callie felt like she hadn't heard the whole story.

Jeff smiled sadly. "I'm hoping we can bring it back. I just applied for another loan, but you know how difficult loans are these days. I've decided to start looking at other options, too, like investors. Jane Willoughby said she might even invest. That would be great but still, she wants us to have a complete financial assessment first. I don't blame her, but I hate to give up Minette's Chocolates. It's like giving up a huge chunk of my life – and Minette's life, too, of course. She's pretty upset about it, as you probably noticed the other day."

Callie nodded encouragingly, making sympathetic noises.

Jeff looked at his shoes. "Even if we have to leave Crystal Bay and start somewhere new, as long as we can have our business, that would be fine with me. Minette says – well, that there's nothing to keep us here anymore. In fact, I'd really like to get away if we could and make a fresh start. Maybe even head up to Madison — where we fell in love."

Wowza. Jeff was romantic and handsome, too. He was obviously a regular at Bodies by the Bay, if his muscled physique was any indicator. When she had hit his chest, it had been impressively broad and unyielding.

"I'd miss you both. But whatever you decide, I'll support you. We're friends, we need to stick together." Callie smiled at Jeff.

"True enough. Well, I'll let you get back to whatever it is you're doing. I know you've been through a lot lately."

"Thanks. Keep in touch, okay? Have Minette give me a call when she's up to it."

"You bet." Jeff nodded. "See you, Callie."

Callie watched Jeff walk in the direction of the rock climbing wall – a fitness club amenity that Minette and Jeff loved and that she had always wanted to try but had never had the nerve to do. Then, she scurried out of the fitness center before she could bump into anyone else.

Ten

Despite her unaccustomed exercise routine, Callie faced another night of insomnia that had her straggling into work early the next morning. She felt lonely, scared and sad.

Samantha had finally called her on her new cell phone the previous afternoon. For the first time, her friend and lawyer had sounded grave. "Callie, the fact that they want your knives is concerning me. Let me see what I can find out. There was nothing you could do if they had a warrant, but from now on, I want you to call me immediately before you speak to the detectives or give anything to them again."

"No problem," she'd answered Sam. "But do you really think they'll want more from me?"

Sam had paused for a very long time. "I just don't know. Let's hope not." Not reassuring.

What Callie needed was some time with Olivia, Viv and George. A dinner at home with the family would be the perfect time to tell her daughter that Hugh and Raine were going to take her out of school for a few days. OK: she had a plan. Time to get cracking, as Viv would say.

Callie decided to check her freezer for some prepared meals to take home to her family. Ironically, she was becoming her own target customer — someone with no time to cook for herself. After looking over what she had already made, she decided she would take some of Olivia's favorite Greek chicken with cinnamon-scented tomato sauce and some lemon potatoes, plus a salad and some warm pita bread, a very similar dinner to the one she had offered Steve Willoughby the other night. Callie felt hungry just thinking about it. After eating almost nothing during the stress of the last few days, her appetite was returning.

Looking around her warm kitchen filled with delicious cooking fragrances, Callie squared her shoulders with resolve. True, her clientele had dwindled to almost nothing. But if she could clear her name, she knew she could find a way to bring them back. They were afraid, that was all. And she didn't blame them. Still, doubts pulled at the edges of her brain. Maybe she was delusional – she'd never known anyone in Crystal Bay to be in this position. She could be finished and just not know it yet.

No! Those thoughts weren't going to help. Just cook, she told herself. Cooking always helped her to think.

Callie was crumbling feta cheese into a Big (Low) Fat Greek Salad to take home to her family that night, when her new cell phone started bleating.

"I'm so glad I caught you. Something's happened," Samantha said in response to Callie's greeting. Her friend sounded out of breath.

An icy fist gripped Callie's heart. "They're going to arrest me? Or no, it's not Olivia is it? Is she OK?"

"She's fine. So are George and Viv. And so far, no one is charging you. No, I'm calling about your client Lucille, from the bank."

Callie felt her sunny kitchen begin to spin as Samantha delivered her next phrase. "Lucille is in the hospital. Somebody tried to kill her."

As she took in this news, the rich scent of soup on the stove and lemon cookies made Callie feel queasy.

"What? How? I just saw her yesterday!" Why did people always say that they just saw a dead person or victim of an accident?

Samantha's usual ebullience was subdued as she delivered the details. "A worker found her unconscious in the whirlpool at Bodies by the Bay. They think they scared off her attacker – she had been hit in the head and it looked like someone had planned to drown her – or boil her to death. The heat in the whirlpool had been set to dangerous levels. But whoever it was escaped before anyone at the fitness center could see them. You'd think in-shape people could run a little faster, wouldn't you?" Samantha often turned to sarcasm when she was most upset.

"That's terrible! I just can't believe it." Callie ran the faucet for a glass of water and took a long drink.

"This is getting crazier by the minute," Samantha said, sounding exasperated." Does Lucille's attacker have anything to do with Drew's murder? That would make the most sense, but who knows? Or is it a completely separate killer running around Crystal Bay?" Samantha paused and her voice was calmer when she spoke again. "Of course I want you to tell me what you've learned, especially if it can clear my favorite suspect. We can meet up and discuss the rest later."

"OK. Just let me interject something I forgot to tell you yesterday. I found out that Drew had financial problems and guess who let me know about it? Lucille. Jane Willoughby is not herself – in fact she seems pretty depressed and out of it. Plus, she doesn't really like Lucille. There's more, but let's wait until we see each other. But forget about all of that for now – is Lucille going to be OK?"

"I haven't spoken to anyone at the hospital – family members only. But we can visit her at home at some point, maybe once she's released."

"What time did this happen?" Callie asked. "I was at Bodies by the Bay yesterday morning for the first time in months."

"Lucille was attacked late last night. She went to Lakeside in the early evening and worked out for an hour. The place closes at 9 but they start clearing the customers at around 8:45. The staff is limited by 8:00 pm. According to workers, the pool area was clear – no one was even swimming laps. It is getting colder outside. I wouldn't feel much like swimming." Samantha snorted before continuing.

"Anyway, Lucille said she was in the whirlpool after her workout and the next thing she knew she was being dragged out with a massive bump on her head and a splitting headache. It looks like somebody hit her and tried to drown her but was interrupted before they could finish the deed."

"But someone must have seen something!" Callie protested. "If there weren't any people in the pool area then whoever did this must have been visible!"

"I did speak to one of the workers there this morning. They weren't letting anyone inside, of course, since it's a crime scene. Still, plenty of people were milling around outside. The person I spoke with told me – I think her name was Piper – told me that when Lucille got bonked on the head, the workers were already beginning to clear out the locker rooms and were on their cleaning rounds. It was the end of the evening, the place was nearly empty and nobody was really paying attention."

Piper again. She seemed to know quite a lot about the fitness center for a part-time worker. Still, what she had told Sam seemed plausible. Callie remembered that there were no lifeguards at the indoor pool – one reason that she always accompanied Olivia to any parties her classmates had there when she was very young.

"What about security cameras?"

"I don't know. I've never seen any in there. Maybe."

Callie thought for a minute. "Why don't you come over tonight?" she asked her friend. "I feel funny talking about this at work." As they were speaking, Callie had felt that same prickle of fear on the back of her neck that she had when going to her car the other night, as if she was being watched.

"Let's see," Samantha said, and Callie could hear her tapping on her smart phone. "I've got a late client. But I can stop by your house after work at around 8:30 if that's OK. Maybe I'll even have some more info for you by then."

"Fine by me. I'm asking George and Viv to dinner. Let's not share this news about Lucille in front of Olivia. She seems OK regarding Drew's murder, but now this? I don't want to push it."

"I won't say a word," Sam said. "I don't really feel like dwelling on it either."

Callie decided to change to a better subject – food. "We're having dinner courtesy of Callie's Kitchen. I'm going straight for my own wares tonight — no extra cooking for me. Anything special you'd like?"

"I probably won't make it for dinner, but I wouldn't pass up some dessert. How about those Greek cookies you make – with the powdered sugar."

"*Kourabiethes*? I'll bring home two dozen – they're small." Sam chuckled and rang off.

Callie put her head in her hands after she hung up the phone. Hugh was right, unfortunately. Olivia would be safer with him right now. She had always prided herself on being able to provide a good home for her daughter, with lots of loving family around her. With a killer on the loose – maybe two killers and one of them possibly gunning for her, she was forced to admit that Olivia might be in danger, too.

A tap on her shoulder made her jump.

"Sorry." Max looked sheepishly at Callie from underneath his spiky haircut. "I didn't mean to scare you."

Callie put her hand on her heart. "Where did you come from? You're not on the schedule."

"I know. I came by to thank you." Max's eyebrow ring lifted as he offered Callie a broad grin that crinkled his eyes to slits.

"Thank me for what?" Callie finished blowing her nose on the tissue and then walked to her hand-washing sink, Max on her heels.

"I heard you offered my friend Piper some work at the shop. She's so excited! I know she'll do great work." Max leaned against the counter and folded his colorfully tattooed forearms.

"Word travels fast." Callie observed, drying her hands and tossing her paper towel in the trash. "Piper seems like a smart young woman. And by the way, she even helped me on the treadmill. Offering her some work was the least I could do for preventing me from flying off the machine."

"Yeah, she told me that you'd met. I was in the area so I thought I'd stop by and say thanks. Hey, I also wanted to let you know that it looks like somebody is inside Drew's bistro. It's still closed but I saw some movement in there."

Seize the day, Callie told herself. This was her chance to check out Drew's bistro. She was desperate for a look inside – maybe she could find something to help her lose her suspect status.

"Max, would you mind keeping an eye on my food – and an eye out for any customers, should they arrive." Callie was already removing her kitchen apron.

"Sure," Max said, uncertainly. "Is everything all right?"

A plan was formulating in Callie's mind. "Not exactly. I'll tell you all about it later."

Max gave her a knowing look. "Gotcha. No problem, go ahead. I'll hold down the fort."

Eleven

Callie ducked out the back door and headed down Garden Street towards Drew's bistro, elegantly named "Drew." It used to bother Callie that there was no apostrophe "s" – it seemed an affectation. But Drew was adamant and thought that the name of his restaurant struck just the right note. She felt sad once again when she thought of all of Drew's plans and hard work dashed by a crazed killer.

Caught in her own thoughts, Callie was startled when she looked up and saw she was standing in front of "Drew." The signage was written in tasteful script on the bistro's front window. That window had been a coveted spot among couples on a date. Callie and Drew had sat there a few times and received excellent service and curious glances, something they'd joked about at the time.

Putting those memories out of her mind for the time being, Callie peered in the front window. She thought she saw a large figure moving around inside the building. She had a strong suspicion as to who it could be – but what was he doing there if the restaurant was closed?

Callie decided to walk around the back door to the kitchen delivery entrance. She really didn't want anyone to see her going into the restaurant. "Chef!" she called, banging on the steel door. "Are you there?"

After several minutes, the door was opened by a harassed-looking man in his late thirties: Chef Johan. Callie remembered him from previous visits, rosy-faced and smiling, his large, meaty hands presenting an elegant plate of food while she and Drew beamed at each other.

Now, the chef's sandy brown curls were in disarray. His impressive belly strained the front of his blue work shirt and Callie noticed large circles of sweat underneath his armpits. At 6 foot 4, he loomed over her. Callie remembered Drew telling her that Johan was from a long line of German Wisconsinites, which accounted for his large size – and his name.

"Yes? What are you doing here – Callie, is it? What do you want?" Johan all but growled.

"I lost a key to my shop and I'm retracing my steps." Callie fibbed, looking up at the chef, smiling sweetly. "May I come in and look for it? Drew might have had it in his office."

The chef eyed her for a minute and ushered her in, quickly closing the door behind them. Callie noticed that the dark circles under his eyes were deep. Was no one in Crystal Bay sleeping anymore? The whole town should do a commercial for a sleep aid.

"I'm not even supposed to be in here," Johan confessed, "So hurry up! We've got to get out of here, soon." He looked at Callie with disgust. "Your boyfriend was a crook. He hasn't paid me in two months! I'm clearing out my things and getting out of here for good. I don't care if this place never opens again. If it does, it will be without me."

Callie went for sympathy, anything to get him talking so that she could stay. "Johan, I'm sorry. I didn't know."

"Yeah, yeah. Right. Someone was funneling money his way but he wasn't giving it to me." He peered at her more closely. "Are you rich or something?"

"Not exactly." The understatement of the year. "I wasn't giving him money. My business has barely been surviving and I've got a daughter to take care of." Not to mention a demanding Yorkie. "What are you talking about?"

"You really don't know?" Johan sighed. "Some investor. Sorry, I didn't really think it was you. I know your story. We all know each other's stories in Crystal Bay, right?" Johan rolled his eyes. Callie realized she knew less of people's stories than she had previously believed, but she allowed Johan to continue his rant. "As you probably know, he was a hot commodity with the ladies."

Callie felt her color rise but kept her voice calm. "Truly, it doesn't matter to me, Johan," she replied. Inwardly, she was stung. How many women was Drew seeing and was she truly the only one who didn't know details? And by the way, Callie hated it when guys referred to women as "the ladies."

The arrogant chef had irritated her enough that she forgot about his intimidating manner and size. "Did you ever see him with anyone specific?" she persisted.

"Oh, you know," Johan said walking briskly into the kitchen. Callie followed, taking two strides for each one of his. "He had women to dinner here sometimes, but usually in groups. Last week The Chamber of Commerce was here for lunch. Jane Willoughby was here and that lady who runs the chocolate shop. Minette, that's it."

The chef stopped and stared up at the ceiling. "Let's see, who else? A few other women who I think were from Crystal Bay College, and that rich older woman who lives near the water."

"Mrs. DeWitt?" Callie asked.

"Yeah, I think that was the name. Maybe she was his investor."

"Then there might have been a conflict of interest," Callie said slowly, trying to digest the information Johan was flinging her way. "She was one of the prime financial backers for The Taste of Crystal Bay, for goodness sakes."

"Is that right? What planet do you live on? Everybody you know is honest and above board? It must be nice!" The chef wiped his sweaty red face with a dish towel and threw it back on the countertop.

Callie laughed lightly, hoping to diffuse his anger. "Not at all, I'm just surprised to hear that about Mrs. DeWitt. If you'll let me into Drew's office, I'll be out of your hair in few minutes."

The chef grumbled to himself as he took a big ring of keys off of a hook and walked with a heavy tread toward the office. "If you left your shop key here, you're lucky that Drew didn't break in and steal all of the cash from your register. Good luck!" Turning the key into the lock, he flung open the office door. Callie sped inside before the disgruntled chef could change his mind.

Once she was alone, Callie opened the pack of rubber gloves she had brought with her and put them on. She didn't want to leave her fingerprints for the police to find and misconstrue. Ironically, the more she had to prove she wasn't a criminal, the more she had to behave like one.

Quickly and quietly, Callie opened each drawer. Nothing. No laptop on Drew's desk, either. Carefully, she looked in each drawer and each nook and cranny in his office as best she could. Still nothing. The police must have taken the computer. Or maybe the killer had this computer, too.

Drew's office was as clean and neat as his home. He had a few decorations, including a small Eiffel Tower on his desk, probably in tribute to the French bistro cooking that showed up on the menu at the restaurant. A few odds and ends, some sticky notes but nothing much else was left on the desk. Drew was as tidy here as he was at home.

Surely the police had already been here, so what was left for her to find? Realizing that time was short, Callie racked her brain and suddenly she remembered how she helped Olivia find things she thought she had "lost." Her daughter spent a lot of time sitting on the floor reading or working on art projects, so things always wound up under her bed or dresser.

It was worth a try. Callie crouched down and started peering underneath the desk and cabinets. She saw some dust but not much else. The police had obviously been thorough in their search. Not ready to give up, she decided to sweep the room again. She pushed at the bookshelves and opened the desk drawers as quickly as she could, but found nothing of interest.

Well, that was that. Callie was ready to leave when the realities of the situation suddenly hit her once again. Drew's presence seemed to be everywhere, from his desk décor to the many books he kept in his shelves. She was bemused to see that Drew had a sizable French cookbook collection, including some wonderful vintage titles. Callie picked up an old book on French patisserie, blinking back tears as she thought of Drew's passions and talents, now wasted. The tears came faster and she decided to prop the book open on his desk while she searched for a tissue.

As she reached into her purse, she spotted a printed book plate that read: "To Drew: With Love, from Kitty."

Kitty?

Suddenly, the sound of raised voices made her look up.

"That jerk wasn't killed by a chef," Johan was saying. Loudly. Callie stepped up to the door and listened. "You're not accusing me, are you? Whoever did it can't have been a chef." Oh no, Callie thought. Was that who she thought it was?

"Calm down, friend," came a familiar voice. Detective Sands. Callie felt sick. What was he going to do when he found her here? She looked around for an escape route, but there was none. Carefully she opened the door a crack and peeked out, straining to hear their conversation.

"I'll tell you exactly what I told the police the first time they came around the question me," Johan said. His rosy cheeks were turning a decidedly unhealthy shade of purple.

Callie saw Sands take a small step back, but Johan pushed his face into the detective's nose, his wholesome features taking on a frightening leer. "No chef would disrespect his tools in that way. No respectable chef would use his chef's knife to kill someone. Our knives are sacred. We'd find another way. Personally, I would have beaten the crap out of him."

The chef took a step back and Callie watched Sands carefully. He looked disappointed, like he'd have loved a reason to book the angry chef. The Angry Chef – it sounded like a show on The Food Network.

Callie decided the only way out of this mess was to stick to her original story. Rearranging her features into what she hoped would pass for a calm expression, she sailed out of Drew's office cheerily. "Thanks, I couldn't find my key," she said, then feigned surprise when she saw Sands. "Why, Detective. What are you doing here?" Miss Innocent.

Sands cocked his head to the side. "Well, well. I'm sure I'd like you to answer the same question. I'm running a murder investigation. You must know you don't belong here, so whatever could your excuse be?"

She smiled as graciously as she could. "I'm just leaving. I was looking for an extra key to my business. Drew had a spare and I thought maybe it was still here." She looked at Johan who was eyeing her and Sands, a smirk on his face. "I didn't find it though." She nodded at Johan. "I appreciate your letting me in."

He grunted. "No problem. I was just leaving, too." Both he and Callie made for the door but Sands' sardonic laugher cut through the air as he stepped in front of them.

"Not so fast, you two. Ms. Costas, do I need to remind you that this is a very serious matter indeed. No more poking around offices where you don't belong. Johan – I've not ruled you out either. If I catch the two of you in here again, I'll let you both have a nice overnight stay at the Crystal Bay police station." Johan rolled his eyes, but Callie simply nodded at Sands. "You're absolutely right, Detective. You won't see me again."

Sands looked like he wanted to say more but just then, his phone rang. He looked at the two of them. "I've got to take this. Ms. Costas, meet me outside in a moment. I'm going to make sure that you leave the premises. Chef, we'll speak more later."

"I can't wait," Johan retorted as Sands walked toward the dining room. He stayed there, facing the kitchen, his eyes narrowed in concentration.

"Tell you what," Johan said, and started back to an area of the kitchen that wasn't visible from the dining room. "Come on," he said when Callie hesitated. With a glance at Sands, she followed him and

watched as he reached to the top of a tall kitchen cabinet. "I'm really sorry I snapped at you like that before."

"Don't worry about it." Callie answered. What did Johan want now? "You're under a lot of strain," she said in a soothing tone, hoping to keep him mollified.

Uneasily, she eyed the countertops in Drew's state of the art stainless steel kitchen. As usual, a knife block rested in one corner. The chef grunted as he shifted his considerably bulky torso. Reaching again with one of his long arms, he felt along the top of the cabinet, searching blindly for an item he had presumably hidden there.

Finally, he found what he was looking for and thrust it at Callie. "Drew left this at the restaurant and I was going to try to sell it to recoup some of my pay. Since I don't like that detective, I'm giving it to you. You never know, it might help. Anyway, I wouldn't trust this Sands guy if I were you."

Callie refrained from telling the chef that what he was doing was illegal when she saw the item he casually passed to her with his callused hand.

Twelve

Holding the unexpected gift tightly to her chest, Callie smiled and nodded to Chef Johan as she slowly backed away from him. "Thanks," she said over her shoulder as she headed out to the dining room and went to join the detective who was placing his phone in his jacket pocket. He gave her a reprimanding look that made his hazel eyes crinkle up at the corners and motioned her outside.

Sands waited until they were a several feet away from the building before speaking. "What the bloody hell were you doing alone with that guy? He could be very dangerous." Callie was surprised to see that Sands looked a bit shaken. "I'd prefer not to have to Taser any suspects today, thank you very much."

"I didn't mean any harm. Anyway, I thought I was the one you suspected."

Sands raised his eyebrows. "True. But as I told you before, everyone is a suspect until further notice."

"I'm trying to help, not that you seem to think so," Callie insisted. "For example, look what I have for you." She proffered the iPad to Detective Sands. "I think this belonged to Drew. The Chef gave it to me just now."

"What?" Sands' eyes blazed. "Just now?"

"Yes. And he said he's been selling things off from Drew's restaurant to recoup his pay. He claims that Drew hadn't paid him for two months."

"Oh, he's been selling off Drew's goods has he?" Sands fumed. "I've got to go back and talk to him. But I need to trust you to leave and not come back. I mean it. I don't want to see you snooping around anymore. Searching for a spare key? Nice try. You don't fool me for a minute. Understand?"

"Yes," Callie said. "But I gave you some valuable evidence. So I can't be all bad."

"That remains to be seen," Sands said gruffly. "Now I've got to talk to that Chef and you've got to walk away from here. Got it?"

"You bet," Callie answered. Sands gave her one last stern look and then turned back towards the bistro. Johan was outside, locking up and muttering to himself.

"I'd like another word, please," Callie overheard Sands say, as he approached Johan.

"Well that's just great!" Johan cried. Callie scurried down the street and didn't look back.

Garden Street was buzzing with the usual amount of tourists and local shoppers. It all looked so normal, as if Drew hadn't been murdered and Callie wasn't a suspect. If only.

Just then, an eerie feeling of being watched prickled the back of Callie's neck. She told herself not to be so spooked. Her sudden chill was no doubt due to a brisk breeze blowing through Crystal Bay, letting everyone know that summer was officially on its way to becoming a distant memory.

As Callie headed back to work to pick up her car, she passed Minette's Chocolates, still with its "Going Out of Business" sign. Jeff was inside, alone, diligently polishing display cases. He didn't notice her.

Callie realized that she'd forgotten to tell Sands about the Kitty note in Drew's book. If she was going to display a cooperative attitude, she'd have to let him know about that right away. Put it on the to-do list with everything else.

* * *

Despite the tragic events of the last few days, the tone at home was lively that evening. As it had so many times before, the combination of George, Viv, Olivia and Koukla warmed up the room. Callie found that she could hardly hear herself think in the din created by George telling stories about the Olympia and filling drink orders, Viv exclaiming with Olivia over her granddaughter's latest school exploits and Koukla barking at a neighbor's Great Dane who was taking his nightly walk past her home.

Callie couldn't help but wonder what was on the iPad she'd given to the detective. Would he find information that would clear her...or further implicate her? Unpleasant waves of anxiety washed over her. When she'd called to invite them to dinner, she'd told George and Viv about the seizure of her knives and her cell phone, so at least she didn't have to break that news to them this evening.

Still, there was a precarious family peace at hand. George had been wild until she'd told him that Samantha was doing what she could to help. Viv was kindly sympathetic but a worried crease had permanently developed above her nose. Callie swallowed the lump in her throat and put on smile for Olivia.

"Dinner's ready!" Callie called from the kitchen.

The group assembled at the table amidst a lot of laughing and joking that helped ease Callie's heart. Koukla sat patiently by her bowl, situated by the back door of the kitchen. She knew that Callie or most likely, George, would put some tasty scraps there if she gave them puppy dog eyes.

The food looked good and smelled even better. Greek chicken stew really hit the spot tonight. Swimming in a light but rich tomato sauce with the barest hint of cinnamon and bay leaf, it was Olivia's favorite dish and one that Callie's customers clamored for. The idea of adding cinnamon – something most of Callie's clientele thought suitable only for sweet dishes – was a little odd for some of her customers. However, once they took a bite, Callie's clients were hooked. Thinking of her once-bustling food business wasn't going to help her stay cheerful tonight. She decided to put her business woes out of her mind, at least for the duration of the meal.

Callie passed pita bread around the table and dug into her food. As soon as she began to eat, she realized that the aching pit inside her stomach wasn't just anxiety and fear – apparently it was hunger, too. The food was making her feel better.

Callie sipped the white wine that George had brought with him – piney, clean-tasting *retsina* that went well with the hearty meal. Viv stuck to her white zinfandel, which she drank nightly, under doctor's orders, of course.

George smiled across the table at Callie as Olivia told him an elaborate story about one of her friends at school, complete with dramatic hand gestures. Callie decided that this was as good a time as any to let her daughter know that Hugh would be taking her to visit him for a while.

"Olivia, how would you like to stay with Dad this week?" Callie took another sip of wine and waited.

Her daughter ripped off a piece of pita bread and stuck it into her mouth. "What about school?" she said.

"No talking with your mouth full," Callie admonished, but with a smile. "You'd miss one day. I'll talk to your teachers. Your dad wants to take you out on his boat for a mini vacation while the weather is still nice."

George frowned. He wasn't one for shirking responsibilities – work or school – but Callie shook her head at him ever so slightly. She waited until Olivia was intent on more bread and then mouthed "Drew" to her father. His forehead slowly unwrinkled as he lost his stern expression. Now, he nodded at his daughter, looking sad.

"Well, I like to go out on the boat. I always miss something important, though, even when I don't think there's anything special going on! Like the time we went to Chicago and I missed the author who came to school with a dog. "

Callie tried not to show her exasperation. Olivia had talked about the dog who came to school for over a week. "I know you hate to miss any action, sweetheart, but Dad and I agreed that a break might be nice for you. I'm sure you'll have a wonderful time."

Viv chimed in. "When I was in school, I would have loved to play hooky in the early fall. It's my favorite time of year, still warm, with the leaves just beginning to turn."

Olivia's eyes sparkled at her mother. "Grandma is right. Fall is my favorite time, too. Tell Dad I'll go."

Callie beamed at her wise grandmother. "Then it's settled. Why don't you call Dad after dinner and tell him to pick you up tomorrow after school. You can stay through the weekend."

Olivia speared some more chicken with her fork and dunked it in sauce. "Do you think he might take me up to Madison, too?"

"Ask him. I'm sure he will if he can." Whew. Once Olivia warmed to a subject, she really warmed to it.

The rest of the meal passed peacefully, at least outwardly. Koukla finally got her wish when George mixed some un-sauced chicken in with her kibble and then gave her a bite of pita bread. Callie had never known a dog that liked pita bread before Koukla.

After everyone had eaten their fill of stew and bread and Olivia had eaten half a dozen *kourabiethes*, Olivia and Viv cleared the table while George ran water in the kitchen sink for the dishes. It was wonderful to have a nice, normal family evening for a change, especially when they cleaned up after themselves so readily.

Callie checked her mobile phone for the time: 8:00. She had some time before Samantha arrived and she wished she could have some time alone before her friend arrived, to collect her thoughts as much as anything else. As much as she appreciated having the clean-up done by others, Callie decided to boot everybody out of the kitchen. All she wanted to do was lie motionless on the sofa for 10 minutes.

"Are you sure we can't finish for you, darling?" Viv asked.

"No, Grandma. Thanks, though. I'll probably leave this until a little bit later. Sam's coming over soon and I just want a few minutes alone. Sorry. I'm just feeling really overtired."

"Of course you are, after all you've been through! And besides, you work too hard." Viv shook her finger at her granddaughter. "No sense burning the candle at both ends."

Callie shrugged. "I won't. I don't think I have much wick left to burn!"

After making Viv promise she wouldn't do any more cleaning, Callie went looking for George, who was cooing over Koukla in the living room. "Dad, thanks for coming over. I'm going to rest for a minute before Samantha gets here and then I'll put Olivia to bed. I'm exhausted."

George straightened up and put both of his hands on his daughter's shoulders. "Are you sure you shouldn't stay with Samantha or me, just for a while? You might be worried about your own daughter, but you are my daughter and I'm worried about you!"

"I'll be fine. Really. But thank you, Dad." George meant well but he fussed around her like a mother hen. That is, when he wasn't offering what she called "lectures," but which he felt were simply normal conversations. In any case, she didn't want to put him in harm's way. Sam was a dear friend, but Callie couldn't imagine living with her for even a few days. Their schedules were completely at odds and besides, Callie felt like she needed the comfort of her own home around her.

"Just remember, *hrisi mou*, I'll be watching you." George's eyebrows furrowed into a thick line over his nose as he frowned at his daughter.

"I know, Dad. I know." Possibly George's sentiments weren't as comforting as he had intended.

Thirteen

Finally, with much fanfare, Callie had seen everyone out the door. She'd even handed a container of rice pudding to George, despite his protests. She loved rice pudding as much as her dad but after Jane's unkind remarks about her weight at Bodies by the Bay the other day, Callie had no appetite for dessert.

As soon as she'd locked the door behind her and called up to Olivia who yelled back that she was out of the shower and in her room, Callie staggered to the sofa and fell onto it. Her head swam with fatigue and tears filled the corners of her eyes.

Though she tried very hard to prevent it, Callie's thoughts turned to the iPad. Who knew what secrets it contained – if any? And why was Chef Johan so quick to unload it? Had he looked at it first? He could have been spooked by what he'd seen there. Not a comforting thought.

Even worse, what if Johan was the killer and he'd taken it from the crime scene? But if that were the case, why would he give it to Callie? Her heart pounding at this possibility, she realized that while the chef might not be a genius, he probably wasn't too stupid to do that.

So much for resting. Callie decided to check on Olivia.

Her daughter was in her room, combing out her long wet hair with her eyes glued to a book. Kissing her daughter on the top of the head, Callie heard the doorbell ring. She walked tiredly down the stairs and peered through the small window at the top of her door.

Instead of Samantha's well-groomed, expertly coiffed personage waiting on her doorstep, it was Detective Sands who stood there, wearing casual clothes instead of his usual suit. He looked different, younger. Callie felt her muscles tense in alarm. What was he doing here?

For a second, Callie considered ducking down and pretending that she wasn't at home. Unfortunately, Sands had seen her peering through the small window at the top of her door. He gave her a jaunty wave and Callie had no choice but to let him in.

"Hello, Detective," Callie said trying to suppress her worried thoughts. "I'm surprised to see you." She stepped aside to let him in the house.

"I'm not here on an official visit, don't worry," Sands said. He gave her what appeared to be a genuine-looking smile. Callie noticed that his front tooth was slightly and somewhat charmingly crooked.

"Oh." Callie was taken aback. "Just so you know, my attorney is due here any minute so if you have any questions for me, maybe we should wait for her. I don't know if I should really be talking to you on my own anymore." She peeked behind him, hoping that Sam was striding up the walkway but no such luck.

"I understand your concerns. Might we sit down? I'll explain why I'm here."

Callie nodded and stepped back, allowing Sands into her living room. "Have a seat," she said, gesturing. "Like I said, I do have a friend on her way over and it's an early day for me tomorrow." Trying to reel customers back in, that is. But she didn't share that thought.

"Of course." Sands waited before Callie was seated before he sank into her sofa. She chose a nearby chair and tried not to fidget. If he noticed her edginess, he didn't comment on it.

Koukla ran from the kitchen and jumped around the floor near the new visitor's feet. "A Yorkie!" Sands noted cheerfully and patted Koukla's head. She wagged her tail and then jumped up next to him on the couch looking for more love. Callie just shook her head. Sands continued to pet Koukla while he spoke.

"Callie, I don't know if you heard, but there has been another murder attempt. Lucille from the bank was attacked. I believe you know her."

Callie exhaled. So, this wasn't going to be about her knives. "Yes, Lucille is a client of mine. I'm very happy to hear that she will recover."

"Yes. Do you know anything about this attack?"

"No. Just what I've overheard."

"I understand you are a member at Bodies by the Bay."

"Well, I guess you could call me that. I hardly ever go there." Exhaustion overtook Callie and she blurted out. "You can't think I had anything to do with this, Detective? Lucille is practically the only client I have left."

"Ah," Sands said, crossing one leg over the other. "Well, just so long as you don't continue snooping around, I want to thank you for the information on Johan and for the iPad he gave to you."

This was so unexpected that for a minute, Callie couldn't say anything. She didn't trust Sands, though in other circumstances she would probably have liked him.

"You're welcome," Callie replied. "Any news on that? Or my knives? Or my phone?"

"I can't discuss the investigation with you. I can only tell you that it's proceeding." Sands leaned forward. "I also want to suggest that you be careful, especially because you do have a young daughter."

"Well," Callie said, and stopped. What did that mean? That he thought she was endangering her daughter with her criminal ways, or that he was not sure if she might be involved anymore? Was that why he showed up at her home? Or did he do that just to unsettle her? She wished she'd paid more attention to Samantha's stories of crime and police procedure.

"I almost forgot," Callie said, determined not to hold anything back. "I found a note when I was at the bistro today. It was inside a cookbook and it said "To Drew: With Love from Kitty." I don't have it – I must have left it at the bistro. I would have told you about it then, but Johan giving me Drew's iPad threw me. And before you ask, I have no idea who "Kitty" is."

"How interesting," Sands replied. "Kitty." He made a note. "Could it have been another girlfriend? No offense."

"It could have been," Callie admitted. She felt her face grow warm at the possible betrayal. "I just don't know."

Sands stared at her a moment. "OK, another question. How well do you know Lucille?"

"Not terribly well. She's a good customer. Most people really like Lucille. Still, it's fairly well known that she can be something of a gossip."

"So it's possible she may have been sharing some information that could have gotten her into trouble?"

"At this point, I'm willing to believe that," Callie answered. "And before you ask, I had nothing to do with this. I wasn't anywhere near the fitness center at that time – ask anyone."

"I plan to," Sands replied. Wonderful.

The doorbell chimed.

"Excuse me," Callie said, nearly leaping from her chair in her enthusiasm. She collected herself in time to prevent her body from breaking into a full sprint, and opened the door with a queenly grace that was purely for show. Callie couldn't put her finger on it, but the detective definitely seemed different tonight than he had at the police station. More relaxed, a bit nicer, but still, almost unbearably observant and alert. It put her on her guard.

"Sam!" Callie greeted her friend as if they hadn't met for years. "Come in, please."

She led Samantha by the arm, possibly a little too enthusiastically. "Okay, okay, I'm here," Sam protested, pulling herself from Callie's grasp. "No need to pull."

Callie shot Sam a desperate look and ushered her further into the room so she could see the unexpected guest seated on her sofa with her traitorous dog. "Samantha, you know Detective Sands."

Sands had risen from the sofa and Callie noticed Sam taking in his long blue-jean clad legs and crisp white shirt with an appraising eye before her mascaraed lashes suddenly started blinking. Or was she batting them at Sands? Was Sam flirting?

"Detective Sands. What a surprise." Sam looked from one to the other.

"Nice to see you too, Ms. Madine," Sands offered smoothly. "I'm just following up on a few things."

"Oh, really? Well, I hope you have some good news for us. This has gone on long enough."

"Sam, please. Have a seat. The detective was just telling me to watch my back, especially now that Lucille from the bank has been attacked."

Sands stood up abruptly. "I've said all I need to for now. I'll leave you to enjoy the rest of your evening. Ms. Costas, I'm sure we will need to speak again."

Wonderful. That was probably going to involve an "official visit."

Callie shrugged at Sam, got up and saw the detective to the door. He had a gentle, loping walk, probably because he was so tall. "Thanks for stopping by," she said. "But truly, I can take care of myself."

"Yes, I suppose you can." Sands stopped just outside the door. She was surprised at the warmth she felt when their eyes met this time. "Please make sure that you remain cautious, especially with a young daughter."

Callie was reminded of the picture of the little girl on Sands' desk she'd observed during the horrible trip to the Crystal Bay police station.

"Yes, of course. Good night," she said and closed the door. Her breath, which she hadn't realized she'd been holding, let out with a whoosh. Was his purpose in visiting to confuse her? If so, Sands had done a bang-up job.

Fourteen

"What was that all about?" Samantha sounded amused.

Callie flopped on the couch next to her friend. "I have no idea. I thought he was you."

"It's difficult to mistake him for me," Sam said, kicking off her heels. "He's much taller than me and much more handsome."

"Very funny," Callie answered. She decided to quiet her inner turmoil by playing hostess. "Sam, what can I get you? I've got so much food and those cookies you wanted. I've got wine, too."

"Thanks, I'll have a glass as long as you're already up. But you know you don't have to wait on me." Sam sounded weary.

"Don't worry about it," said Callie already on the move to the kitchen. "How about food?" she called out to her friend.

"Nah," Sam called back. "I'm not that hungry. Too tired."

Callie had learned that people always refuse food at first and then end up wanting to eat. To save a trip to the kitchen later, she put together a hummus and pita bread plate with some raw veggies and dug a half-full bottle of Riesling out of the back of the refrigerator. Placing everything on a tray, Callie sauntered back into the living room where Sam was flicking through her android phone, a frown creasing the well-preserved skin between her eyes.

"Sorry, no phones allowed. It's time to relax." Over Sam's weak protests, Callie gently removed the phone from her friend's manicured hand and put it on a side table.

"Anyway," she said, placing the tray within Sam's reach and handing her the glass of chilled Riesling, "since Sands was just asking me about it, let's start with the attack on Lucille. Anything new on that front?"

"Not really." Sam took a sip of wine and raised it in half toast to Callie before continuing. "Bodies by the Bay doesn't have security cameras. If you think about it, why would they?" Sam put her wineglass on the table in front of her and leaned back on the sofa cushions. "The fitness center is very low crime. Heck, the whole town of Crystal Bay has been low crime. Petty crime, yes. Kids stealing bicycles. Some DUIs. Murder and attempted murder, not so much." She started munching on the goodies that Callie had placed before her.

"I'm guessing they will install them now," she said through a mouth of food. "Sorry, I'm starving after all."

"That's disappointing about the security cameras," Callie agreed. "What I can't figure is who would risk trying to kill Lucille with people still in the vicinity? Maybe whoever did it was desperate."

"Jane Willoughby is high on my personal list of suspects," said Samantha. "Something weird is going on at Bodies by the Bay." Samantha shook her head.

"I agree that something strange is going on there," Callie finally said. "But I'm not sure it has to do with Lucille's injury in the whirlpool."

Samantha leaned eagerly towards Callie. "What?"

Callie picked up her wine and put it down again. "Max has a friend named Piper. He recommended her to me regarding social networking for my shop. The other day I was at Bodies by the Bay and I met her. Piper shared with me that they are having a rash of strange thefts regarding syrup of ipecac. It makes you, uh, toss your cookies."

Samantha abruptly dropped the pita chip, laden with luscious garlicky hummus, that she'd been about to pop into her mouth. "Callie, wait a minute..."

"I know. It's disgusting," Callie continued before Sam could finish. "Piper, Max's friend, said it had become a problem. She was wondering why Jane even stocked it anymore. It used to be an over-the-counter drug and was used for poison control, you know. In case someone had an accidental ingestion of something. Now, Piper is claiming that people are using it to purge."

"Callie, you're not going to believe this. The word at the office is that a strange substance was found in the food at Drew's house: syrup of ipecac."

Callie felt her mouth fall open in disbelief as Samantha came over and sat next to her on the sofa. Sam faced Callie. "I don't know why he would have done that, so don't jump to conclusions. We don't even know that he was the one that did it."

"Who else would have done it?" Callie replied, feeling her cheeks burn with humiliation. "Maybe he planned to prank me or something. I guess I never believed that he was so mean-spirited." Tears stung her eyes and she angrily wiped them away.

"I don't understand. Why make both of us sick? And when I, uh, found him, he hadn't been sick." Callie gulped as the image came back to her. "So obviously, he hadn't eaten the food. The only thing left is that he wanted to make me sick. I guess that's why he invited me over."

Sam took another sip of wine. "It's just a piece of the puzzle. I can't figure it out either."

"I know. It makes no sense." Callie put her face in her hands. "Nothing has made sense for days." Sam patted her on the back.

Finally, she raised her head and took a shuddery breath. "I realize now that I really didn't know Drew at all. For example, the head chef that worked for him told me that Drew hadn't paid him in over two months. He was furious."

"Where did you see Drew's chef?" asked Sam.

"Today. In fact, Sands caught me in the act of snooping. By the way, I found a note in a cookbook. 'To Drew: With Love from Kitty,'" she recited in a sarcastic singsong.

"Oh no," Sam groaned. "Well, whatever you were able to find, you've got to stay away, I'm serious. You're lucky you're not calling me from the station right now."

"I know, but I wanted to see if I could find any clues after they took my knives. Which brings me to my big question: why did they take them? The murder weapon was on the scene." Callie felt queasy just thinking about it.

"I couldn't find out much. Obviously, the detective isn't going to tell me anything. However, I kept my ear to the ground and spoke to a few crime lab colleagues, off the record, of course. It looks like the police assume that the killer brought their own knife, a professional grade. So it's possible that they're trying to match up different knives to see if they could have been contained in a set."

"Why not take my knives from home?" Callie wondered. "Is that next?"

"I don't know," Sam fretted. "I suppose it could happen but don't give them anything without calling me. Where do you get your knives, by the way?"

"The tools I use at home are good but cheap. A lot of stuff I've gotten from basic kitchen departments and such. But at work, I've got the professional-grade stuff. I guess I got carried away when I opened my own business and ended up spending a bundle."

Sam nodded. "Well, I'll let you know the second I hear anything."

"OK," Callie decided to change the subject. "Getting back to this latest incident with Lucille, I was thinking of visiting her when she gets out of the hospital." Callie started clearing Samantha's clean plate, mentally congratulating herself on correctly anticipating her friend's hunger. She walked to the kitchen and placed the plate on the counter, eyeing her knife block as she did so. She shuddered.

"Yeah, OK, but why?" Sam asked when Callie returned to the living room and flopped back down on the sofa.

"She's a good client, Sam. I'll bring her some cookies or brownies, something. Her assault may have nothing to do with Drew's murder, but what if it does?"

"Tread lightly," Samantha advised. "I don't know about this. If you do visit her, keep it breezy. You don't want it to seem like you're trying to tamper with a witness. As your lawyer and friend, let me tell you that you can't be too careful. Promise?"

"I promise to be careful. But maybe she will remember something that will help me."

"All right, Miss Marple. Don't say I didn't warn you. Speaking of cookies, how about you give me some for the road? I'm beat and I know you have to be at work early tomorrow, too."

Callie packed up some *kourabiethes* for Sam and saw her to the door with hugs and promises to keep her snooping to a minimum.

Hauling herself upstairs to bed, Koukla hot on her heels, Callie wondered about the spiked food, Lucille's attack and especially, Detective Sands and his impromptu visit. Better watch out for that guy, she thought, but with regret, recalling his hazel eyes and sandpapery voice. He was dangerous in more ways than one.

Fifteen

Callie dreamed of the ocean that night, not a peaceful vacation-friendly ocean, green-blue and white with froth, buoying up swimmers as they swam happily in the calm waters. The ocean in her dream was angry and dark, with cold black waves that threatened to pull her under. It took all of her strength to fight the powerful current; it was dragging her down, further and further into the cold, deep water.

Struggling to swim to the top of the imaginary ocean, Callie woke up. No wonder she couldn't breathe. Her head was under her pillow, the fluffy cotton fabric right near her open mouth. Her blankets and sheets were twisted around her legs and Koukla had retreated to the far corner of the king-sized bed. When she saw her mistress sit up, she ran to her, licking her face. Koukla had a way of making even the worst dream seem ridiculous.

Still, the nightmare left Callie feeling uneasy. Deep down, she believed that she was simply missing something and if that elusive "something" occurred to her, she would be able to figure out who had killed Drew and why Lucille had been attacked.

Suspects were everywhere: Chef Johan, for one. But was he angry enough to kill? Even Mrs. DeWitt didn't escape scrutiny. Chef Johan had mentioned that she had been at Drew's bistro shortly before his death. She was strong, physically fit and she lived near Drew's home.

And what about Jane Willoughby? She was hiding something and she had a link to the substance found in Drew's food. And Minette. Johan said she'd been at a lunch held at Drew's bistro. Then there was Jeff and even Jane's husband. What did he know about the fitness center and the odd goings on there?

What about Piper? And Lucille? Could they somehow be involved? Callie frowned as she thought about them. Each young woman seemed to know a lot of information that they really shouldn't.

Thinking back to her nightmare, Callie realized that she loved the seasonality of the lake and the bay, the beauty and the peace. Was she simply unexciting or was she smart to play it safe?

Play it safe. Ha! These days Crystal Bay was anything but safe. And speaking of safety today was the day for Olivia to be picked up by her dad. Hugh was leaving work early and arriving at Callie's Kitchen by four, after Olivia's school day ended. Callie looked at her clock. It was only seven o'clock, but she had to hurry. Max should be there now, but she wanted to put some extra time in to make up for all of the errands she'd had to run lately.

Callie called to her daughter as she pulled on some capris and a long-sleeved T-shirt with the Callie's Kitchen logo. Koukla sat on the edge of her bed watching her, no doubt wondering why her usually calm and cuddly owner had been thrashing about earlier like a trout in a net. "It's time to get up."

Silence and more silence. "Olivia!" Callie called again, quickly gathering her hair into a ponytail. She peeked into the mirror. These nightmares weren't doing much for her under-eye circles – and hurriedly put on some concealer, blush, powder and lip gloss. Not ready for a photo shoot, but better.

Callie sat on her daughter's bed. "Come on, honey. Don't dilly dally today. We've got to get going."

Olivia buried her head under her covers. "I don't want to go to Dad's." Uh-oh, thought Callie. Not now, I've got to go! Inwardly, she fumed but she tried to keep the frustration out of her voice when speaking to her daughter. After all, the kid was as shaken up by Drew's murder as she was.

"Why not, Olivia? You seemed fine with it yesterday. Aren't you looking forward to a break from school?"

"I guess," her daughter said, sitting up. "But I like school. And anyway, Raine is kind of a pain. Hey, that rhymed!" She giggled and rubbed sleep out of her eyes.

Callie hid her smirk from her daughter as best she could. Samantha would love that one: Raine the Pain. "What do you mean? I thought you liked her." It couldn't be true. Was she really going to have to convince her daughter to like her father's new wife? Apparently so. Ex-wife of the Year Award, here I come, thought Callie.

"Oh, she's all right, I guess. But she's always asking me how I AM and what do I want to DO. She doesn't just let me sit and read a book, like you do. She doesn't just let me BE." Olivia scowled.

"I see. Well, at least she's thinking about you and wants you to have a good time. It could be worse, you know."

Olivia did not look convinced. "Anyway, Mom, what about you? Will you be safe? I don't like you being all alone." So that was it.

"I'll be fine." Callie smoothed her daughter's tangled hair. "I've got Koukla, *Pappou* George and Grandma Viv to keep an eye on me." And, Callie silently interjected, I've got Detective Sands on my trail like a bloodhound.

Callie smiled at her daughter's sleepy face. "Look, when you get back, I promise we'll have a great time together. You can have a friend for a sleepover. Rent movies. I'll take you bowling. Whatever. But right now you've got to get ready to go. You'll be late for school and I'll be late for work." Callie stood up. "I'm making coffee. Want a waffle?"

Olivia brightened at that. "Lots of syrup?"

"Sure."

"OK. I'm up." Livvie had lowered her feet to the floor, so Callie left the room. The house rule was that you had to have your feet on the floor to truly be "up."

* * *

Callie tried to relax as she drove to work, taking time to appreciate the route. She smiled as she passed a hand-painted sign that read "The Sweet Corn Lady" and made a mental note to buy some ear corn before it was no longer available for the rest of the season. She passed The Cove Skating Rink, with peeling paint and a weather-worn statue of a bearded pirate looked like he'd seen better days – and he had. The place had been around since George's day and Callie had spent a fair amount of time there as a middle-schooler and teenager.

In those days, there just weren't that many places in Crystal Bay to go, but Callie recalled that she had always enjoyed herself at The Cove. No doubt, when her time came, Olivia would go there too unless a new business popped up and knocked the old pirate out of his spot. In the current economic environment that didn't seem likely.

Cool air blew through the window as Callie passed Lake Shore Drive and turned onto Main which led directly into the Garden Street business district. Rolling up her window, she looked at her car's digital clock. Not too late. Hopefully, Max could serve the customers while Callie stocked lunches and dinners in the main freezer section at the front of the shop. Max had said he would do some baking this morning, too.

Callie parked behind her shop and noticed garbage piled high in the alley behind Minette's – were they moving out for good? If she ran into Jeff, she'd ask him but she hoped not. He'd seemed so optimistic at the fitness center the other day.

Opening her door, a sugary smell of homemade cinnamon rolls wafted out, the scent making Callie's mouth water. She'd been eating so little lately, surely one cinnamon roll couldn't hurt? Or how about half a cinnamon roll with some fruit? That sounded much more virtuous, but not nearly as satisfying.

Callie nodded a "hello" to Max who stood at the front of the shop arranging muffins, banana bread and today, cinnamon rolls. Unfortunately, he was not joined by the usual slew of morning customers. Only two or three unfamiliar faces, tourists, probably, waited to be served. Well, maybe they had friends. Customers or not, her morning baked goods presented a tempting array.

Callie walked back to the kitchen where she poured herself some coffee and pulled a hot roll from a tray in the kitchen. She popped a piece in her mouth and sighed. The rich cinnamon flavor, flaky pastry and rich creamy frosting dispelled the last remnants of her horrible dream.

"Hey, how's it going?" he greeted her. "Aren't these great? I made the dough when I got in and have been baking them all morning."

"Thanks, Max. There IS something about cinnamon, isn't there? Especially when it gets chilly outside." Shuddering, Callie remembered the cinnamon coffee cakes she'd baked for Lucille's meeting at the First Bank of Crystal Bay. That had been her only big order in quite a while.

Customers or no, her business was still officially open and there was food to prep, an activity that was normally quite soothing to Callie. It required concentration but it also served as a balm to frayed nerves. Cut up the fruit and vegetables, cube the butter, peel the potato, and stir the soup. The work you did with your two hands had an immediate result – a delicious finished dish. Comfort food could be just as comforting to prepare as it was to eat.

Caught up in her food prep work, it took Callie a minute before she realized that Max was no longer ringing up their meager amount of customers. He'd rejoined her in the back of the shop to clean up the cinnamon roll ingredients and dough scraps.

"Max," Callie said adding salt and pepper to the *avgolemono*, aka Greek egg-lemon soup, she was stirring. "I'd like to meet with Piper about social media. I don't know if it will help attract customers in the current climate, but maybe I can create some more positive buzz around Callie's Kitchen. At least I'll feel like I'm doing something."

"Sweet. Great idea. Why don't you get in touch with her and arrange a time? She'd love to help, I know it."

"That's wonderful," Callie answered, feeling her shoulders relax a bit. "I have to pop out later, but I'll be here by 4:00 pm. My ex-husband is stopping by to take our daughter to his house for a few days. You know, just until things settle down around here."

Max nodded. "Piper has school and work today, so I'll text her and see what she can do."

That settled, Callie wrapped up some kitchen duties, and glancing at her wall clock, decided if she was going to visit Lucille today, she better do it now.

Callie packed up some *kourabiethes* and a few of the cinnamon rolls for Lucille. She would skip the flowers in the interest of time. Food would have to be enough of a gift for her injured friend and client. Telling Max she would be back within the hour, she hopped in her VW and set off in the direction of Lucille's apartment.

Callie took the long way to Lucille's in an effort to calm down and focus. Lucille lived on the outskirts of town, near Crystal Bay College. Scenic Lake Shore Road, while not the most direct route, offered a pleasant view. The trees along the lakefront were some of the most colorful in town, and Callie enjoyed their beauty as she cruised purposefully along.

Soon she pulled up to a modern townhouse in a newer development set back from the main road. A small park with playground equipment and benches had clearly been designed to attract families with children. The semi-attached one-story home had six concrete steps leading up to the front door, which held a pretty wreath of dried summer flowers and a sign that said "Welcome."

But would she be welcome? Callie wondered if she should have called before stopping by, even though one of the bank tellers had told her over the phone that Lucille was resting at home today.

Hoping that she wasn't interrupting a peaceful nap, Callie rang the doorbell and waited. She heard soft footsteps approaching almost immediately and she let out her breath with a whoosh of relief.

"Oh! Hi, there," Lucille greeted her with most of her usual perkiness, but her eyes looked tired and she seemed pale. "What a nice surprise. Are those for me?" she asked, taking the cookie boxes.

"I thought you might enjoy some sweets. Plus, I wanted to stop by and see how you were feeling. Is it OK if I come in for a minute? Or am I disturbing your rest?"

"Are you kidding? I'm so bored I could spit. My head is killing me or I'd be at work today. Nothing is on TV and my head hurts too much to read. Please, come in." Lucille ushered Callie into the townhouse and closed the door. Callie looked around the room and spotted a slim console table. "Mind if I leave my purse here, right by the door? Otherwise, I might forget it. It's been that kind of week."

"Sure." Lucille shrugged. "I don't mind."

Slowly, the young woman padded down the short hallway in front of Callie. She wore big pink fuzzy slippers that clashed with her fashionable, slim-fitting terry sweatpants and sweatshirt. Callie stifled a smile – big pink fuzzy slippers were exactly what she would expect Lucille to wear around the house.

Lucille's sunny living room had a comfy looking sofa that was currently occupied a large gray cat. It looked balefully at Callie, and then went back to napping.

"Before I sit down, can I get you anything? I'm going to put these goodies in the kitchen and I was going to make some tea."

The idea of caffeine was too tempting for Callie to resist. "I'd love some tea. Thank you. Sure I can't get it?"

"No, I've been sitting around way too much as it is. Why don't you have a seat?"

Lucille padded into the kitchen, which was right next to the front entryway and Callie sank down onto a chair. A table in front of the sofa was littered with newspapers and magazines: People, Us Weekly, Food and Wine, The Food Network magazine, various fashion magazines and The Wall Street Journal.

"I didn't know you were so into food," Callie called to Lucille.

"Oh, I am," Lucille called back. "I love to bake, especially. I really admire what you do, in fact."

"Well, I'd like to sample some of your creations," Callie said, picking up the Food Network magazine and flipping through an article about making your own candy corn. Fascinating. Would she have patience to make her own candy and sell it at the shop? It could be a nice thing to offer, but it would depend on how time-consuming it was. What about homemade caramel apples for fall? That might work.

Lost in her shop-improvement thoughts, it took a minute before Callie realized that Lucille seemed to be taking a very long time in the kitchen; was she feeling weak and was just too proud to say so? She knew the feeling.

Callie stood up to offer her friend some assistance, but just at that moment, Lucille returned from the direction of the front hallway, holding two mugs. "I thought I heard the door." Lucille looked puzzled and her pretty face was decidedly paler. "This head injury has me seeing and hearing things, I swear!"

"You'd better sit down." Callie held Lucille's elbow to steady her. "You're not looking very well."

Lucille didn't appear to hear; she was talking to her cat. "Come on, Matilda," Lucille said, placing the two cups of tea on a side table and resuming her reclining position on the sofa. Callie returned to her chenille-covered chair facing the window. The cat looked up and went back to sleep by Lucille's feet. "That cat," said Lucille. "She loves to snuggle usually, but today she seems wary of me. She's mad that I left her when I went to the hospital, I think."

That provided Callie with the perfect opening. "I'm so sorry to hear about your attack. I'm just happy that you're going to be all right."

"You and me both," answered Lucille. "I was certain I was a goner there for a minute."

An awkward silence ensued and Callie broke the ice first. "Lucille, what happened exactly? Do you feel up to talking about it?"

"I guess so," said Lucille. Matilda finally crept up on her lap and she sat absently stroking the cat while it purred contentedly. "I've been driving myself crazy trying to figure out who would have wanted to hurt me and I truly have no idea."

"Did the assailant say anything when they, uh, hit you?" Callie asked.

Lucille blanched a bit and didn't answer right away. "Sorry," Callie said. "I know this is emotional for you."

Lucille shook her head and looked pained. "Ouch. I keep forgetting not to move my head too much," she said, smiling weakly. "It's not you. The whole thing was just so strange. There I was, relaxing in the hot whirlpool and the next thing I know, someone has a death grip on my neck. I mean, really squeezing. Then, they whisper in my ear 'You're dead.'"

Sixteen

"Lucille, that's awful!" Callie cried.

"Tell me about it," Lucille replied. "Then, before I can blink, everything goes totally black. I woke up on the side of the pool, my skin on fire and my eyes all cloudy and feeling woozy." She gave Callie a self-depreciating grin. "I'm just sorry I wasn't at my best for the paramedics. Some of them are so hot in this town, you know?"

Callie had to laugh and Lucille shrugged and giggled along with her. "So obviously you told the police about your attacker and what was said to you," Callie said, determined to get a straight answer.

"Yep. Including that one detective with the accent. I asked him how he wound up in Crystal Bay and he said 'The usual way a man winds up anywhere. A woman.' He was really nice, funny too. Like he wanted to put me at ease."

Callie took that in. Sands was charming, no doubt, especially if he didn't suspect you of foul play. Then again, Drew had been charming too, and look where that had gotten him.

"Lucille, did the voice sound male or female?" Callie asked.

The young woman stretched and shifted her body. She yawned before answering. "The detective asked me the same question. It might sound weird, but I just don't know. Sometimes I think it was a woman and sometimes I think it was a man. They were whispering, so their voice probably sounded different than if they had been speaking at full volume."

Drat, Callie thought. "You've been through some serious trauma. I can see that you're getting tired, so I won't stay." Callie stood up and gathered up her bag. "Is anyone looking after you? I could drop off some food after work if you like. Ready-to-eat meals – how about it?"

"The doctor told me to eat light with a head injury. I don't know – do you have any chicken soup or anything like that?"

"Yes," Callie answered, thinking of her special *avgolemono* soup. "I've got just the thing for you. I'll drop it off later."

Lucille yawned again. "That would be great, thanks. My mom is coming by today but she can't cook. Don't tell her I said so." The young woman reclined back on the sofa, seemingly exhausted. "I'd see you to the door but I'm getting really tired. Thanks so much for stopping by. I'll look forward to the soup. Can you just slam the door really tightly when you leave? It will lock behind you."

"You bet. Take care of yourself, Lucille. Hope you're back to your old self soon." Lucille nodded and then sank down in the pillows contentedly, the cat asleep on her lap.

Callie retrieved her bag from the front hallway, carefully closed the door behind her and then tried the lock. It didn't budge, so she walked down the steps, thinking.

Lucille had been indiscreet about several people. However, Callie had always considered herself to be one of Lucille's special confidantes for no other reason than the young bank worker was very free with her information. What if this chatty young woman viewed others as special confidantes, too? She was very friendly and just about every business person in town had an account at the First Bank of Crystal Bay. Her attack did not sound random. Or did someone simply think she knew something, based on the fact that she was viewed as a busybody?

Hardly anyone was on the road, so Callie was back at work shortly. She washed her hands at the separate hand-washing sink and checked on her *pastitsio* or Greek macaroni, as Olivia called it. It was baking on low heat – Max had obviously kept an eye on it while she was at Lucille's house and it gave off a tantalizing aroma.

"Thanks for watching the oven," she called to Max as he returned to the kitchen. If nobody showed up, *pastitsio* would freeze well, but after today, Callie might have to start watching her use of fresh ingredients. She chewed on a pencil as she debated canceling a few orders with suppliers. But would that do more harm than good?

Just then the bells over the door jingled and in walked Olivia with Hugh and oh, goody, Raine. Telling herself to be nice, she walked out to greet her daughter.

"Hi honey," she said greeting Olivia first and bending down to give her daughter a hug. "Hi, Hugh, Raine," she said straightening up and tugging her T-shirt more firmly over her waist. "Where's George? He was bringing Olivia to me."

Hugh opened his mouth to answer, but Raine, laughing, cut him off. "Oh, we all got here at the same time, isn't that just so funny? So we thanked George and said we can take it from here."

Raine looked straight into Callie's eyes. "Your dad is just so wonderful. And what a character!" She sighed and tossed her long blonde hair over her shoulder. Callie knew that Raine's father had died a few years previously, so perhaps she was sincere in her effusive admiration for George.

Raine was a striking woman, something that Callie realized anew each time she came into contact with her. And she couldn't be more unlike Callie. Raine was tall and buxom, with a large frame and a pretty, girl-next-door face. Her long blonde hair hung in waves and her fashion choices were a dizzying array of colorful team sweatshirts and holiday-themed sweaters.

Today Raine was resplendent in a bright yellow and green Packers hoodie, jeans and Nikes. She looked a bit like an overgrown cheerleader, the complete opposite of Callie's darker, more ethnic looks.

Not a bad person at all, thought Callie. Just, a little much at times. But apparently, her bubbly nature was a hit with Hugh. He beamed at Raine. "Yes, I've always liked George myself. He's a good guy."

Pleased to have her sometimes difficult father praised, Callie smiled faintly and addressed her daughter. "Do you have everything you need?"

"We packed last night. Remember?" Olivia was bouncing around, looking ready to go. In her heart, Callie was glad her daughter was excited once again. She would hate to send her off miserable, even though she was missing her already.

"Hugh, I think I've got all the asthma meds and stuff in there. You guys can call me any time if you have questions or need anything. I'll leave my cell phone on." Callie stopped herself when she realized that she sounded a bit desperate. Things would be fine. Her daughter would have fun. Raine would eventually change into a sweatshirt that wasn't so neon.

Hugh hugged Olivia to his hip. "I think we'll be OK, but thanks. You ready to go?"

"Yes!" Olivia said enthusiastically and everybody laughed. Raine sounded like a bubbling brook.

"Sweetie, why don't you take Livvie to the car," Raine addressed Hugh. "I just want to look at all this good food! I might pick up some food for us to take home."

Hugh looked more closely at his wife, suspiciously, it seemed to Callie. "I'll see you out there. Bye, Callie." Olivia hugged her mother and then skipped out of the shop before Callie could say "Don't forget to take a shower tonight!" Maybe that was just as well. She got the feeling she was nagging her daughter too much lately.

Callie was so engrossed in thinking about how quiet her house would be that night without Olivia that she wasn't immediately aware that Raine was gazing at her with an intense, sympathetic look on her face. She had stepped closer to Callie and frankly, she was invading her personal space.

"Raine, let me show you some of our specials for today," Callie offered, taking a step back. What was up with this woman?

"Oh, sure, maybe in a minute. That was just an excuse to talk to you. I wanted to tell you how sorry I am about your boyfriend. What horrible news! We read all about it in the paper."

Raine put her hand on Callie's shoulder. "Hugh and I were so happy that you'd found someone. And now he's gone." If Callie weren't so annoyed, she was sure she would have found this statement moving, along with the tears that were beading on Raine's long-lashed blue eyes.

"We were so happy that you were moving on," Raine said, looking down and dabbing at her eyes with a Kleenex she apparently kept stuffed in the sleeve of her sweatshirt. "You know, like Hugh and I have moved on." The odd thing was that Raine seemed totally sincere, not intentionally nasty or mean-spirited.

Raine was sobbing in earnest now. "You seem like such a wonderful mother and you have so much style. Look at you!" Raine blew her nose and gestured at Callie's outfit which consisted of her Callie's Kitchen t-shirt and slim-fitting capris. Maybe if you were used to dressing in team apparel, this was the height of fashion.

"In fact, your daughter is such a dear and you two are so close, that you have inspired me! Hugh probably didn't tell you, well, why would he?" Raine's bell-like laughter swept through the room. "We're trying for a baby ourselves."

Callie gasped and tried to hide it with a cough. If only life had a "delete" button. She would have just deleted the last 10 minutes and then she would never have to be stuck replaying this crazy conversation in her head ever again. Callie tried to formulate a response, but found that for once, she was speechless.

A baby? That made her think about things she usually tried very hard not to think about. Had Raine bought Hugh matching green and gold boxer shorts to match her Packers sweatshirt? She remembered hearing that men's fertility increased if they wore boxer shorts. Don't go there, she told herself.

Luckily, Raine appeared to have misconstrued her distressed look. "You look like you've seen a ghost!" said Raine. "I'm sorry; I shouldn't have brought up the topic of Drew. Really, I just wanted to offer my sympathies."

Finally, Callie found that her voice had returned. "I'm fine. Really. Thanks for your kind words of...sympathy. It's just difficult to talk about Drew right now." And to hear your husband's new wife talk about their plans for procreation!

"I had something else I wanted to tell you." Callie wanted to plug her ears, but Raine plowed on, relentlessly. "I don't know if Hugh shared this with you, but we were both interviewed by the police about the murder." She spoke the last word in a loud stage whisper that was probably heard on the sidewalks outside.

"You were?" Now that was interesting. If she was a suspect, her ex-husband would be one, too. After all, as far as anyone else knew, Callie and Drew were having the hottest love affair since, well, since Hugh and Raine. Hugh could have been a jealous husband. A jealous, murdering husband. That is, if he cared anymore, which he obviously didn't. According to Raine, Hugh was well on his way to making new Green Bay fans and his former wife was not on his mind.

"Yes. But we were at an ABBA cover band concert with some friends and lots of people saw us, so we were off the hook right away." An ABBA cover band concert? Oh boy. Callie stifled a laugh at the image of Hugh, a notoriously bad dancer, shaking it to "Dancing Queen."

Raine leaned in closer and Callie noticed a streak of mascara under one of Raine's teary eyes. They sparkled at her next question. "What about you? Have you been cleared of suspicion?"

"Um, well. I'm not really authorized to talk about the investigation." No one had come out and told her that, but it sounded good. Sands would be pleased. Sands kept turning up like a bad penny but she'd rather see him right now than converse with Raine another second.

"Thanks so much for chatting and for taking Olivia for a few days, but I really should get back to work." Callie tried to assume an air of extreme busyness by bustling about the front of the shop,

"It's our pleasure!" Raine said. Callie decided not to mention the mascara smear. "You hang in there, now. You're a tough cookie!" Raine glanced down at the artfully arranged cookie display case and giggled again. "A tough cookie! That's fitting!" She laughed to herself as she walked to the door, then turned back to Callie and waggled her fingers at her. "Goodbye! We'll have Olivia call you!"

Callie forced the corners of her mouth into a smile, nodded and waved back. As soon as Raine had disappeared out the door, she sank against the display case, drained. Well, you had to say one thing for Raine: she was more upbeat than a brass marching band. But all that talk about reproduction with Hugh? That had to stop.

To soothe her frayed nerves after the unexpected encounter, Callie finished some more kitchen tasks. Max came up to her in the kitchen, all smiles. "Piper is going to meet us here in about 15 minutes. He looked around and lowered his voice. "She said she would be happy to be your social media consultant."

"That's great!" Callie said. Then she remembered that she'd left her new cell phone in the car. Even though her daughter had just left, she wanted her phone on hand in case Olivia needed her. As an afterthought, she grabbed her purse. Maybe she'd stop by Minette's Chocolates and see if they had any of those truffles Lucille liked so much. Her friends would probably appreciate the business, even at this, their eleventh hour. She could drop off the indulgent candies later, after she delivered *avgolemono* to the bank worker, as promised.

"I'm going out for a minute," she called to Max. "Be right back."

A rush of air in the alley startled Callie about the same time that she heard footsteps running towards her. Before she could turn around, a sharp crack on her head turned everything black.

Seventeen

Callie felt very cold. Why was her mattress so uncomfortable? She knew it was probably time for new one, but she didn't understand how her bed could turn into a slab of concrete overnight. She tried to roll over and find a more comfortable position, but wait. It was time to go to work. No, she was too tired.

A muffled voice said "It looks like she's coming around." Callie wanted to open her eyes, but her head hurt so much she couldn't do it at first. Finally, she forced her eyelids open a crack and the light made her whimper in pain.

"Oh my god, oh my god," a female voice kept saying. She tried to place the voice. Was it Livvie? The thought of her daughter needing help made her grit her teeth and force her eyes all the way open.

Two faces stared down at her. At least Callie thought it was two faces – or maybe she was seeing double because the light was so bright and her eyes didn't want to open all the way. As she concentrated on focusing her eyes, Callie realized that Max and Piper were peering down at her.

She was not in her own bed but instead, she was sprawled on the pavement in the alley behind her shop. Callie slowly turned her head to the left and then to the right and found herself staring underneath the dumpster of her business. Max had told her he'd seen a rat back there the other day but thankfully, Callie had not seen any of the rodents herself. The thought of them made her shudder.

As she struggled to sit up, Max and Piper each took a shoulder and tried to make her lay back down. "Not so fast, huh Callie?" Max's worried voice pierced her painful brain fog. Piper had removed her cardigan sweater and had bunched it up as a pillow. The sweater was as soft as a cloud under Callie's aching head and for a moment, she relaxed until she remembered that she was lying in an alley. "Let me up," she croaked.

Max looked at Piper and shrugged. "Let's get her up, I guess. On the count of three we lift her, okay?" Piper nodded. "One, two, THREE!" Callie was grasped tightly, one person hoisting her under each armpit into a sitting and then a standing position. She felt herself swaying forward in their grip and tears of humiliation and pain came to her eyes. "Let's get her inside," Max said. "Callie, we'll keep hold of you. Can you walk?"

"I think so." The trio made their way slowly and carefully into the kitchen and Callie was helped to a chair. "You guys can let go. I can sit on my own." Max and Piper backed away from her, but stood nearby.

"What happened? You say goodbye to me and then next thing I know, I'm taking out the trash and I nearly trip over you lying next to the dumpster. Did you hit your head?" Max appeared extremely worried and in her fuzzy state, he came across as a bit impatient, too.

Callie struggled to remember the exact chain of events. "I don't think I fell and hit my head. I think someone hit me and then I fell. That's it. Someone hit me on the head. They must have knocked me out for a minute."

"Oh geez, Callie, you're going to need to see a doctor. Now. You could have a concussion. Any nausea? Can you see how many fingers I'm holding up?" Max held three thick fingers in front of Callie's face.

Piper, on the other hand, was as cool as the Greek cucumber-yogurt sauce Callie's clients clamored for in the summer months. She smacked his hand away. "Max, you're not helping." She gave Callie a worried look. "I think we should call an ambulance, that is, unless you want Max and me to drive you over to the hospital ourselves."

Callie squinted at Piper, her head aching in the bright lights of her kitchen prep area. No, she didn't want Max and Piper to take her anywhere. Maybe she was grumpy and out of it from being hit on the head, but why did she have the feeling that Piper was always seeing her at her worst?

"I think I'll have my father drive me. I'm up and I'm talking, I'm not nauseated." As a seasoned mother, Callie knew the warning signs of concussion. "I think I need to see George right now." Her throat constricted and she felt like crying. She knew he'd chew her out for finding herself in the middle of a dangerous situation – again – but his strength would be comforting right now. Callie was frightened to the bone.

"If one of you will just give him a call," she continued, swallowing the lump in her throat. "My dad's number is... Uh. It's...."Callie couldn't remember. Her head was still too foggy. She looked at Piper who was still gazing at her with a concerned expression. "Will you get me my purse? I had it with me when I got hit. It might still be in the alley."

Piper nodded and dashed towards the back door of the kitchen.

"Max, why do bad things keep happening?" Max looked at his sturdy black shoes and didn't reply. Callie rubbed her face. "I'm just glad that Olivia wasn't here. She could have gotten hurt, too."

"Everything's been screwed up since Drew got himself killed," Max muttered.

"Got himself killed?" Callie was aghast. "Are you blaming him for being murdered?"

Max didn't want to seem to meet Callie's eyes. He was about to speak again when Piper rushed in from the alley.

"Your purse – it's gone!"

"Oh no," groaned Callie. There went her driver's license, credit cards, health insurance cards, card for the money-dispensing "Tyme Machine" aka ATM – pretty much everything.

As reality dawned, Callie felt a cold chill begin at the top of her head and ran slowly down her spine. She'd been attacked, just like Lucille. She was lucky to be alive! Callie started to stand up and felt her knees buckle. Quickly, she returned to her stool.

"What was in it?" Max and Piper asked in unison.

Callie looked from one to the other. "All of my cash, credit cards, driver's license, health insurance. You know. Nothing big." Pain and fear turned Callie's voice bitter and she instantly regretted her tone when she saw Max's eyes narrow. "But I'm lucky I'm not hurt worse than this." Pain shot through her forehead. Maybe she'd spoken too soon.

Max faced Piper, his hair even spikier in profile. "Let's go look outside. Maybe the thief dropped Callie's purse in a dumpster or something, or left some evidence behind. You never know."

"Good idea," Piper said. They started for the door and then Piper looked back. "I don't know if we should leave you alone."

"I'll look on my own," Max said. "You stay with Callie. I'll call her dad when I'm done looking for her purse."

Max left and Piper peered closely at Callie. "Do you want some water?"

"Sure." Callie's headache was extremely painful but at least she wasn't seeing double anymore. She accepted a glass and took a cautious sip. Well, what to talk about? Why was Piper here? Oh yes, computers and social media.

"Max says you're quite the computer expert."

The young woman looked pleased. "I love computers. As a kid, I got kind of good at cracking codes and that hooked me."

Callie looked at her. "Cracking codes?"

"Oh my goodness, nothing serious! I never went after government files or anything. No, I just loved to figure out passwords, codes, etc. It was kind of a game to me. But I stopped – I won't do that here!

Now I'm really interested in the Internet and social media. Anyway, cracking people's passwords is just too easy."

Really? "I'm just curious. How do you go about hacking into somebody's personal computer or iPad?"

"If you know what you're doing, it's not that difficult. I mean, some people even have passwords that are ridiculously easy to figure out. Like, did you know that the word "Password" is one of the most commonly used?"

"I guess people are afraid they'll forget their password so they use something they are sure to remember." Callie began to shake her head and thought the better of it as a sharp pain raced across her cranium. Touching it as gently as she could, she was alarmed to feel a tender bump growing.

Piper charged on, warming to her subject. "Right. So a lot of times, people go for the obvious: their street name, pet's name, kid's name, their middle name, something like that. Or they go for really simply numerical codes: Literally 1, 2, 3, 4. If you know something about the person, it's usually easier to decipher the code. A lot of people choose something that's important to them, but something they think others won't figure out." Piper's eyes flashed with excitement. She looked like a fresh, blooming flower and Callie knew she looked like a wilted weed. Still, Piper hadn't just endured a concrete nap in an alley after a blow to the head. Fair was fair.

"You enjoy cracking codes," Callie prompted, taking another sip of water. It tasted metallic, so she set it down on the counter.

"I do. Basically, I really like puzzles. And don't worry. Like I said, I don't use this skill at work."

"I'll be sure to remember that," Callie replied, closing her eyes. She opened them when Max returned to the kitchen, out of breath and with dirty stains on the front of his shirt. The aroma of garbage clung to him, and Callie felt her stomach turn over.

"Sorry I was gone so long, but I looked in every dumpster and trash can near the shop. Nothing. I guess whoever took your purse wanted money and credit cards." He walked over to the wall phone. "Your dad's number is right here, Callie. I'll call him now."

She nodded gratefully at Max and continued to ponder the attack. How many times had she entered that alley – even late at night – and been as safe as Koukla in her doggie bed? Hundreds of times. It seemed like too much of a coincidence.

Callie was starting to get sleepy, not a good thing with a head injury. She had to stay awake. Maybe if she stood up and took a walk, she would feel better. As she rose from the stool, Piper jumped up and grabbed her arm. "I'm getting tired, I think I need to walk," Callie said. Suddenly, she really, really wanted to be rid of Max and Piper. Hurry up, Dad, she thought to herself.

"I'll take your arm." Piper grabbed Callie's left bicep and Callie let her, but decided she was going to give the orders from now on. "Let's go back to the alley. I want to see if anything looks amiss."

"Are you sure you should?" Piper asked, but Callie was already pulling her in that direction so the younger woman let her take the lead.

Stepping out into the alley, Callie peered left and right. Everything looked normal and she could faintly hear the usual buzz of the after-work crowd that descended on the local shops before heading home for a quiet evening. Well, some of them were heading home for a quiet evening. At least one of them was a killer still on the loose and the other was a purse thief.

The only difference that Callie could see was that the trash from Minette's Chocolates was no longer there. Someone must have tidied up – so maybe somebody had seen her attacker.

Callie turned to go back to her shop when suddenly she heard her name being called. Carefully, she turned in the direction of the voice.

"Are you hurt?" It was Mrs. DeWitt and Minette. Callie nodded but that gesture made the cobblestones of the alley seem to spin. She groaned and held her hand to her head.

"Get this girl back inside right now," commanded Mrs. DeWitt. She and Minette followed Callie and Piper into the kitchen and re-seated Callie.

Once Callie was settled again, Mrs. DeWitt spoke. "We were walking in the back door of Minette's and we saw commotion in the alley." When Callie filled her in on what had happened, Mrs. DeWitt narrowed her eyes at Max. "Why didn't you call 911?" she demand-ed.

Max and Piper looked sheepishly at each other. "Callie didn't want that. She wanted her dad to take her to the hospital. I just got off the phone with George Costas and he's on his way." Max sounded a bit defiant and Callie recalled that he had never seemed to like Mrs. DeWitt all that much. Apparently, she had told him that his piercings didn't look "appetizing" for someone in food service.

"Are you two crazy? Callie can't wait."

Piper was flushed, obviously embarrassed by being criticized by the formidable older woman. "Max and I were helping her."

"Well!" Mrs. DeWitt exclaimed. She motioned to Minette who had been standing helplessly by her side. "Minette, you and I will take Callie to the hospital. Max," Mrs. DeWitt said his name as if the syllable were a dead mouse she was holding by the tail. "You call George Costas and tell him to meet us there."

Before she could protest or speak, Callie found herself being led to the back seat of Mrs. DeWitt's navy blue Mercedes, with Minette next to her, holding her hand.

"Callie, I'm so sorry!" Minette was tearful. "You could have been killed. Like Drew!" At this last, Minette was unable to control herself and burst into full-blown sobs.

"Minette, dear, you're supposed to be comforting her, not upsetting her. Get a hold of yourself!" Mrs. DeWitt's words were harsh but her tone was soft. "There, there. We'll get Callie taken care of and she'll be fine!"

"But my purse," Callie mumbled, feeling groggy but not quite as badly as before. "I don't have my health insurance card. Everything was stolen."

"Not to worry," Mrs. DeWitt sounded nearly cheerful. "I donated a lot of money to the hospital last year. They'll be only too glad to admit you once I'm done speaking with them."

The ride to the hospital passed in a blur. As Callie was whisked from the emergency waiting room and into the hospital's inner sanctum almost immediately, she realized that it was far better for Mrs. DeWitt to have accompanied her to the hospital rather than George. The registration nurse had apparently taken Mrs. DeWitt's suggestion about checking with the company for proof of insurance and Callie was certain things wouldn't have gone as smoothly without her.

"Callie! *Hrisi mou!* What now? I get a call that you're hurt and now I think – no! She's getting into trouble again. How could you?" George Costas burst through the doors of the hospital room like the hounds of hell were after him. That was all he had said though. George wanted to interrogate Callie, she knew. It must be killing him to stick to just that one short rebuke. However, out of deference to Mrs. DeWitt or the hospital setting, he was keeping calm, at least for the time being.

"How can I thank you two enough?" Callie asked Mrs. DeWitt and Minette as they sat with her. They'd insisted on staying, Mrs. DeWitt perhaps sensing that her presence was preventing George from erupting into a million questions and admonitions.

"Nonsense!" Mrs. DeWitt replied. "No thanks are necessary. What are friends for?" Minette nodded and smiled at Callie. Her tears had stopped once they entered the hospital.

"Yes," Minette echoed. "She's right. You'd do the same for us."

Callie was touched that Minette was waiting with her. Surely, she had bigger things to occupy her time. For example, earlier today it had appeared as if she and her husband were removing all of their equipment and furnishings out of the shop. Fleetingly, she wondered what had happened with their attempt at another bank loan. It couldn't have been denied that quickly, could it?

Mrs. DeWitt's influence was apparent in the quick arrival of a brisk young ER doctor who was prematurely bald with a kind face. He examined Callie briefly and then sent her for a CAT scan. Once it was determined she was not suffering from a concussion, she was released to the care of George who decided it was time to vent some of his fear and frustration.

"Callie, I'm glad you are all right. But I warned you to be careful. And do you listen? No!"

George pointed a finger at his daughter and took a breath, obviously gearing up for a long, loud tirade. Mrs. DeWitt frowned at him and stepped between him and Callie, who was holding her head in her hands and bracing herself for the onslaught. When Mrs. DeWitt stepped in, she looked up in surprise.

"George Costas," Mrs. DeWitt sounded like ice. George raised his shaggy eyebrows and was surprised into silence. "I know you're worried about your daughter, but I'll not let you stand here and scold her. She needs you right now. Now, are you going to behave yourself and take your daughter home to watch over her tonight as the good doctor has suggested? Or do I have to?" Mrs. DeWitt's eyes flashed with fire and even the ER doctor looked impressed.

George's olive skin flushed like a ripe tomato but he held his tongue. Callie knew him too well: there was no way he was going to let someone else take care of her. She was his project and his alone.

"Very well," her father said, attempting to smile at his errant offspring. "Callie, dear, you come with me. We will speak no more about this for the time being."

Callie gave a weak nod to Mrs. DeWitt who nodded back at her. To George, "the time being" probably only meant about half an hour, but at least it was a small reprieve. Who knew? He might even cool down, at least a little bit.

Once the ER doctor saw that the family drama was played out, he told George to watch her that night and wake her up every few hours, just in case. Callie was thrilled not to spend the night in the hospital, but too late she remembered her promise to Lucille. As she, George and her friends left the hospital, she relayed her visit with Lucille and her promise to bring soup to her injured friend.

"I'll call Max at the shop and he can deliver it," George reassured her. "With some soup for you, of course. The doctor said you should not eat much until you feel better."

"No problem there," Callie answered. "All of this drama and trauma hasn't left me with much of an appetite."

The four parted ways in the hospital parking lot with thanks and promises to check up on Callie in a few days.

George seemed to have absorbed the fact that he was needed by his daughter and he maintained a respectful silence as he drove along the lakefront. Callie shook her head at this new mood shift and quickly stopped. It hurt.

"We'll go to your house, Callie," George said as they drove out of the hospital parking lot. "I can sleep on the sofa. It will be better for you to be surrounded by your own things and anyway, there's Koukla to look after."

"Thanks, Dad. I know it hasn't exactly been our top priority today, but I should probably report my stolen purse to the police."

"Now, now, no worrying about trivial matters. You'll give yourself a bigger headache." George smiled at his daughter, his brown eyes crinkling up at the edges in the way she loved. "When Max initially called me, he told me that he would report the stolen purse and the assault while you were en route to the hospital. It's likely already been taken care of. Of course, you'll get questioned by the police again, though." George frowned at this last.

Despite zero desire to be questioned by the police, Callie felt that her stolen purse was the bigger problem at the moment. "My purse had everything in it! But you're right. I can replace most of it. At least they didn't get my new cell phone. That was in the car."

"See? It's not all bad news. Just remember that things can be recovered. People cannot." He paused. "Do you think your attack is related to Drew's murder? I think you should reconsider moving in with me until the killer is found."

Callie sighed, but quietly. George meant well, but she needed her freedom. Not that she minded the company tonight, though. Her head was pounding and George's presence would be supremely comforting. That is, if he kept up his promise and refrained from scolding her.

Once George had gotten her into the house, fed her some soup and given Koukla food, water and attention, he announced that it was time Callie got herself to bed. She was in no position to argue.

"I'll just stay down here," George said, settling on the couch with Koukla on his lap. He flicked on the TV in her living room. "But I will be checking on you from time to time, so don't let me startle you. I'll try to be quiet but I am going to have to wake you up, just to be sure you're fine."

"Thanks. Sorry for all of the trouble lately. I'll be more careful." Callie gave her father a hug.

George focused his deep brown eyes directly on his daughter's face. "Of course. But you must be careful, for the sake of the people who love you. Whoever is behind these actions, it isn't a game. No, this isn't a game at all," he repeated stubbornly. "This is your life."

As Callie lay in bed cocooned in her thick white comforter, her father's words echoed in her aching head. "This is your life."

Indeed: This was her life and she wasn't going to be a victim. Yes, this violent attack had made her more concerned for her physical safety. Alright, she was afraid, down to her bones. But Callie also saw it as progress. Maybe this latest attack meant that she was getting closer to finding the killer. If she was so close, how come she still didn't have any firm notion about who could have wanted Drew dead?

Or maybe there were two criminals on the loose: the one who killed Drew and the one who was running around Crystal Bay hitting women on the head. But why? To steal a purse? Lucille had nearly died and nothing had been stolen from her.

No, the three incidents – Drew's murder, Lucille's attack and Callie's assault outside of her shop had to be linked, she decided. If someone thought a head injury was going to stand in her way of finding out the truth, they were wrong. She wasn't giving up. What if the attacker had harmed her daughter? Or her father?

Somebody had to blink first. And that somebody wasn't going to be her. Let the killer think that he'd knocked her down and out. She was just getting started.

Eighteen

Callie woke up to the scent of English Breakfast Tea brewing in the kitchen. She lay blissfully on her pillows for a moment, enjoying the sweet fragrance, as well as the yellow sunshine that was peeking through the blinds of her bedroom. Her head still hurt a bit but it was no longer throbbing. Not quite fully awake, Callie forced herself to sit up as she became aware of the low murmur of masculine voices that wafted up the staircase along with the aroma of brewing tea. Oh no. She struggled out of bed and got to her feet.

Softly, so as not to leave the sounds of her footsteps on the creaky floorboards, Callie tiptoed to the top of the staircase and listened. Along with the deep rumbling of her father's Greek accent came the attractively raspy baritone of Detective Sands. The back of her neck prickled with anxiety. She dashed back into her room, unsure if she could face either of them.

"Callie!" called George from the foot of the staircase. She heard him coming up the stairs. Luckily, it was just one pair of feet that she heard. Seconds later, her father entered the room.

"Ah, good. You're up. How are you feeling today?"

"Better, I guess. Who were you talking to?" Maybe she was still dreaming.

"That police detective stopped by to discuss your attack. He agreed to interview you here rather than at the station, since I told him you'd probably feel a little bit under the weather." George came over to his daughter and kissed her on the cheek. Callie appreciated the affectionate gesture but was starting to feel like a truant teenager who was late for school.

"He wants to talk to me right now?"

"Well, why not now? You're up." George motioned with his hands, his "hurry up" gesture. "Just get dressed. I'll cook you some breakfast after he leaves."

"Okay, Dad. Give me five minutes." She smiled at George and castigated herself for any impudent thoughts. It wasn't George's fault that Sands was here. Pulling on a light sweater and blue jeans, Callie brushed her hair and splashed cold water on her face. She frowned at her disheveled reflection in the mirror before carefully navigating the stairs on shaky legs.

Detective Sands was sitting at the kitchen table, looking completely at ease in Callie's home. How did he manage to appear so in control, no matter what? This time he was dressed in his usual charcoal suit, not the white shirt and jeans that Samantha had found so attractive the other night.

One leg crossed over the other, the detective was drinking his tea calmly while Koukla sat at his feet, begging for scraps. The little dog ran to Callie, wagging her tail as soon as she saw her. Callie bent down and scratched the dog behind her oversized ears, then slowly stood up and faced the detective.

"Good morning," Sands greeted Callie before she could say a word. "I hear you got a nasty bump on the head. You should have called us straight away, you know." He put down his cup and frowned at her.

Callie decided to pour herself a cup of tea before answering. As she stepped toward the kitchen table, Sands got up and held out a chair. Trying to appear aloof, she sat down, thanked him and picked up Koukla, who nestled on her lap.

"I know. I'm sorry. Didn't Max call you? He said he would, while I was at the hospital. My purse was stolen when I was attacked."

"Max. You mean that young fellow who works for you? We haven't logged any calls from him. I found out about your being attacked from the hospital – they called the police when you told them that your injuries had been sustained by an anonymous assailant."

"What?" Callie was well and truly stunned. "Max and Piper – well, let me start over." Why wouldn't Max have made good on his offer to call the police? Something must have happened to prevent him. Callie took a sip of tea and added more sugar.

"My employee Max has a friend, Piper," Callie said wearily, willing herself to become alert. "She goes to Crystal Bay College and works at the fitness center part-time. Anyway, the two of them found me in the alley after I was hit – or whatever. I'm still not exactly sure what happened. Max was working with me yesterday and both he and Piper said they would take me to the hospital."

When Sands didn't interrupt, Callie continued.

"I wanted my Dad – George – to take me instead. Somebody had to stay at my business and run things, so I felt it was probably better for Max to stay at work." She decided not to mention that she had wanted to get away from Max and Piper. Callie looked up at her dad who was leaning against the sink, watching the exchange. Unfortunately, he took her glance as a cue to enter the conversation.

"Callie's friends – a Mrs. DeWitt and Minette from Minette's Chocolates – arrived on the scene and they volunteered to take her to the hospital. I met them there. Max did call and tell me about the change of plans." George worried a kitchen towel in his gnarled hands, twisting it over and over. "That's really all I know about it."

"Mr. Costas," Sands said abruptly. "Thanks for the tea and breakfast. It's been most kind of you. If you don't have anything to add right now, I think I should talk to Callie alone. I'm sorry to be forward but I would really appreciate it."

Callie could see her father's color rise – never a good sign. "What is the meaning of this?" George sputtered. Callie cut him off.

"It's OK, Dad. Really. I'll be fine." Callie's father looked nonplussed, but he complied. "I'll take Koukla for a walk. Come, Koukla!" Looking at the pair sitting at the table, he started to say something, but thought the better of it. "I'll be back soon," he said in a gruff tone. Cooing to Koukla, he took his time leaving the house.

Once the front door had clicked shut, Sands leaned forward.

"Callie, what's going on? This attack could have been random, but something tells me it wasn't. For example, what was Piper doing at your place of business during that time of day? Was she a customer?"

"Piper has agreed to do some social media for Callie's Kitchen in exchange for college credit," Callie managed not to croak out her words. She was exhausted and craved dark roast coffee, not tea, but this was not time to be picky about the choice of caffeine on offer.

"Piper and Max are dating," Callie explained, taking a sip of her now tepid tea. It was better than nothing. "He recommended her services to me. I don't know if I should be telling you this or if it has any relevance, but she claims to be a pretty good computer hacker. Reformed, that is."

"Right." Sands sat back and looked at Callie a bit warily, it seemed to her. "So these two didn't drive you to the hospital and you didn't call the police. Why?"

"I told Max to call the police." Callie swallowed. "But I just wanted my dad to take me to the hospital. Even though we don't always see eye to eye, we are really close and we always have been, especially since my mom died when I was a kid. After the attack, I was in pain and I was scared and I wanted to be around someone I could trust. True, he can be tough, but I know he cares about me, especially when it counts the most."

Detective Sands looked at her a minute. "Sorry about your mother." He cleared his throat and continued. "But he didn't drive you. Mrs. DeWitt and a woman named Minette drove you?"

156 | JENNY KALES

"Yes. Minette was in the process of moving out of her business yesterday. At least, I think she was. There were all of these big cardboard boxes in the alley behind Callie's Kitchen when I got to work yesterday. I didn't get a chance to ask her about it, I just assumed." Sands raised his eyebrows and Callie trailed off uncertainly. The detective nodded at her to continue.

"Anyway, Minette and Mrs. DeWitt, you know her." Sands bobbed his head briefly. "She's got a foundation and the business school is named after her family. Plus she was – is – involved in choosing the winner for Taste of Crystal Bay."

Sands cleared his throat. "I'm not sure I could forget her if I wanted to. Why was Mrs. DeWitt in the area? Do you know?"

"I have no idea." What was she doing there with Minette? Good question. "I didn't think to ask her. I was in pain and I was upset about losing my purse – and everything in it."

"So did these two ladies see anything of interest?"

"They didn't see anybody hit me, if that's what you mean. At least, that's what they told me."

"Now, what about the purse?" Sands asked, switching gears. "What all was in your handbag?"

Callie took a sip of tea. "The usual stuff. My wallet, some makeup. Luckily, my house keys and business keys were in my pocket." Callie sank back in her chair. "I may as well tell you, I had to get a new cell phone, but that was in my car. Whoever hit me didn't get it." She paused. "Anything of interest on the cell phone you took from me? Or Drew's iPad?"

"Hmm. We'll see." The detective's expression was bland and Callie couldn't read anything into it. Were they building a huge case against her but just didn't have enough evidence yet? She rested her elbows on the table and hid her face in her hands.

"Listen, just relax, Callie. One step at a time," Sands said. "Don't get upset. Regarding your purse, you should know that we probably won't recover it. You'll want to cancel your credit cards and call your bank of course."

The bank. Just hearing about it made Callie think of Lucille and how both of them had shared a similar assault. "Do you think that the same person attacked both Lucille and me?"

Sands looked right back at her. "Right now, Ms. Costas, I just follow up and try to find how and if things fit together. It could have been a random theft, or not. I don't know."

Sands looked down at his notes and then passed the paper over for her to sign. "Your official statement on the assault and theft," he said, handing her a pen. She signed quickly and handed the pen back to him. Their fingers brushed.

"Well," he said, standing up. "I'd better go. Lots of things to follow up on." He raised one eyebrow at her.

Callie stood up with him. "I'll see you to the door."

Sands suddenly turned to her. "Callie, remember the last time I was here? I told you to be careful." He narrowed his eyes at her meaningfully. "For example, don't get any ideas about playing Nancy Drew. It's dangerous."

Callie was surprised at his concern and also a little confused. If he thought she was guilty, why warn her to be careful? If he thought she was innocent, then why not return her items to her? "I'm being careful. I even sent my daughter to stay with her dad and his wife for a few days."

"Good." Sands seemed pleased, but then he frowned. "Were they around yesterday near the time of the attack?"

"Now that you mention it, yes. My ex-husband and his new wife had just picked up my daughter from my shop. They wouldn't hurt me! They had Olivia with them. My daughter," she clarified. "We've had an amicable divorce. My ex's new wife loves me!" Callie said the last sarcastically, and Sands gave her a sardonic smile.

"Lucky you." Sands leaned in closer and put his hand on her shoulder. "I'm glad you weren't seriously injured. Just remember, next time you might not be so lucky." He removed his hand, touched his fingers to his forehead in a mock salute and was out the door.

Not that Callie wanted to admit it, but her shoulder felt warm and tingly where he had touched it for about 10 minutes afterwards.

* * *

When George and Koukla returned from their walk, George wanted a full rundown of the conversation.

"Why did I have to leave? You know, I almost didn't. I'm your father. I have a right to stay and hear what this detective is saying to you."

"Dad, don't worry. He just wanted to clarify a few things and take a statement about my attack."

"I know this incident might seem like a simple robbery to the police, but you could have died when you hit your head on the pavement." Callie shuddered, as she'd been trying very hard not to think about that.

George put his arm around his daughter and gave her a squeeze. "I'm sorry to be so blunt, but there it is. But now, it's a beautiful day and you're just fine. Let's eat breakfast." She couldn't argue with that. George made a mean feta cheese omelet.

"Coffee?" Callie asked hopefully.

"Of course!" George sounded gruff. "Greeks don't drink tea in the morning. I just served that to make the detective feel at ease." He bustled back to the kitchen to fire up the coffee pot with Koukla hot on his heels. She'd perked up as soon as she'd heard the word "breakfast."

Even as Callie laughed at her father's comment, she wondered about Max. Why hadn't he reported the attack and theft?

Nineteen

The September sky looked slate blue against the golden leaves of the oak tree in her front yard and the breeze coming through the window was cool. Usually, autumn was a time that Callie enjoyed. The kaleidoscope of colors provided by the leaves' changing hues invigorated her and gave her that first-day-of-school feeling, a fresh slate when anything could happen.

Or it would have, if not for the constant presence of her father. He'd called his restaurant, The Olympia and told them he was taking some time off. It looked like he intended to spend all of it with Callie.

"Do you feel up to helping me make a *spanakopita*?" George materialized in the door of the living room, wiping his hands on a dishtowel. Callie was touched by his question. He knew that *spanakopita* was her favorite comfort food. Paper-thin phyllo generously brushed with melted butter, wrapped around a salty, savory mixture of spinach and feta cheese – it never failed to help her forget her troubles, at least briefly.

"If I can sit down," Callie offered, struggling out of her position on the couch. George extended his strong hand and helped her up, leading her into the kitchen where he settled her into a chair near the stove. The warmth from the oven made Callie feel drowsy and content. Already, the *spanakopita* was working its magic.

Callie watched as George squeezed the moisture from his thawed frozen spinach and started chopping a brick of feta cheese that was nearly the size of a text book. How many spinach cheese pies was George planning on making?

"We need to talk," George said, dropping several sticks of butter into a pan on the stove.

"I'll watch the butter," Callie offered, scooting her chair closer to the range, where it began to melt in a golden, fragrant pool. Nothing smelled as good as melting butter. "What is it, Dad?"

"Why do you think Drew was killed?" George said facing her, his thick brows furrowed. "How could you have gotten involved with such a person? I'm trying to understand how this happened to you. You have always been such a sensible girl, even though you've done things I don't agree with."

Callie's cheeks burned and her head started throbbing again on cue. "Dad, I'm not sure I have any answers for you. Drew isn't what he seemed, that much I do know. It feels like I only knew the very public side of him, but he obviously had enemies. I'm trying to piece things together, but it's not easy." She paused. "You know I'm an official suspect, right?"

George narrowed his eyes. "Yes. That detective told me, even though you didn't. When will you learn – you can't hide anything from your father?" George grunted at Callie's expression and continued. "I tell him – I didn't raise my daughter that way. And I raised you on my own, without your poor mother. I am insulted that this man is questioning you. You are not the criminal and I tell him, he is wasting time."

Callie smiled, despite herself. "That must have gone over well."

George gave the spinach a vicious whack with his kitchen knife. "I tell him – why do you not find the real killer? My daughter is the one in danger. And he only says: That's what I'm trying to do. Find the real killer." George gave the spinach a final chop and dumped it into a huge mixing bowl. He crumbled the book-sized brick of feta cheese and started sprinkling it on top.

"He's just doing his job, Dad," Callie said with a sigh. "I want to help him find the real killer, too. The sooner that happens, the sooner I can get back to a normal life."

"That may be. But you're not the one. Are you?"

Callie's head swiveled to George. His eyes were shut tight and he was trembling. Callie smelled the butter starting to scorch and she turned off the flame and removed the pan, struggling with her emotions. He couldn't possibly think...but he had asked. Slowly, she got up and put her arms around her father. "No Dad. I didn't kill Drew. I promise you. You are a wonderful father. I would never do anything like that. You taught me right from wrong – you and Grandma Viv. So don't worry."

George returned her embrace, then drew back and busied himself by cracking several large eggs over the top of the spinach-cheese mixture. "I didn't think so," he said, grabbing a wooden spoon and stirring the contents of the bowl, a small smile on his lips. "But I had to ask. I was thinking. Maybe you are afraid of this Drew. Maybe he threatened you and something went wrong? So now I know." He turned to her. "You go and rest. I'm baking this pita and then I have to go to The Olympia for a bit. One of the cooks is out sick and I said I'd fill in if you were doing better. I'm just a phone call away, though." He kissed Callie on the cheek and helped her back to the sofa.

* * *

Callie shifted position and Koukla gave a grumpy little grunt before nestling her small body back onto her owner's lap.

"You don't know how easy you have it," she told the pint-sized Yorkie, who pricked up her comically oversized ears, no doubt hoping that a beef-flavored treat would suddenly materialize. When none did, she put her head back down. Callie petted the dog in consolation, for the dog or for herself, she didn't know.

She couldn't believe George had even entertained the thought that she had it in her to stick a knife in someone. However, in George's defense, he had thrown out the idea that she could have done it in self-defense. Still! Did George really believe she'd gone that far astray?

Life was spiraling out of control and Callie couldn't stand to think about her troubles another minute. She glanced at the side table and languidly picked up the Julia Child book that Viv had lent to her. As long as she was in an enforced rest period, she may as well read. Flipping through to where she had left off, Callie was soon engrossed in the lively writing about Julia's time in France. Nothing seemed to get her down, not even her first lame attempts at cooking or her freezing cold Paris apartment where everything seemed too small for her tall frame. Just as she finished a section about Julia's equally height-endowed sister joining her in Paris for a lively visit, she fell into an exhausted sleep.

What seemed like hours later but what was probably only several minutes, she woke up with a start and rubbed her eyes. Callie shook herself like Koukla and considered her next steps. First: She'd call the shop and find out how things were going. Max was on the schedule this morning and she needed to find out why he'd never called the police.

"Hello?" Max's husky voice crackled through the line.

"Hi, it's me. How's it going?"

"Callie! It's good to hear your voice. You must be doing better." When Callie murmured her assent, Max continued. "Well, it's pretty quiet. You know. Not so many customers. But don't worry about that right now." Max's despondent voice took on new urgency. "You could have been hurt much worse."

"That's what people keep telling me but it looks like I'll be fine." Now, now, she told herself. Don't take it out on Max. She sighed and started over. "I appreciate your concern, truly I do. But I have to ask you about something."

Callie fidgeted. "Can I ask you something? Why you didn't report the assault and theft like you said you were going to? I spoke to a detective this morning and the hospital called it in, not you."

Max gave an anguished cry. "I completely forgot!" he wailed in an uncharacteristically dramatic fashion. "Piper had to go to work at Bodies by the Bay and she said she had a lot of homework to do. And, I'm not gonna lie." Max sounded worried and hesitated before plowing ahead with his story. "We got into kind of a fight. I don't know if she's going to work for you after all."

"A fight?" Callie said. "Oh no. What about?"

"I'd rather not say," Max said sheepishly. She could almost see him blushing to the ends of his spiky hair.

"Okay, fine. So you were distracted."

"Yes. I'm sorry to be so irresponsible. By the time I remembered I had promised to make the call for you, it was late. I figured by then you or your Dad had reported the crime. I admit it: I dropped the ball."

"Max, I" – Callie began, but he cut her off.

"Are you going to fire me? I'm sorry I let you down but I love this job and I need this job. Especially now...Oh, never mind. I just really need this job. Give me another chance?"

"Max, settle down. Nobody is firing you. I just wondered what happened. You know, the police have been questioning me again and I thought I'd check with you. And honestly, I'm still really upset about getting hit on the head behind my place of business."

"Sorry I flew off the handle. I'm just worried. If we don't get more customers in here, then..." he trailed off.

"I know. It's not going to be good. Listen, I appreciate everything you're doing. I'm going to rest up today and come to work tomorrow."

"Really? That would be great. I know we'll think of some way to get people back in here. Anyway, Piper probably will help you. She seemed pretty interested. The least I can do is smooth things over with her, if that would help."

Callie felt a warm glow of gratitude. "Thanks. It would help."

"Oh, and before I let you go, I almost forgot. Foot traffic hasn't been good, but we just got another decent-sized order for The First Bank of Crystal Bay. Lucille is coming back to work and her boss wants to welcome her with our mini coffee cakes."

Lucille. Now there was someone Callie would like to see. It was just after visiting Lucille that she had received her own whack on the head.

"Max, let me deliver those tomorrow. What time do they need to be there?"

"Let me check." Callie heard the comforting noises of her shop as he referred to his notes: the clink of ceramic plates, the ding of the oven timer. Max must be working while he talked to her on the phone. Even though business was slow, she wanted to be back in the heart and hearth of her business. She could almost inhale the lemony, rich scent of *avgolemono* soup and the warm aroma of cookies baking. It made her feel homesick.

"10 a.m.," Max said returning to the phone. Then, hesitantly: "You're sure you can drive?"

"I think so. If not, I'll let you know."

"Okay. Well, I guess I'll see you tomorrow. And hey, please..."

This time Callie cut him off. "I know, Max. I'll be careful." See you soon." She hung up.

Feeling a little unsettled from her interchange with Max, Callie decided she had a few more calls to make. Sitting down at the kitchen table, she grabbed the phone and cancelled all of her credit cards. She'd figure out her driver's license later. But what if she got pulled over? Well, she'd just have to make sure that didn't happen. Sooner or later her luck was going to have to get better. Wasn't it? Of course, Drew had thought his luck was changing too. And now he was dead.

Twenty

Speaking of luck, Callie still had her checkbook and she would be able to use it for cash. She could do that tomorrow at the First Bank of Crystal Bay when delivering the cakes. Tired of phone calls, Callie sank back into a kitchen chair and groaned when the phone rang again. She was tempted to ignore it, but what if it was one of her creditors? Reluctantly, she answered it.

"Are you kidding me?" Samantha said loudly into the phone. "I have to find out about my best friend getting attacked from a colleague at work? Not from my best friend – or shall we say, the attackee?"

"Please," Callie protested. "My head hurts. You were my next call, I promise."

Sam softened her tone, but not much. "I don't know what the heck is going on, but something is. Have you been snooping around even though I asked you to stay put?"

"Not really. At this point, I just want to get on with running my business. I've missed so much time due to Drew's death, that I don't even have the luxury of sitting out the rest of the week. I've got to get back to work."

"I know." Sam of all people knew what was at stake. "What you need is a police escort to follow you around town, to make sure you're not endangered by anyone. I know just the guy!" Sam said suggestively with a low chortle.

"Don't. Even." Callie protested. "He was already here again this morning. Sands, that is, if that's who you're referring to."

"Oh, I bet he was. And I hope he told you to be careful."

"He did. How did you know? That's all anyone says to me these days. He also told me, and I quote: 'Don't go playing Nancy Drew.'"

"He didn't!" Sam's chortle turned into a full-blown laugh. "I'll bet you loved that."

"Not exactly. In fact, he inspired me to do just the opposite."

"Hmmm," Samantha said. "Seriously, Callie you've got me worried. A killer is still out there. You and Lucille – and anyone else even slightly involved – need to watch your back."

"Funny you should mention Lucille. I'm delivering coffee cakes to her at work tomorrow."

"Look at you two. You can't keep good women down. Still, watch your step. Somebody out there took a risk and hurt both you and Lucille. Put the two of you together and I don't like your chances."

"Not to worry," Callie answered, more glibly than she felt. Lucille might be less of a victim and more of a participant, but she'd save that theory for later. If everyone had their way, she'd be bedridden until further notice.

Placing the phone back in its cradle, Callie considered what to do next. She desperately wanted to speak to Jane Willoughby. It seemed to her that Jane had to know more than she was saying. For example, in his moody rant, Chef Johan said that Jane had been at the bistro frequently, a fact that Drew had never shared with her.

Sands hadn't said anything about Jane beyond his initial questioning the night of the murder. As someone involved in the Taste of Crystal Bay, Callie reasoned that Jane had to have talked to the police at least once. And then there was the whole syrup of ipecac debacle. Like it or not, Callie was going to have to visit Jane again and find a way to get her to talk. Unfortunately, a cookie bribe probably wouldn't do the trick.

She picked up the phone and dialed Bodies by the Bay. "Hello, can you put me through to Jane Willoughby's office?" Callie asked the receptionist. Koukla just looked at her, impatient with anyone who wasn't prepared to offer their lap as a cushion.

Jane answered, somewhat breathlessly, on the second ring. Callie's heart started to pound. "Jane, it's me. Callie Costas."

"Hello, Callie. What's up? I heard you were attacked the other day. Sorry about that. Trouble seems to be following you around." Jane spoke evenly.

"Yes, it does. I'm doing better, though. I wondered if we could meet up and chat. You knew Drew for a long time. I just have a few things I'd like to chat with you about." Like how syrup of ipecac got into the romantic gourmet meal Drew was preparing for me.

Jane sighed in exasperation. "Like what? I'm not sure I understand what you think I know."

Impatience gave Callie confidence. "You and Drew conducted a lot of Chamber business together. You may just have details that you observed and they might be relevant – but you might not even know that they're relevant. I've been suspected of his murder and I'm trying to gain perspective on why I may have been attacked."

"I'm sure I don't know why you were attacked," Jane replied hotly. "And I don't really like what you're implying."

"I'm not implying anything." Callie decided to try a different tack. "We're both businesswomen. I'm struggling to keep my business afloat and take care of my daughter. You're great at what you do. But now my business is in danger – like a lot of others in town. I just want to have a friendly chat, nothing more. It would be nice to talk to someone who understands what it means to run a business." It was an obvious attempt at flattery, but it just might work.

Jane didn't sound all that mollified. "Callie, I'm sorry. I'd like to help you but things are really busy for me. Mrs. DeWitt and I are trying to figure out what to do with the contest money now that Drew is...gone. Plus, work is really hectic and we have our hands full here trying to reassure our clients that they won't be attacked like Lucille was."

Jane let out an exasperated sigh. "So, as you can see, I don't have a lot of time right now. Anyway, I'm glad you feel better. We'll talk soon, when things aren't so crazy." Jane rang off.

Callie was dejected but not surprised. The way things were going, when were they not going to be "crazy" as Jane put it? Obviously, Jane didn't want to talk to her. Fine. She'd just have to work around her. But how?

Fatigue overtaking her, Callie sat back down on the living room sofa with her feet up. That was all the encouragement Koukla needed. Overjoyed, she jumped on her owner's lap and curled her body into a ball. Absently patting the dog's head, Callie drifted off again as she envisioned ways of trying to snoop around Bodies by the Bay without alerting Jane.

The nap refreshed both Yorkie and her mistress. Callie awoke to a rumbling stomach and a barking dog that needed to be let out. After releasing Koukla into the back yard, Callie found that George had left a foil-wrapped pan of *spanakopita* on the stove. She grabbed a piece and ate it out of hand greedily, thankful to have a father who was an expert cook.

Callie shared a few pita chips with Koukla and realized that she was feeling much better. She'd call her daughter later, but then what? She couldn't bear to sit still. She imagined her picture on the wall at the Crystal Bay police department, the circumstantial evidence piling up around her.

Koukla gave a little yip. The dog needed to be walked, that was for sure. However, Callie didn't feel like running into her neighbors who may or may not have heard about her attack. The idea of reliving her ordeal for the neighborhood was not appealing.

What about heading into another neighborhood? Callie wolfed down another piece of *spanakopita* while she considered her options.

Suddenly, Sands' derisive warning about "not playing Nancy Drew" rang in her ears.

That was it. The call to Olivia would have to wait. Callie was going to play Nancy Drew – and Koukla was going to help her.

* * *

The sun was beginning to set by the time Callie had finished crafting her plan. Carefully stretching her limbs and rotating her neck, Callie evaluated her physical strength. She wouldn't be able to perform a 20-minute Greek folk dance, a staple at every Greek wedding she'd attended (including her own), but she could probably handle walking and snooping. The brilliant orange rays were beginning to sink below the horizon and Callie realized that she'd better hurry.

Quickly, she changed into a long-sleeved navy T-shirt and dark blue jeans. The night was cool, so she threw a black cardigan over the outfit. Black and blue – fitting, considering her injuries, but more importantly, her attire would blend into the dark. Stowing her cell phone and a small flashlight into her pocket, Callie clipped Koukla's leash to her harness.

She was just grabbing Koukla's kennel when the doorbell rang, making her jump. Cautiously she peered out of the peephole and groaned when she saw who it was. Viv was standing on the stoop, shifting from foot to foot in her comfortable walking shoes, with a concerned look on her face. Callie opened the door.

"Darling, how are you?" Viv crooned, patting Callie on the shoulder as she moved smoothly into the entryway. "I thought I'd better stop by and see with my own eyes that you are on the mend. George called me and asked me to check on you. Turns out, he got stuck at the diner and he's frantic about you! But wait a minute," she said, taking in Callie's clothing and purse that was slung over her shoulder. "Are you going somewhere? In your condition?"

Viv narrowed her bright blue eyes into slits. Callie offered the first excuse that came to her.

"I've got a couple of errands to run," she began and Viv started waving her arms around. She held up a palm to her granddaughter.

"Not so fast. Anyhow, my dear, you're dressed a bit oddly for errands," she said, taking in Callie's monochromatic outfit. "Besides, it's getting dark. Can your errand wait?"

Callie shook her head vehemently.

Viv's cheeks colored a bit. "Oh I see. Perhaps it's a feminine product you need to buy? No need to be embarrassed in front of your grandma. Let me go instead. I'll just be a minute and you can get right back to the sofa for a rest...."

Callie held up her hands to stem the tide of words. "No," she said, with a small laugh. "It's an errand only I can do. I might as well tell you, but you can't tell anyone. I mean no one. Promise?"

Viv folded her arms across her chest and pinned her granddaughter with blue eyes that looked like laser beams. "I promise. What is it? "

"I want to revisit the scene of the crime and see if it helps shed any light for me. But first I'd like to visit Mrs. DeWitt's property. She and Drew were such close neighbors. I just want to take a look around."

Grandma Viv's mouth fell open as if to scold her and now it was Callie's turn to silence her grandmother. She raised her arm like a traffic cop.

"Please," she pleaded. "I can't stand sitting here. My life could be falling apart as we speak. I've got to see if I can find any detail that can help me figure this whole thing out – before I'm attacked again, or lose what's left of my business or even – go to jail! I promise to be careful but I have to do this." Callie found herself gasping after she delivered this speech.

Viv shook her head slowly. "Callie, what will George say if I allow you to run off in the dark to a murder scene and something happens to you?"

Callie was ashamed to feel tears start and she blinked them back.

"I'm running out of time. The day I found Drew, I was too upset to think straight. If I go back, I might see something that the police have missed. Or maybe something will occur to me now, something new that's triggered by being back there. I waited until evening because I don't want anyone to see me. And I'm bringing Koukla, so it looks like I'm just out walking my dog."

"All right, darling," Viv said with resignation. "You can go and bring Koukla. But you get an old lady in the bargain. I'm coming too."

After making Viv promise that she would stay in the car so as not to arouse even more suspicion, and leaving a note for George so that he wouldn't call out the Marines when he found her not at home, she bundled her grandmother and Koukla into the VW. Callie turned just past the library, passing the police station – the thought of her time there made her heart beat faster – until finally she made the turn onto Lake Shore Drive.

The lake sparkled in the early evening sunset, the water glittering like the crystal of its namesake. Actually, that wasn't exactly true – the town had not been named for crystal but for ice. In the old days prior to electric refrigeration, the winter ice on the water was a sought-after commodity, sold to the neighboring cities each year. Fleetingly, Callie wondered what the past residents of the nearby towns had done in the summer, when they really needed the ice.

"Almost there," Callie reassured both her disapproving grandmother and her wiggling Yorkie. She passed Mrs. DeWitt's long winding driveway and parked on the side of the road under a thick coverage of trees that still held much of their colorful foliage. She appeared far enough away from Mrs. DeWitt's home that no one there would spot her trespassing.

"Grandma, I won't be long. Just sit tight."

"Humph." Viv answered, clearly miffed at not being part of the team. "I'll be here if you need me," she finally relented.

As she made her cautious way to Mrs. DeWitt's pier, autumn leaves crunched under Callie's feet, a cheerful sound that reminded her of favorite Wisconsin pastimes for fall: bonfires and fall picnics. Other than the leaves and Koukla's jingling dog tags, not a sound could be heard. Coupled with the darkening sky, the silence seemed eerie.

The night was so still and so reminiscent of the evening she found Drew's body, that for a minute she panicked and became short of breath. She kept walking, watching the prancing trot of her little dog who was thrilled at the change in scenery. It helped. Her breathing slowed and she stolidly continued to her destination.

Mrs. DeWitt's house was dark, except for a bright light over the door and flood lights that illuminated the tall, stately trees and abundant autumn flowers Callie had admired on her previous visit with Grandma Viv. Could she really be so fortunate? Maybe nobody was at home. Callie felt herself relax a little more.

Koukla pranced about, finding spots to stop and sniff, a telltale sign of things to come. Callie reached in her pocket for a baggie. Even while on a snooping mission, she wasn't one to leave dog waste on other people's lawns.

The pier, lit by a single light at the end of the dock, beckoned. Gently pulling on Koukla's leash in one hand and holding the waste bag in the other, Callie made her stealthy way toward the pier. Glancing behind her, she nervously took in Mrs. DeWitt's stunning floor-to-ceiling windows.

The curtains were drawn, but one of the windows was open to the warm night and Callie noticed a gentle breeze lift the curtains up, and back down, like a gentle sigh. She stopped, looked around again. When she was certain she wasn't being observed, Callie stepped more boldly onto the lawn and looked out at what she had come to view.

On her previous visit, Callie had noticed that Drew's home was visible from Mrs. DeWitt's gorgeous, window-walled sitting room. While he did have a pier of his own, no boat bobbed in the calm waters tonight. Drew had often spoke about buying a boat and what a good time they would have together, taking trips on the bay. Clearing her throat, she narrowed her eyes and focused on the task at hand.

The vantage point from Mrs. DeWitt's back lawn presented a decent spot to watch the comings and goings of Drew and his guests. Drew had a side door that he often used. Like all of the other homes on the bay, no fence obscured either his view of the water or his neighbor's view of his home. Sheltering trees on the side of his home and in the front provided color and shade, but his back yard leading to the pier was open for all to see. To maximize the view, Drew's kitchen and most of his bedroom faced the water.

In other words, Mrs. DeWitt could have seen many of Drew's activities and those of his guests, if she were so inclined. What this meant, Callie wasn't sure. But it seemed likely that Mrs. DeWitt would have seen something or someone that night.

Numbed and horrified as she had been the night of Drew's murder, her own safety hadn't been more of a passing thought. But now she realized that if she'd been in the way, she may well have faced the same fate as Drew.

"Come on, Koukla," she whispered. "Let's go."

Koukla ignored her and pulled more firmly against the leash. She had something in her teeth and was shaking it in a playful manner. Callie fervently hoped that it wasn't a field mouse, as she had a minor but pesky rodent phobia. She peered down to see what was in the dog's tiny but strong jaws. No rodent, thankfully. Koukla had found what looked like a thick piece of rope. In fact, it looked very similar to the rope toys the dog had at home by the boxful.

"Drop it!" Callie said more firmly and more loudly than she intended. Obediently, the dog released the rope into Callie's palm and sat at her feet waiting for more play time.

"Just a minute, Koukla," she said, inspecting the rope to make sure it was long enough that the dog wouldn't choke on it. The things she did for her pampered pet.

The rope was a little stretchy, shiny and relatively thick. In fact, it seemed more like a bungee cord than a rope. That was odd. Then again, maybe it had something to do with docking boats, though usually a different kind of rope was called for in that case. She decided that Koukla could have the strange object. Maybe it would pacify her as they continued to their next destination. She was just bending down to give the rope to her dog when a voice made her jump.

"Hello? Who's there?" The voice came closer. "Callie Costas? What are you doing here?"

Twenty One

Ava, Mrs. DeWitt's housekeeper, walked toward her, holding garden shears and a basket of freshly cut flowers. Callie realized how silly she looked and slowly rose from her protective crouch. She looked more closely at the blooms and saw that they were beautiful roses, in shades of red and pink.

"Hello?" Callie realized it came out more like a question. She eyed the garden shears and Ava followed her gaze, giving a tiny trill of laughter.

"I know it's late to be gardening, but I heard a frost report and I simply had to bring the roses in. Gertrude loves her roses and she'd be so disappointed if they didn't make it through the night." Ava chuckled again. "But, why are you out here? Did you ring the bell and I didn't hear you?"

Just as Callie had planned, Koukla provided the perfect excuse. "I was taking a walk with my dog. We've been cooped up at home all day." Callie shrugged and smiled in what she hoped was a natural way. "I also wanted to stop by and thank Mrs. DeWitt for helping me the other day."

Callie felt someone walking up next to her and froze. Turning, she saw that her worst suspicions were confirmed.

"Ava!" Viv trilled in a tone that suggested they were all gathering for a garden party.

"Viv? Why, what are you doing here?" Ava looked from one to the other, confused. Callie could relate and desperately tried to cover her dismay. Any minute now, Ava was going to transform from confused to angry at the fact that two non-neighbors were ambushing her on Mrs. DeWitt's lawn.

"Oh, I'm just accompanying my granddaughter on a few errands. You know she's been hurt, so I've been keeping an eye on her." Callie cast Viv a grateful glance.

Ava's little bow mouth pouted in sympathy. "I heard all about it." She turned to Callie. "You must have suffered a terrible ordeal. Should you be out walking around in the dark?"

She looked at Viv. "No offense, but if you faint, your grandmother isn't the best person to assist you. How would she carry you to the car? You must take care of yourself, you know." Ava took Callie firmly by the shoulder and began leading her up the hill towards the house. Viv followed, complimenting Ava on her beautiful roses all the way. Callie decided it was best to appear weak and submissive, so she posed no resistance as the petite Ava guided her forward in a surprisingly firm grip.

"What an adorable little dog," Ava commented as they completed the climb. "What's her name?"

"Thanks," Callie smiled at the Yorkie, who was always useful as an icebreaker. "Her name is Koukla. That means "little doll" in Greek."

"She's so cute!" Ava enthused, bending down to pet the dog. Callie nearly jumped a mile when Koukla began a low growl. The diminutive housekeeper retracted her hand.

"Koukla!" Callie admonished. "Stop that." She looked at Ava apologetically. "Sometimes she smells her "prey" on people who've been working in the garden. You know, chipmunks, etc. Yorkshire Terriers were bred to hunt rodents, so sometimes her instinct kicks in. She's really very gentle." Koukla barked once, loudly, and Callie winced.

"Yes," Viv chimed in. "She's very protective of her owner." She gave a significant glance to Ava, who merely gave a bemused smile in return. Koukla might be a terror with small rodents but she was no match for a human being.

"Oh, I'm not offended," she said. "Anyway, it's getting dark," Ava continued. "Many animals are afraid of the dark, just like people. But I suppose we humans are a species of animal, aren't we?"

"Uh, yes." Callie clenched her fist more tightly around the "doggie bag." Unfortunately, Ava noticed.

"Why don't you hand me that bag?" Ava asked. "I'll just toss it in the trash."

"Oh, no." Callie was a bit mortified at being caught clutching a bag of dog leavings in addition to trespassing. "I don't want to put you to any trouble."

"No trouble at all," Ava said, taking the bag. Too late, Callie realized she'd handed over the bungee-looking rope along with the bag.

"What's this?" asked Ava, looking straight at Callie. Her eyes were really quite a piercing blue, with a sharp intelligence behind her jolly exterior. With her petite figure and bright blue eyes, she looked much younger than her years.

"I don't know," Callie answered. "Just something Koukla found on the grass."

Ava examined the rope briefly. "I'll toss that out, too."

"Thanks," Callie repeated. She decided to keep her ruse going. "Please give my regards and thanks to Mrs. DeWitt for the other day."

"Yes, please tell Gertrude I'll call her soon," Viv gushed.

"I will," Ava answered. In the quickly diminishing light, she was gazing at Callie with an odd look on her face. "I'm sure she would have loved to see you in person, but she's at a meeting tonight with the Chamber of Commerce, regarding the small business contest and what they'll do about a new winner."

"Oh," Callie was taken aback. "Is she meeting with Jane Willoughby, do you know?"

"I don't really know. She just said she was going out to a Chamber meeting. I assume the usual people will be there. And now, if you'll forgive me I need to get back to the roses. And you should get some rest." Ava looked impatient for her impromptu and uninvited guests to leave.

"Of course. Sorry to keep you," Callie answered, tugging once more on Koukla's leash. "And sorry about my dog," she called to Ava, who was rapidly walking toward the house. "I don't know what got into her tonight."

"No trouble at all. Good night you two! Get home safely!" Reaching the front step of Mrs. DeWitt's expansive home, Ava abruptly stopped, turned and faced Callie and her grandmother, her basket of roses clutched firmly in her arm. The garden shears gleamed in the fading light.

"Good night!" Callie and Viv sang together. They began a rapid walk back to the car, not speaking and not even looking at each other. Callie might be mistaken, but she thought she'd identified the expression on Ava's unlined face. It was fear.

Once the canine-human trio was safely inside the car, Callie whirled to face Viv. "Why did you come out there? Now Ava is bound to be suspicious. She's probably going to tell Mrs. DeWitt we were out snooping around. And she's going to tell Detective Sands, which means he'll want to speak to me again in an 'official capacity'. Just what I need!" she huffed.

Viv was defiant. "You don't think I'm going to sit idly by and not protect you when I see a woman with huge garden shears conversing with you on a dark lawn? I saw her basket of flowers and the points of the shears sticking out – the moon is especially luminous tonight, thank goodness!"

Viv was developing a good head of steam as she kept on with her lecture. "I'm not leaving you alone in the dark with anyone after a man was stabbed to death. What kind of grandmother would I be if I did that?" Viv tossed her head and straightened the smartly tailored but casual jacket she wore.

"Okay, okay," Callie relented. "But I'm trying not to attract too much attention to myself. Let's just keep that in mind."

"Anyway," Viv said as Callie started the car. "Ava didn't seem to think anything of it."

It was no use arguing with her. But could Ava really be a threat? "I hope not, Grandma," Callie said with resignation. She touched her grandmother's forearm. "Thanks for protecting me."

Viv pouted for a second longer and then decided to accept Callie's gratitude. Patting her granddaughter on the knee, she asked "What's next?"

"One more stop," Callie told Viv. "This time, let me make sure the coast is clear before you get out of the car. I don't know if police are patrolling Drew's house, so let's be careful. I'm not going to park right in front – we'll walk a bit."

Reviewing her run-in with Ava, Callie felt that it was entirely possible that she or Mrs. DeWitt knew something about Drew's visitors the night of his murder. However, she was willing to admit that it was equally as possible that neither woman knew anything. Mrs. DeWitt was a busy lady, not often at home, just like tonight. However, Callie found it strange that Ava would still be on the premises. Wasn't it going a little bit above and beyond the call of duty to hang around at night just to bring roses in?

As she pondered Ava and Mrs. DeWitt's work arrangement, she realized that employee loyalty was nothing unusual in a town like Crystal Bay where the good jobs were held by people for years and years, much to the chagrin of the young Crystal Bay College grads who wanted to stay in town and find jobs close to home.

Callie pulled up to the curb a safe distance away from Drew's house, stopped the car and leaned her head against the steering wheel a minute. Being so close to the murder scene was making her feel shaky all over again.

"Darling, what is it? I knew this was going to be too much for you," Viv asked gently.

"It's just difficult to be here again. I haven't been, since..." Callie swallowed the lump in her throat as she thought about the last time she visited Drew's home. Worse still, his death was uncovering a side of him she hadn't even known and yet, still she missed him. Or maybe she missed the idea of him. Either way, her heart pulsed with grief and she sat for a minute allowing it to wash over her. Silently, she wished him peace.

The night sky was almost entirely black, the trees making huge, looming shadows that resembled gigantic prehistoric beasts. No kidding, Ava, she thought. I'm one of those humans scared of the dark.

"Well, what are we looking for?" Viv asked, practical as always, as the two of them got out of the car and began walking slowly down the street with Koukla walking slightly ahead of them on her leash.

Practically tiptoeing now, Callie and Viv approached Drew's home. "Do you see any police cars?" Callie whispered to Viv. The two of them looked around but nothing looked unusual. Callie tugged Viv's arm and they walked halfway up the walkway before she was brave enough to turn on the flashlight she'd brought with her. Bright yellow crime scene tape glowed garishly as she ran the beam up, then down.

Various debris were scattered on the porch, some propped up against the front door, while other tributes simply lay limply upon the ground. It was an astounding and odd assortment of objects.

A stuffed teddy bear lay next to a vase of silk flowers. Several greeting cards and notes were carefully placed against the door jamb. Someone had tied balloons to the door and a few were beginning to deflate. A small Eiffel tower was tipped on its side and unthinkingly, Callie bent down and set it right. Where had she seen one of these before? Oh yes. Drew's office. Was this tribute from someone at the Bistro? Chef Johan aside, Drew had always seemed popular with his co-workers. He had to have been paying at least some of them.

Callie hugged Viv's arm closer to her then bent down to pet Koukla who was starting to whine. It was all so unbearably sad and strange, this little hodgepodge shrine on Drew's porch. To Callie, however, it was not surprising. People in Crystal Bay needed to find something to do when tragedy struck. If someone was sick, they sent food. If someone in the family died, they sent food and attended the funeral. If someone lost their job, they offered food and moral support. George was right when he had said that people always needed to eat.

What happened when a single, attractive man was murdered, one who had provided some of Crystal Bay's finest dining to both locals and tourists? Having no precedent to guide them in this specific case, her fellow Crystal Bay residents simply did what they had always done: they made a gesture of goodwill toward the deceased, if only a bunch of balloons or silk flowers. Crystal Bay people were good people, Callie thought.

Well. At least most of them were.

"Grandma, let's go around the back." Viv nodded as Callie led the way.

"Such a shame. Drew had his whole life ahead of him. Who would think that a random murder would hit Crystal Bay? Honey, let's be careful, it's so dark back here," Viv kept up a constant stream of chatter that Callie found oddly soothing as they walked through the long grass, although she no longer believed that Drew's murder was random.

Brandishing her flashlight, Callie decided to walk the perimeter of the house exactly as she had done the night of the murder to see if it triggered any memories. She ran her flashlight around the back patio and saw that the ceramic pots had been smashed, the cheery yellow mums scattered across the flagstones.

Koukla started growling low in her throat again and Callie feared that an animal had done the damage and was waiting to do more – maybe a fox or one of the huge raccoons that loved to raid the area. Callie was afraid for her loyal companion. A larger animal trying to defend itself could do away with Koukla in one swipe of its sharp claws. "Hush, Koukla," Viv said softly and the dog gave a short, sharp bark in reply. So much for being silent.

Callie swept the beam from her flashlight around the perimeter again looking for glowing eyes. Thankfully, she saw nothing. She walked around the entire house, trying to take in as much as she could in the dimness, her eyes darting anxiously in every direction.

Callie switched off her flashlight and closed her eyes, trying to re-call details from that terrible night she'd found Drew. She'd crawled in a window and called the police when she'd seen his body. Food had been cooking and nothing had really looked amiss.

Callie decided to scan Drew's side door, the one visible from Mrs. DeWitt's house. She started a slow trek around the back patio one more time and decided to look out across the water to see if she could spot Mrs. DeWitt's home in the distance. Koukla panted alongside of her, obviously tiring of her role as doggie detective. Viv's chatter had died away and Callie knew she was growing tired. So was Callie. It was time to go soon.

Peering out across the water, Callie stopped short. The lights were on in Mrs. DeWitt's home and a silhouette could be seen in one of the windows. Short, curly hair, petite frame. It had to be Ava.

And she appeared to be staring directly at them.

Viv had followed Callie's gaze. "Is that who I think it is?" she stage-whispered and Callie nodded briskly. "I think so," she said, al-ready starting to walk in the direction of the car. "Let's go."

"You got that right," Viv answered. "I'm getting the creeps out here."

Keeping the flashlight pointed only at the ground to keep the light low, Callie led Viv along the other side of Drew's house, Koukla straining the leash at the end of Viv's arm. Her flashlight shone on a few more "tributes" and Viv stopped to look. A piece of thick white notepaper lay upon a bouquet of red roses. Freshly cut, the large blooms were not encased in florist's paper, but simply arranged in a small, neat bundle.

Viv started to bend down as if to grab the note, but Callie yanked her back, as gently as she could. "Don't pick it up!" she said. "You don't want to touch it – it could be evidence!"

The two of them crouched down to get a closer look, Callie keeping Koukla far away from the paper. The notepaper was crisp and fresh and it contained a message, obviously printed from a computer. Excitedly, Viv read it out loud: "Dearest Drew, I'm sorry. Love always, Kitty."

Twenty Two

"Who's Kitty?" Viv asked. "Do I know her?"

"Grandma, let's talk about it where we're safe. I'm calling Detective Sands right now." The two women made a beeline for the car, Koukla scurrying along at their heels.

Viv soothed the dog while Callie dug out the detective's business card and called him. What would she do if he didn't answer? She'd just have to call the regular police non-emergency line. She clenched her jaw as the phone rang several times. Finally, Sands picked up.

"Hello, Detective. This is Callie Costas. Listen, I've found something at Drew's house that I think you should see. Can you drive over?"

"What exactly are you doing at Drew's house?" Sands asked, sounding genuinely perplexed. "I don't know if you're extremely clever or just extremely reckless!"

Callie had to half-laugh at that. "Me either. Seriously, you'll want to see this. It's a note, from someone named Kitty. I saw a note by the same person in Drew's office the other day, remember?"

"All right. I'll be there soon. Where are you?"

"In my car."

"Stay there, please, just to be on the safe side."

"One more thing. My grandmother is with me." Callie figured she may as well tell him everything.

"Wonderful." He hung up.

"Callie, do you know this Kitty person?" Viv persisted after Callie let her know that the detective was on his way. "I'm thinking....I knew a Katie, but not a Kitty."

Kitty. Callie grimaced, her previous warm feelings toward Drew turning into a stony feeling that gathered in the pit of her stomach. Had there been other women, or just this Kitty?

"I don't know anyone by that name," Callie admitted. "But it's odd. I've seen the name on a note I found in Drew's office, just recently."

Viv sighed. "Strange. And you have no idea who she is?" Viv said sitting up straight and peering out the window. "Well. I find it all very interesting. It's kind to leave tributes for Drew but how do people have the nerve to just walk right up to that house? Just standing outside gave me the willies!"

Callie smiled at Viv. "Yes, but you did it anyway. You're one tough lady."

"True," Viv agreed. "I try not to let my fears keep me away from my duties. Tonight my duty was to keep you safe and protected." The two exchanged smiles, but Callie wasn't so sure she'd be safe and protected once Sands arrived. Maybe he'd be angry instead of grateful that she was the one who'd found a clue.

It seemed only a few minutes before Sands' car pulled up in front of Drew's house. The two women, accompanied by the now thoroughly disgusted Yorkie, got out of the car and walked over to meet him. He must have been speeding the whole way here, Callie thought.

"All right, what do you have to show me?" Sands looked skeptical. He nodded at Viv as she introduced herself and said "Pleased to meet you," then allowed the duo to lead him to the Kitty note. He crouched down and read it aloud, then stood up and looked at Callie. "Kitty again. Just like the note you found in Drew's office."

"I know." Callie felt her blood pressure skyrocket. Was it now going to look like she had killed Drew out of spite, a woman scorned? Why oh why hadn't she just gone home the minute she'd seen this stupid letter?

"You didn't leave this note, did you?" Sands crouched down again and took a closer look. "It looks recent."

"She did not," Viv piped up. "I was right here. We were walking around and found it together."

The detective turned back to Callie. "Can I ask once again – what are you doing here? You must know it doesn't look good."

"I could lose my business, my daughter and recently, someone attacked me. It's not that I don't trust you to do your job, but you seem to think I'm involved. I thought that if I came back here, I'd remember something about the night I found Drew, something that would help. I also visited Mrs. DeWitt's house and she has a pretty good view of Drew's home. Did you speak to her?" she demanded.

Sands looked slightly taken aback by her tirade. "I understand that you want to clear your name. However, unless you want to get into deeper trouble than you already are, crime scenes are officially off-limits. And I can't discuss any conversations that I may or may not have had with any other witnesses."

"Callie is innocent!" Viv chimed in. "Please believe her."

Sands looked from one to the other and then down at Koukla. "You even dragged your dog into it. You all make quite a team." He shook his head.

Just then, a black and white car showed up and two officers emerged. Sands directed them to the letter and "tributes" and they began placing the items in clear plastic bags.

"Right. You two are coming with me. I need you to make another statement – both of you. Callie, you're going in my car where I can keep an eye on you." He addressed Viv in a gentler tone. "Can you drive Callie's car to the Crystal Bay police station? I need a statement from you as well."

Viv agreed and took Koukla with her. Knowing it was pointless to argue any further, Callie got in the car without protest and Sands began the drive back to town. Callie texted Samantha to let her know what was happening and asked if she could meet her there. To her relief, Samantha agreed.

Near the water it had been so still that you could hear the lapping of gentle waves against the rocks and the whisper of bat wings. Closer to town, the cool but clear weather had energized the populace. Indian summer was an all-too-brief event in Wisconsin where you could begin the morning at 40 degrees and end it at 80 degrees. Or even more likely, vice versa. You couldn't blame Wisconsinites for living it up outside when they could.

"Look at Garden Street," Callie said, just to make conversation. "It looks like Christmastime out there! Maybe the economy is improving. Or maybe it's just the nice weather."

"It is quite lively," Sands agreed. As they drove past Callie's Kitchen, she felt a pang. It looked snug and warm, the windows darkened for the evening. Callie envisioned them dark forever, if she had to close up shop. She looked the other way, not able to cope with that feeling at the moment.

A pedestrian crossing forced Sands to stop the car as he waited for a large group to pass. One of them, tall and heavy-set, looked familiar. Chef Johan. Based on their last meeting, Callie would have expected him to be long gone by now. He was speaking animatedly to someone next to him, someone much shorter because he was looking down. He was also smiling broadly in an obvious effort to be charming. When he smiled, he looked somewhat attractive. His teeth were straight and white and he had a dimple in his strong chin.

The group near the chef cleared out and Callie could see Johan's companion. She gasped. Sands heard her sharp intake of breath and stared at her. "What is it?" Callie just shook her head, her eyes transfixed on Lucille, who was teetering along, in her usual pencil skirt and spiky heels. As Callie watched, she stumbled a little on her heels and Johan caught her arm. They kept walking and jabbering away, totally oblivious to Callie's interested gaze.

"I'm just surprised to see Lucille with Drew's chef. Johan. I had no idea the two of them were an item. You questioned him the other day," Callie reminded him.

"So I did," Sands said, eyeing the pair with interest. He glanced at Callie, but he didn't say anything more.

Well, well. Lucille seemed to have recovered nicely. Samantha was right. You couldn't keep a good woman down. But what was the young bank worker doing with Chef Johan?

* * *

Callie was getting used to giving statements at the police station. Too used to it. She and Viv were interviewed separately, while a young officer entertained Koukla. By the time it was all over, Callie and Viv promised Sands that they wouldn't return to Drew's house, or in Callie's case, Drew's bistro. Callie couldn't tell if Sands suspected her more or less after her attack and if this recent evidence helped her or hurt her. Samantha was trying to remain calm but Callie could tell she was furious that she had been called to the police station once again. Overall, this combination of worries didn't make for a restful night.

The next morning, Callie tried to get back to business as usual. She fed a grateful Koukla, applied lipstick (bright pink, to give some color to her haggard face), rushed about her house, tidying up and all the while she thought about her sighting of Lucille and Johan out on a date.

She remembered the abundance of food magazines in Lucille's apartment the other day – if she was dating a chef, maybe she was trying to educate herself on the latest food news. Though, she had admitted to Callie that she was a "foodie" herself – so maybe that was part of the attraction with Drew's moody chef. When it came to romance, who was she to judge someone else's taste?

Chef Johan was volatile, though apparently he could also be charming. He was definitely a thief. He was a disgruntled employee, absolutely. But did that make him a killer?

Callie and Lucille had both been attacked recently – they had that in common. Was that all they had in common? Lucille was close with the chef or even "just friends" with him, which would have given her proximity to Drew. Was she another of Drew's conquests? Maybe, maybe not. After all, she'd told Callie that Drew was "weird." Still, maybe Lucille was in a greater position to judge Drew's personality than she'd let on. Enough! Callie was getting a headache just imagining another potential deceit on Drew's part. And what about Kitty?

As she gathered her purse and gave Koukla one last belly rub before she left for work, Callie was unenthusiastic about being Lucille's delivery person. Experiencing an unusual amount of worry and stress early in the morning was not helping her to motivate for a day of trying to win back customers and keep her business afloat. She prayed that people were finally coming back to Callie's Kitchen.

Blinking in the late September sunshine, Callie thought ruefully that the weather had never been more beautiful than in the days following her horrific discovery of Drew's body and subsequent interrogation by the police. Somehow, slogging through ice, snow or sleet under slate grey skies would have better fit her mood. Nature, however, was indifferent to her troubles.

Putting on oversized sunglasses against the glare, what Samantha called her "Jackie O. look," Callie prepared herself to face the day.

At Callie's Kitchen, Max was busy cooking and baking, but Callie noticed that he'd scaled back a bit. Usually he made enough for an army. A couple of what appeared to be tourists and one or two regulars were sampling apple-pumpkin breakfast cake and braided Greek butter cookies. Still, just a few people compared to the large crowd that usually arrived in the morning wasn'td a good sign.

 Callie slipped into the kitchen to inspect the coffee cakes that Max had supposedly made for Lucille. Thankfully, Max had been diligent in his preparation. The cakes appeared to be boxed up and ready to go; her signature blue-and-white "Callie's Kitchen" boxes were marked with a note saying "First Bank of Crystal Bay."

Based on the low number of boxes, Callie deduced that this was just a small party and didn't require the massive amount of cakes Lucille had ordered for the head honchos of the bank's parent company in Madison.

As Callie began taking boxes to her car, Max appeared from the front of the shop looking glum.

"Hi," Max greeted her, but without much enthusiasm. Callie peered more closely at him. Even the spikes of his haircut seemed to be drooping. "Are you feeling better?" he asked.

"Thanks, I am. Well, mostly. I still have a headache and am a little achy, but generally, I feel all right, considering. What about you? Is everything okay?"

"Oh, yeah. It's still slow, but the people that do show up seem to enjoy the food." Max blushed. "I didn't make as much food as yesterday. I'm trying not to waste ingredients."

"I noticed. Thanks. Let's stick to that policy for the time being, at least until things pick up. If they ever do."

"Hey, here's something!" Max seemed to want to cheer her up. "Those crème brûlée cupcakes you had last fall? One of the tourists asked when you would serve those again."

"Really? Well, that's a positive piece of news. I've got to find my kitchen blowtorch and then we can make them. They were *trés magnifique*, weren't they?"

Callie leaned against the counter, her arms crossed in front of her. "You seem a little down," she said to Max, noticing that his glum expression had returned. "Is anything wrong? Well, besides the usual worries about work." *And the fact that your boss is a murder suspect.*

"I'm fine. Well, not really. It's a little embarrassing." Max didn't seem to want to meet Callie's eyes.

"Just a second," Callie said, checking the front of the shop. Her few customers had departed. She sighed and turned back to her employee.

"I'm grabbing some coffee. Want some? And then you can tell me all about it. I want to try that apple-pear coffee cake, too. I've got a couple of minutes before I make my delivery." She started bustling around looking for coffee cups and sugar.

Max pulled up a stool. "It's just that...." he hesitated and took a sip of the coffee Callie had handed him. "I don't think that Piper wants to go out with me anymore."

"Oh?" Callie replied. "Were you officially 'going out?'" Whatever that meant to people Max's age. She tried to not think about the free social media expertise that she might be losing and put an understanding look on her face.

"Yeah, I guess." Max smiled. "I just don't know what's wrong with her. She seems distant these last couple of days. I'm almost afraid to ask what's wrong because I don't want her to dump me."

Obviously the poor guy was desperate if he was asking her for love advice. Callie began slicing pieces of breakfast cake for each of them. Unable to resist, she took a huge bite. The cake was so moist and flavorful, redolent of cinnamon and brown sugar, with a tender crumb.

Callie devoured another bite of cake before deciding to answer. "Don't be afraid to talk to her. Likely, it's not you at all. She's probably just busy. She works and goes to school, right?"

Max nodded. "So don't worry about it," Callie reassured him. "If you just started going out, you're still getting to know each other." With a failed marriage and a dead boyfriend to her credit, Callie wondered if she was committing a sacrilege by giving relationship advice.

Max gave her a hint of a smile. "You're probably right." He sipped more coffee and set down his cup with a decisive click. "Well, I've got more stuff to bake and then I thought I'd start a new batch of Greek chicken stew. It's on the menu for the week. I checked the walk-in and we've got the ingredients. Is that okay with you?"

"You bet, but don't make the usual large batch. Until customers return, anyway." Max looked worried at the thought of fewer customers but agreed. Callie gathered up the small order of coffee cake boxes for Lucille and picked up her car keys. "I'm off. See you in about half an hour."

Callie found a space right in front of the bank this time and set off in the direction of Lucille's cubicle. Seeing the bank tellers reminded her that she needed to write herself a check for cash until her new debit cards arrived.

"I heard you were mugged," Lucille said quietly as Callie reached her desk. "Let me help you with those." She started grabbing blue and white cake boxes.

"They're not heavy," Callie protested.

"It's no trouble. Thanks for bringing the food," Lucille enthused. "You know how much I love them. Everybody has been so nice to me since I came back to work, and now you've brought my favorite cakes." She opened one of the boxes and inhaled deeply. The scent of cinnamon, brown sugar and vanilla wafted out.

"Yum!" she said, beaming at Callie. "I also wanted to thank you for the soup delivery the other night. I couldn't believe it when I found out that you were attacked, just like me. What's happening to Crystal Bay? It's not a safe place anymore."

"That's just what I was thinking," Callie stammered, trying to figure out a way to ask about Chef Johan without appearing nosy. "I don't even want to step out at night without a big, strong guy on my arm!" She blushed to hear herself speak that way, but it just might work. Anyway, she had stepped out with Viv and little Koukla only the night before – and to a crime scene no less.

"Oh, I don't know," Lucille said slowly, inspecting her nails, shiny with red lacquer. "You and I are both strong and fit. Even so, I'm definitely reviewing my self-defense training after my attack at Bodies by the Bay. If anyone comes after me again, I'm ready for him. Or her!" Lucille held up her arms in a mock karate chop and Callie couldn't help but laugh at her antics.

"Well, what I mean is," Callie said, trying again, "there *is* safety in numbers. And having someone bigger and stronger by your side will really help deter a would-be attacker, wouldn't you say?"

Lucille opened her eyes wide. "Callie. Are you already dating someone again? Who is he?"

Impressed at Lucille's ability to turn the tables, Callie was momentarily stunned into silence. "Uh, no," she finally answered. "But it would be nice to have a bodyguard, especially with a killer still on the loose."

Lucille looked at her, puzzled. "I didn't think so. I mean, it would be kind of soon." She chewed on one of her perfectly manicured nails for a second and then seemed to regain her usual buoyancy. "Hey, Callie. I've got this. Thanks for delivering the goodies, but I'll unload them myself. You go get off your feet or something." She started arranging the boxes on a table next to a coffee urn.

Callie's shoulders slumped as fatigue washed over her. Lucille's offer was tempting. "Well, I can't do that, but I do have an errand to do here at the bank. And I have been missing way too much work. Sure you don't mind?"

"Nope. Go on, now!" Lucille playfully waved her away, so Callie thanked the young woman again and headed for one of the bank teller stations.

As she wrote her check for cash, Callie decided that gossipy Lucille had suddenly become a pretty good poker player. She wasn't giving anything away.

* * *

Callie returned to her shop where she hoped she'd be greeted by a throng of Greek-stew loving customers. No dice, as George liked to say. Maybe now was a good time to finally call Olivia. She dialed Hugh's cell phone, telling herself it was perfectly fine that she didn't feel like interacting with Raine at the moment.

"Hi, I was going to call you," Hugh said by way of greeting. He sounded worried.

"Why, what's up?"

"Olivia's been having a lot of wheezing. We're trying to figure out what's going on. Raine gave her a breathing treatment and she seems better, but I'm concerned. I didn't want to bother you unless absolutely necessary."

"Of course you're not bothering me. Can I speak to Olivia?"

"Sure. Here she is." Callie was relieved to hear her daughter's voice on the line. She sounded pretty much like her usual self, if a little tired.

"Hi Mom! How's Koukla?"

"Hi. Well, she's just fine. Keeping me great company. I hear your asthma is acting up again."

"Yeah. I did a treatment and it helped but I swear, every time I'm around Raine it gets worse."

"You're probably imagining it." Was Olivia now experiencing anxiety-related symptoms due to Raine? How was she going to fix that problem? Raine not only wasn't going anywhere, she was seeking to produce progeny – aka, new "Raines." Callie let out a sigh, feeling defeated.

"Drink lots of water and don't overdo it with the exercise. I'm going to call the doctor and ask for advice. I miss you and love you."

"Love you, too, Mom. When I get home, will you let Koukla sleep in my room?"

Callie smiled. "Sure. Now let me talk to dad again. Bye!" She heard the phone exchange hands and Hugh was back on the line.

"Just let her rest. I don't want to treat her like an invalid but I don't like the asthma kicking up, even on medication. I'll call her doctor and keep you posted. Maybe she'll have to come home before the weekend is over. If there's an emergency, take her to the hospital. Promise?"

"Yes, I'll take care of her." Hugh sounded a little impatient, but then softened his tone. He knew better than anyone else how scary it could be to watch a child have a serious asthma attack. "Don't worry, Callie. She's in good hands."

"Hugh," Callie wasn't quite sure how to broach the topic. "Do you mind giving her the breathing treatments next time? It's nice of Raine to offer to help Olivia, but maybe she'd feel better if you were the one to do it."

Hugh blew air out of his nostrils in an exasperated gesture that used to drive Callie bananas and still did. "Raine's great with her, Callie. You don't have to worry. But yes, I'll be happy to deliver the medicine if it's needed."

Fair enough. Callie rang off and sat down on a chair, her fatigue returning. As much as she trusted Hugh to take care of his daughter, she felt slightly apprehensive about not being near Olivia when she clearly needed her.

What would make her feel better, Callie asked herself? Besides eating a pound of chocolate or a dozen crème brûlée cupcakes, the only thing that came to mind was figuring out Drew's murder once and for all. She was tired of watching her back and having people think that she had the slightest thing to do with his death. She was tired of people shrugging her off and refusing to talk to her, people she'd known for years. She was tired of suspecting people and having them suspect her.

Like Jane. Well, watch me refuse to take 'no' for an answer, Callie thought. Jane might not want to talk to her, but she couldn't prevent her from visiting Bodies by the Bay as a client, could she? But – Detective Sands had warned her away from any more crime scenes, she thought guiltily. Well, she just wouldn't go near the pool or hot tub.

Callie grabbed a bowl of soup from one of the huge stock pots on the stove and sat down at the staff table, formulating a plan. By the time she finished, she knew just what she was going to do.

Twenty Three

Max and Callie finished their food prep for the day and tidied up. The lack of customers was really becoming a problem. Only one or two brave (or hungry) souls had ventured in for a bite and then, nothing. Callie stepped outside and looked up and down the street, a rush of crisp fall air cooling her face, flushed from standing over stock pots and hot water. Nobody appeared to be headed her way. Maybe it was time to lock up and go home.

Though the air outside was cool, inside, the shop was warm with the homey scent of Greek chicken stew and the tantalizing aroma of crème brûlée cupcakes. Would this food just go to waste, too? Obviously, the people of Crystal Bay had believed that vile newspaper reporter's version of things instead of believing in her. For a split second, she considered what it would be like to be a hostess at The Olympia again. No way. She'd think of something.

Max had worked on the cupcake batter and was monitoring a batch while Callie took stock of her refrigerator contents, making sure that she had the right ingredients for the cupcakes' signature custard frosting.

The frosting was applied to each cake and then caramelized with a small but powerful cooking blowtorch, right before being placed in a refrigerated display case. Looking at the pile of mixing bowls they'd used, Callie filled a sink and started rinsing them, then placed them in the dishwasher. A quick search on her office computer regarding membership policies at Bodies by the Bay and she had everything she needed.

198

Despite her distraction, Callie noticed that Max seemed happier as he worked with the cupcakes, carefully adding just the right amount of batter to each muffin tin and then setting the timer with no question about it, some spring in his step. The first batch came out, pale gold, with a fragrant vanilla scent. Max placed the cakes on racks to cool and it was difficult to resist eating one even without the rich, creamy custard frosting, topped with a crackling layer of caramelized brown sugar.

Callie was in too much of a hurry to even contemplate a cupcake break — she had to get to the fitness center before closing time. She'd barely had time to place a call to the doctor, who had suggested Olivia visit the office as soon as she got back from her father's house.

"Max, can you handle closing up tonight? I've got a pressing errand. If you don't mind storing the cupcakes once they cool, I'll finish decorating them tomorrow morning. They've got to be thoroughly cold before the frosting is torched, anyway." Callie wiped her hands on her apron.

"Sure. You go ahead." Max turned out another batch of cupcakes on a huge stainless steel baking rack. Callie regarded her employee carefully. Had he reached a rapprochement with Piper? Unfortunately, Max's love life woes weren't her concern at the moment. She'd follow up on that later, but in the meantime, she hoped Max hadn't sensed the mixed feelings she had about the young woman.

"Thanks for all of your hard work. See you later!" Callie called to Max as she picked up her purse and waved goodbye before heading out the front door. She wasn't taking any chances with the alley tonight.

Callie powered the VW along Lake Shore Drive until she arrived at the modern structure that was Bodies by the Bay. She could see several people in various stages of exercise through the gleaming glass windows. Patrons of all shapes and sizes were running on treadmills and riding exercise bikes with their eyes glued to flat screen TVs. Some chose to focus on the peaceful panorama the calm waters provided, and some wore ear buds so that they could work out to their own private soundtrack. The place looked as busy as ever.

Callie all but sprinted up the steps. Jane's BMW wasn't there: check one.

Stepping aside to allow a gaggle of young women in brightly colored workout gear to pass by, she strode purposefully through the doors and straight to the customer service desk. A young woman wearing a tight tank top with a "Bodies by the Bay" logo greeted her. "Hi, welcome to Bodies by the Bay! What can I do for you?" She smiled broadly, showing gleaming white teeth that shone from her friendly, freckled face.

Callie was happy to be able to share one piece of truth among all of the lies she was about to tell. "I've come about my membership card. My wallet was stolen and I lost all of my cards."

The young woman's face fell. "I'm sorry, but you need I.D. to have a card here. I can look you up in the computer, but without any I.D. I can't reinstate your card. It's a center policy. We want to have security for our customers. Especially because," the girl lowered her voice to a whisper. "Someone was attacked here recently. You can't be too careful."

Callie pretended to ponder this scenario. "You're right. Well, let me see." Again, she pretended to think this over. "I know." She leaned forward conspiratorially. "I'm a friend and colleague of Jane Willoughby, the owner. Do you mind if I pop in her office? Maybe she can help me."

The friendly young woman looked crestfallen; for the second time in just a few minutes she had to deliver bad news to Callie. "I'm so sorry, but Jane isn't here right now."

"Oh." Callie feigned surprise. "Well, in that case, let me talk to her assistant. They might be able to tell me when she'll be in."

Relief was apparent in the receptionist's voice; finally, this customer was going to let her off the hook. "You go right ahead. I think her assistant is still there." Determined to be helpful now that she had a resolution, the receptionist asked "Do you know where her office is?"

"Yes, thanks. What's your name so that I can tell Jane how helpful – and cautious – you are? I'm sure she'd like to know." Callie decided to make a friend so that if she got caught in the act, at least this young woman might vouch for her.

The young woman beamed. "Why, that would be very nice." She blushed becomingly. "My name is Stacy."

"Got it. Thanks, Stacy."

Slinging her gym bag over her shoulder, Callie headed to the back of the gym where Jane's executive offices were located. A well-muscled young man sat outside the door, looking through a body building magazine. "I'm looking for Jane Willoughby," Callie offered hopefully.

The young man set the magazine down and flexed his biceps before answering. "You just missed her. Can I help you?"

"Well," Callie decided she'd go for helpless and confused and see where that got her. "I'm a colleague and friend of Jane's and I lost my membership card. Actually it was stolen."

"Uh-huh," replied the muscly guy.

"So I wanted to know if Jane could help me get reinstated, since she does know me personally. Stacy said you're all being extra cautious about security, which I completely understand." Callie gave him her best innocent look, but her heart froze when Jane's hunky assistant picked up the phone on his desk. "Let me call Jane's cell. You can speak to her directly."

No, no, Callie fretted. She tried to smile, but inside she was screaming in protest. It was all she could do to stand still while the call was put through. While she considered making a dash for the door, Jane's assistant frowned. "It went straight to voicemail," he said. "Sorry. Can you come back tomorrow?"

Callie tried again. "I work tomorrow and I was really hoping to use the fitness center right afterwards."

"Oh, well, Jane will be back tomorrow at 9 a.m." Suddenly, the guy was all business. Callie gave him her best smile.

"Would you let me in her office for just a minute? I want to write her a note."

"Just a second." The assistant looked down at his own cell phone, which was buzzing away. "Hello?" He smiled hugely, apparently recognizing the phone number, an action that revealed charming dimples. "Hey, what's up? Yeah, we can get together tonight! How about..." he appeared to remember he had an audience. Callie must have perfected her innocent expression because he shrugged and walked to Jane's door, unlocking it. "Go ahead and write a note. I've got to take this call."

Callie was so ecstatic that she nearly hugged him, but she was pretty sure that whomever he was talking to wouldn't appreciate it. Nodding wildly in assent, she entered the office, switching on the light. Silently she thanked the guy's hormones for overriding his common sense.

Half-closing the door so as not to arouse suspicion, Callie knew that she couldn't waste this lucky break. She turned on Jane's computer screen and waited until it warmed up.

What had Piper told her? Most people chose very simple passwords – too simple. In Jane's case, would she pick a tough password or like Callie, would she be too busy to remember anything too difficult? Callie hoped for the latter as Jane's locked screen came up.

"Bodies by the Bay," she typed. No. "Workout." No. "Jane 123" she tried. Again, nothing.

Callie decided to go with a hunch. "Kitty." Still nothing. Darn.

"Chamber of Commerce." Nothing. "Drew." Nope. She was relieved at that, but what was her password?

"Password," she typed, growing desperate. The computer screen stayed locked.

Callie knew that the computer program might shut her out if she tried many more inaccurate passwords, so she took a minute to think. As she considered, her eyes scanned the room. She opened Jane's desk drawers – she could always claim that she was looking for writing implements if someone saw her, she thought. To her disappointment, no envelope saying "computer passwords" leapt out at her. Jane kept a neat and tidy desk, much like Drew. The pages of her notepads were blank.

Callie was struck with a sudden inspiration. "Eiffel Tower" she typed, remembering the tributes at Drew's home and also the tiny figurine on the desk at his bistro. Nada.

Callie started pacing around the room, her eyes worriedly darting to the slightly closed door and back to the computer screen. The wall to the left of Jane's office door was filled with photos of Jane and local dignitaries. There was one showing Jane and Mrs. DeWitt with a Crystal Bay College banner behind them. That must have been taken right around the time they announced the fateful business contest. Callie kept looking.

Near the bottom left row of photos was a picture of a younger Jane, cutting what looked like a ribbon, during the opening day of Bodies by the Bay. It appeared to be a clipping from the local paper with the headline "Crystal Bay's New Fitness Queen."

Callie's gut had the same feeling she experienced while riding on a rollercoaster right before it dropped. She raced to the computer and typed "Fitness Queen." Bingo! Password accepted. The screen opened up to show several folders, including one for the Internet and e-mail.

Breathe, she told herself, almost too excited to focus on the files in front of her. Callie found Jane's e-mails and began quickly scrolling. She kept peeking up, looking for someone to walk in. Dimly, she heard employees saying good night to each other, but her attention was on the e-mails. She clicked a few but they appeared to be all business-related. There was one from Jane to her husband, telling him she'd be late.

Callie kept scrolling, unwilling to admit defeat. She kept scrolling frantically, until she saw it. Drew25@yahoo.com, Drew's personal e-mail account. Now she felt like she was on the first drop of a tall rollercoaster and about to approach an upside down loop. She clicked to open the e-mail.

"Jane,

Why are you being so cold? I promise I'll keep you warm. Think up a good excuse because I don't want to let you go too soon. Can't wait to see you. Love, Drew."

Callie gulped and looked at the date – it was just three months ago. Okay, she and Drew hadn't been together three months ago. But Jane was married. She kept scrolling.

There was another one, dated two weeks before Drew's death. Callie could hardly bear to read it.

"Jane,

I'm so sorry about the baby. Please don't blame me. You know it doesn't change anything between us. Call me later on my cell. I'll be at the Bistro so stop by there if you want. You've made it all possible. We belong together and all of our plans are nearly complete. Don't give up. All my love, Drew."

Callie scrolled down but couldn't find any more. Then again, the tears that had sprung to her eyes at this new discovery were possibly blurring her vision. She assumed that Jane had received and sent more e-mails but why hadn't she erased these? It wasn't discreet of her at all. At the very least, these e-mails implicated Jane and Drew in an affair and a pregnancy, if not Jane herself as a potential murder suspect.

Maybe she couldn't bear to delete them, Callie thought. She remembered how depressed Jane had seemed, a depression she had attributed to the miscarriage. Callie hadn't known the half of it. Not only did Jane lose her longed-for baby, but her lover was dead.

Had Jane killed him in a fit of anger and now regretted it? Callie didn't know and right now, she didn't have time to think about it. She'd been in here long enough. After closing the e-mail and shutting down the computer, Callie bent down to pick up her gym bag and nearly fell off of the chair when she heard a familiar voice.

"Who's there?" Steve Willoughby sounded surprised and not a little perturbed. "What are you doing in Jane's office?" Callie jumped in the chair and felt her face turning bright red.

Steve stood in such a way that his body was blocking the door. Callie had never noticed before how powerfully he was built, even though he wasn't especially tall. He was wearing sleek charcoal grey workout attire that hugged his strong, muscular arms. Callie looked into his light blue eyes. He did not look happy.

"You startled me!" Callie tried to arrange her features into what she hoped was a friendly grin. "I'm just writing a note for Jane. I lost my wallet and I'm trying to get my membership card reinstated. I thought Jane could move things along for me more quickly."

Steve strolled away from the door and walked toward Jane's desk, inspecting it. "Where's the note?" he asked. "Do you need paper or something?"

"Uh, yes. I couldn't find any." Callie felt her heart pounding like a drum in her chest and was amazed that Steve couldn't hear it.

"There's some paper right here," Steve said, opening one of the drawers. "I'm sure Jane wouldn't mind if you looked for paper in her desk. Don't be shy." Steve handed her a pad of pink sticky notes and proffered a pencil.

"Thanks!" Callie scribbled out an innocuous note and left it on Jane's desk. Now Jane would know she'd been here, exactly what she didn't want. Maybe Steve would go out of the room before she did and she could remove the note.

Suddenly, Piper breezed in and stopped short when she saw Steve and Callie at the desk. What was this, the Bodies by the Bay hotspot all of a sudden?

"Hi there, you two," Piper sang. "Callie, you look much better than you did just the other day! Did you bring any food? Max and I are due to go out later, in town, but I'm starving."

"No, I'm sorry. I don't have food tonight. Well, I'd better get going. It was nice seeing you Piper, Steve." Callie got up quickly, nodded to each of them and tried not to look longingly at the note on the desk. She wished that she could take it back. Now Jane would certainly suspect that she'd been snooping.

Piper and Steve stayed right behind her as she walked out the door. Callie watched as Steve closed the door and locked it. Piper seemed oblivious to any tension. "See you soon!" she sang.

"You bet," Callie said, hoping that Piper hadn't seen her discreet eye-roll. She kept her head down, raced past the receptionist's station and out the front door of Bodies by the Bay, Stacy's friendly "Good night!" ringing in her ears. She gave a quick wave and headed to her car. But before she could unlock the door, she saw Jeff and Minette frantically calling to her and waving.

True, her friends were Bodies by the Bay regulars but it was unnerving that she had been seen by so many acquaintances while on her clandestine mission. So much for her career as a spy. Never mind. She'd say hello to her friends and then get out of here and fast.

"Hi," Minette said. "Working out again?" Callie couldn't read her tone. Before she could respond, Jeff interrupted them, his eyes shining. "Did you hear?" Jeff asked. "We've got great news! We're going to be able to keep our business." He beamed at Callie and Minette gave her a toothy smile that somehow didn't reach her eyes.

"But didn't you just move everything out of the shop? I saw all of those moving boxes," Callie said, happy for her friends but puzzled.

"That's new stuff going in," Jeff said proudly. "I had to order more supplies and we're updating our décor a little bit. I've got some new funds, partly a loan and partly a new investor. We want to make Minette's Chocolates more inviting and appealing than ever."

"That's wonderful," Callie said. "Congratulations! Welcome back to greatness!" She hugged each of them and then had a thought. "I'll have crème brûlée cupcakes for sale in the next few days if you'd like to sell those to your customers again," Callie offered.

"You bet we would," said Jeff. "Can you send us two dozen when they're ready?" As Callie agreed, a wave of fatigue hit her and she staggered a little bit. She was doing a lot better after her attack but sad to admit, she wasn't back to her full strength quite yet. She tried to smile, but Minette had noticed.

"Sorry," Minette apologized. "We're probably keeping you – you need to rest."

"I'm just a little distracted as well as exhausted," Callie answered. "I need to call Olivia. Her asthma is acting up again and she's at Hugh's house tonight."

"Oh, no! That is a worry. You go ahead and head home – and keep me posted," Minette said while Jeff bounced on the balls of his feet, clearly anxious to get started on his workout.

It was all Callie could do not to jump in the car. "Thanks, I'll do that," Callie said relieved at being dismissed. Waving goodbye to her friends, she sped out of the parking lot.

Twenty Four

Callie found herself heading back down Lake Shore Drive toward Samantha's house. She had to tell Sam what she'd seen and ask her what to do. She had no proof that Jane was a killer but this was definitely new and interesting evidence. It was a clear link between Jane and Drew – a secret link.

Callie's was overjoyed when Sam's townhouse came into view. Please be at home, Sam, she thought. She parked her car and climbed the steps to ring the doorbell.

She rang the bell again and again, but Sam didn't answer. The house was dark but that wasn't unusual for Sam this time of night. Still, she would call her again later just to make sure. The discovery of Drew's body had probably altered the way she viewed unanswered doors for the rest of her life.

Callie went back to her car and picked up her cell phone. Sam didn't answer her phone which usually meant one of two things: she was working late or with a client. Or, maybe, thought Callie, she was even on a date. "Call me when you can" she tapped into her phone. "It's about the investigation." A few minutes later, Sam texted back: "Wrapping up a meeting. I'll call you in an hour."

Now what? Callie wondered. She didn't know if she could wait an hour.

Should she call Detective Sands? As far as she knew, nobody else was aware that Drew and Jane were having an affair – or what it might mean to solving the case. He'd told her to stop investigating on her own and here she was, breaking into Jane's computer. Still, she knew in her heart that she had to share this piece of the puzzle in the hopes that it would prove that there were others who may have a motive for Drew's death. Like Steve Willoughby, for example. Did he know the truth about his wife?

With trembling fingers, Callie located Sands' card and dialed his number.

"Sands. Who am I speaking to?"

"It's Callie Costas."

"Ms. Costas?" Sands sounded surprised to hear from her. "You again? Is everything okay?"

"Yes, I mean, no," Callie stammered. She took a deep breath. "I'm fine, physically, that is, but I discovered some information that I think I should tell you. It's important," she hastened to add.

"Right, then. What is this 'stuff' you want to tell me? Where are you by the way?"

"I'm in my car," Callie answered, perplexed. "Why?"

"Just curious. Stay in your car," Sands said. "If you have information for me and only me, let's keep it that way. Now, what is it?"

"I just came from Bodies by the Bay and happened to see Jane Willoughby's computer files. I had stopped by her office and I looked at her e-mail – I know I shouldn't have but she has kept refusing to talk to me. I suspected that she'd been hiding something."

"Looked at her e-mail? I can't believe this," Sands let out a strangled roar.

"I had a hunch or I never would have looked. Do you want to know what I found or not? It's big!"

"All right, I'll bite. What did you discover?"

"It looks like Jane and Drew were having an affair – and the baby she lost? It looks like it might have been Drew's."

"I see," Sands sounded grave. "An e-mail revealed this to you?"

"Yes. I had no idea before, I swear I didn't. I want to help solve this, that's why I'm telling you."

Sands gave a deep sigh. "You're a live one, that's for sure. I'll follow up and thanks for the tip. However, any more checking into people's computers without their permission and you may be facing multiple charges."

Callie didn't answer. Total despair washed over her. "I'm not going to be able to convince, you, am I? I had nothing to do with this. I've shared every piece of evidence and information that's come my way."

"True. However, there is such a thing as being too helpful, Ms. Costas."

Callie's voice broke as the full impact of her recent findings hit her. To top everything off, she hadn't been able to shake her worries for her daughter's health after Hugh's phone call the other day. Callie burst into tears before she could stop herself and immediately struggled to regain control. What would Sands think?

"Now, now. Just relax." Sands said this kindly.

"I'm sorry. It's not just the fact that I don't want to go to jail! I'm worried about my daughter. She's having some health problems and she's staying with her father."

"Oh," Sands said. Callie remembered when he cautioned her to be careful for herself and her daughter. She thought of the picture of the pretty little girl on Sands' desk.

"Detective, do you have any kids?" she blurted.

The detective was silent a long time and Callie wondered if he was angry with her. Finally, he spoke. "I do not, not anymore," he finally said in a low voice. "My daughter died when she was young." Callie was too horrified to respond. Why had she asked him that?

"I'm sorry," she finally managed. "So sorry."

"Thank you," Sands said. He cleared this throat and asked again "Anything else you need to tell me at the moment?"

"No," Callie said firmly. She was going to go home and bury her head under the covers.

"You're certain?" Sands persisted.

"Yes." Callie felt drained

"I'm sorry about the discovery you made regarding the 'affair.' Not a mistake I'd make." The detective cleared his throat and his voice changed to steel. "My advice: do not get involved any more than you have. It could be dangerous for you – in more ways than one."

Before Callie could respond, she heard a click and the detective was gone.

What a night, Callie thought as she drove home. She'd thought that finding Drew had been the worst experience of her life, but the bad stuff just kept accumulating. Humiliation made her face feel like it was on fire and there wasn't even anyone to see her blushing.

Blinking and trying to focus on the road, Callie felt overwhelmed with unanswered questions and right at the top of the pile was: Why was Drew seeing her if he and Jane were not only an item, but were potentially about to become parents? What had he wanted with her? As with so many other things about Drew and his life, this made no sense.

* * *

George was peeking out the window, obviously looking for her as Callie pulled into the driveway. As she walked into her comfortable living room, she braced herself for the onslaught and she didn't have to wait long.

"Where have you been? The doctor told me to keep an eye on you and you're not making it easy." George seemed perturbed, but mostly just happy to see that his only daughter had made it home safely.

Callie brightened. Maybe she was going to get off with only a half of a lecture. She knew George was rightly worried for her health and safety but she just didn't have the energy to defend herself. She needed some quiet time to puzzle out all that she had recently learned.

"Sorry to worry you," Callie said, giving her father a hug. "I had some things to do, but I'm staying put for the rest of the night. I actually feel a lot better. Why don't you head home and have a good night's rest in your own bed?"

Taking a closer look, Callie saw that George looked exhausted. His tiredness was confirmed when he didn't offer a vigorous argument to her suggestion, but only nodded wearily.

"I might just do that *hrisi mou*, but only if you promise to double-lock your doors and turn on your house alarm. I've just let Koukla out, so as soon as I leave – lock up! And call me at once if you need anything."

"Will do, Dad. Thanks for everything and *kalinihta*. Good night!" She double-locked her doors and turned on the alarm – a gift from George after her divorce – like a good daughter.

However, Callie's night was anything but good. She sat up cataloguing her worries, unable to sleep. Koukla snored happily on her lap, oblivious to the malicious machinations of humans.

In the middle of the night, anything seemed possible and probable. Thoughts and feelings that would seem silly in the light of day were hulking monstrosities in the dark. All this worry was only clouding her mental capacities when she needed them the most.

Finally, Callie fell into a troubled sleep but all too soon her alarm was bleating in her ear. She groaned as she pushed the "off" button and willed herself awake. With a knot of dread in her stomach, she realized that Detective Sands would probably pay Jane Willoughby a visit at the very least. She cringed when she thought of Jane discovering who had tattled on her.

Forcing herself out of bed, Callie showered, dressed and was finishing the last of a huge cup of coffee when the doorbell gonged. Praying it wasn't Detective Sands dragging her to the station for another official statement – or worse – she unlocked the deadbolt and found Samantha on her front step. It was such a relief that she nearly wept.

"I'm sorry I never got back to you last night," Sam said, stepping inside. "Got any more coffee?" Callie nodded and motioned for Sam to follow her into the kitchen.

"I had a meeting with a client that ran late," Sam explained, sitting down at the kitchen table and accepting a mug of coffee from Callie." I know today is your early day, so I didn't want to disturb your sleep."

"What sleep?" Callie complained. "I barely got a wink. Sam, don't be angry with me, but I discovered some evidence last night and I told Detective Sands."

"Oh I know all about that," Sam sounded grim. "You should have texted me the details. My assistant already called me to share that she heard Jane was brought in to the police station. I can't believe that she and Drew were in a relationship." She paused. "How are you taking the news?"

"I'm just numb. I feel so stupid. It looks like not only were they were having an affair, but Drew was also the father of the baby she lost." Callie looked down into her cup, unable to meet her friend's eyes.

Sam made sympathetic noises. "I'm so sorry. How on earth did you find out?"

"I hacked into Jane's computer." Callie grimaced at her friend, knowing this was going to go over about as well as stale *loukoumades*.

"Callie Costas! What the --?" Sam exhaled loudly, her eyes flashing. "Are you trying to look guilty? Thanks a lot! The goal is to keep you out of jail, remember?"

"Sam, I know that. I promise to never hack into a computer again. Frankly, I'm surprised I was able to do it at all. Someone gave me some, uh, hacking pointers and I just, I don't know, got lucky...."

"Stop. I don't want to hear it. Good gracious, Callie," Sam sputtered. "What am I going to do with you?"

"Okay, okay. Well, there's something else. Looks like Chef Johan and Lucille are having a fling. I don't know what that means but I do know that the chef was no friend of Drew's."

Sam took a thoughtful sip of her coffee as she regained her composure. "No kidding," she said, looking thoughtful. "Here's an odd coincidence: Did you know that Mrs. DeWitt's housekeeper Ava is Lucille's neighbor? They live in the same apartment complex."

"No, I had no idea" Callie was admitted. "Viv and I ran into Ava the other night when we found that note from 'Kitty'." "I knew she lived in town, I just didn't know she lived so close to Lucille. I guess I never really thought about it."

Callie poured some more coffee into her own cup and raised her eyebrows at Sam. "You realize that Mrs. DeWitt's house is right across the bay from Drew's. I know you can see his home fairly well from Mrs. DeWitt's home and back lawn. Maybe those two know more than they're saying."

Sam shrugged and took another sip of coffee, but Callie persisted. "It's interesting, don't you think?"

"I'm not sure what it means," Sam admitted. "But it's definitely interesting. I'm not certain what they'd have to gain from offing Drew, but any new information gives us something to cling to at this point. Getting back to the whole Jane situation, I'll see what I can find out."

Sam leaned forward and looked Callie right in the eye. "In the meantime, please stick to work today. It's safer that way. Believe me, your friends and family will thank you."

Callie smiled. "I think I can manage that," she said, wondering if there was going to be any work to get back to for much longer.

"Good," Sam sipped some more coffee and stood up. "I better get going. It was good to see you," she told Callie. "But no more hacking.

No more spying. You're going to get into trouble – and I'll be there right along with you."

* * *

Callie fortified herself with another cup of coffee and checked her new cell for messages or texts. It was a good thing she had this phone, considering that her old one was still being held by the police. There were no messages, not even from Hugh, which she took as a sign of Olivia's improved health. Still, she made a mental note to check in with him just as soon as she completed her morning tasks at work.

Max wasn't scheduled to begin work until the afternoon, so Callie was alone in the kitchen. Alone, being the operative word. She'd had exactly two customers that morning but now you could hear a pin drop.

Callie opened her walk-in freezer and looked at the piles of banana bread muffins, Greek yogurt coffee cake, *avgolemono*, Greek chicken stew and wondered if she should place it in her refrigerated cases or keep it in the freezer. She hesitated to waste any more food. Checking her mail, she received more good news. The rent was due on Callie's Kitchen. Doing some quick mental math, she realized that she probably wasn't going to have much money left to run the business once she paid that important bill.

Callie closed the freezer and checked her refrigerator, looking for a distraction. The custard-flavored frosting for the crème brûlée cupcakes had chilled nicely. Callie had frosted about two dozen the previous day and placed them back in the fridge to stay fresh. She'd planned to blowtorch them right before she put them in the display case so that the topping would be nice and crunchy.

Remembering that she'd promised these to her friends cheered her up a bit. Perhaps she could create some good karma for herself when the indulgent cakes went on display in the new and improved Minette's Chocolates. She dialed Minette but got voicemail so she left a message: "Cupcakes are ready, so let me know when you want them. And good luck with everything."

Callie was sitting alone, willing customers to walk in the door and not having any success when Max arrived for work about an hour later.

Max greeted her and then gave her a closer look. "You look tired. Still not feeling well?"

"Thanks a lot," Callie replied, but with a smile. "I'm achy, but okay. It's just that the customers are avoiding us. I don't know how much longer things can stay this way."

"I know," Max said. "I've thought the same thing. In the meantime, you're probably hungry. Why don't you take a lunch break? We'll think of something. I know Piper is already coming up with ideas for your social media sites."

The first positive news of the day. Callie packed up what she called her Big (Low) Fat Greek Salad and headed toward a park near the library to enjoy her food, but first she dialed Sam, desperate for any news.

Thankfully, Samantha answered almost immediately. "Jane is still at the police station, from what I know," Sam answered. "One of the lawyers from our firm – not me – has been called. It looks like they are questioning her about Drew's death but she's not admitting to the murder. She did admit to an affair, though. They were able to get a warrant and went to Bodies by the Bay this morning to confiscate her computer."

Callie was silent for a minute, absorbing this news. "I'm keeping my ears open but I don't have much else to report," Sam said. "Jane hasn't been charged, but I don't think she's leaving anytime soon. Your buddy Sands is one of the people investigating her."

"I'll bet. I'm the one who threw her to the wolves. I guess I thought it was the right thing to do. Or maybe I was the one who was jealous and seeking revenge."

"Listen, Callie. You did what you had to do. You had information and you passed it along. Whether he was right or wrong in his personal life, Drew didn't deserve to die."

"You're right. Well, keep me posted. You don't think they'll haul me back in, will they?"

"I hope not. Call me if they do."

Not a comforting thought, but Callie decided to take it one hour at a time today. She couldn't remember the last time she'd felt so low.

Looking up from her half-eaten lunch, Callie wondered if Grandma Viv was volunteering at the library today. It was a Friday, the day that Viv did a lot of her volunteer work. Callie packed up her food and decided to check. Viv could always cheer her up.

As Callie descended the stairs of the library, she spotted the welcome view of Viv reading aloud to a group of preschoolers. Some of the kids fidgeted and one tousle-haired blond girl whined about going to the bathroom, but most of the kids seemed enchanted. When Viv had finished reading, she greeted each child and mother like they were old friends before spotting Callie. She rushed over to her granddaughter and embraced her.

"Hello, dear. It's so nice to see you. But what brings you here? Aren't you working today?" Viv looked at her granddaughter with concern. "You've not been taking care of yourself – have you?"

"I'm doing all right," Callie hedged. "Right now, I'm on my lunch break. I was eating – or trying to eat – in the park and I just thought I'd say hello."

"I'm so glad you did," Viv said while rummaging around in her bag. "How have you been enjoying that Julia Child book I lent to you?"

"Oh, I love it but I haven't had much of a chance to reread it lately," Callie confessed. "Do you need it back?"

"It's not due for another two weeks. I just ripped through it!" Viv patted her granddaughter on the shoulder. "Take your time."

Callie smiled. "I'd love to keep it awhile longer. Thanks."

"Well, dear, I've got to go. I've got an appointment with my eye doctor. If I'm going to stay up late reading at my age, my prescription has to be just right!"

The two women walked out of the library together and Callie said goodbye to Viv, watching her with admiration as she strode in the direction of her doctor's office. She hoped she'd be so sharp, stylish and active at her grandmother's age. And how clever of her grandmother to distract her with a good book – and one about someone who fell in love with food, no less.

Her appetite returned, Callie decided to read while she finished her lunch. The salad was delicious, with crunchy romaine and cucumber, salty feta cheese and ripe, juicy tomatoes, topped with briny Kalamata olives.

As she enjoyed her food, Julia Child's charming non-fiction narrative took hold of Callie at once. She decided to read just one more chapter before heading back to work. The truth was she was reluctant to leave the little bubble of positive feelings that a good book and a tasty lunch had given to her. But as her eyes sped along the page she saw something that made her sputter.

Drew's lover, "Kitty?"

Of course.

How could she have missed it?

* * *

Callie was in a fog as she gathered up her things. Kitty was sorry, but what was she sorry about? Killing Drew? Had Kitty found out about Jane and the baby long before Callie had? If Kitty was involved with Drew and in love with him, it might be enough to cause a jealous rage. If jealousy were the motivation for Drew's murder – especially romantic jealousy – it all made sense in a sick kind of way.

Kitty would have had access to sharp knives. That would explain why there weren't any knives missing from Drew's knife block. Yes, as a chocolatier, Kitty aka "Minette" would have had no problem finding a murder weapon.

As Callie had read the Julia Child book, she came across a mention of Julia's cat in Paris. And suddenly it clicked as she remembered the conversation she'd had with Minette the day she comforted her about the loss of her chocolate shop. Minette was named by a mother who loved to watch Julia Child on television and who often spoke of her love for felines. In French, a term of endearment for "cat" was "*minette*." Minette = Kitty.

Callie recalled that Minette was in the alley the day of her attack. She had appeared to be helpful, driving with Mrs. DeWitt and Callie to the hospital, acting concerned. She'd been emotional and crying. Callie thought it was because she was worried about her mugging and upset about her business, but now she realized that Minette was probably crying for Drew, her dead lover. Were they tears of regret or anguish? Or a little bit of both?

Callie wondered if Lucille had been involved with Drew and not Chef Johan. It would explain Lucille's attack as well as her own. Minette may have been trying to get rid of any former rival for Drew's love.

What about Jane? Perhaps Minette had been trying to frame her with the syrup of ipecac, placed at the scene of the crime. The ultimate revenge wouldn't be murder for Jane, mother of Drew's baby. Life in prison would be a more fitting punishment from that perspective.

But how could she be certain that Minette was a killer? She'd already steered Sands towards Jane, a move that she was now regretting. She looked at Max and wondered if she should confide in him. At the very least, she had to call Detective Sands. She dialed his number and only got voicemail. Now what?

Before she could figure out a course of action, Piper walked through the shop's front door and stood there staring at Callie and Max.

Max's face took on a crimson hue, but then he grinned broadly. "Piper, what are you doing here? I thought you were working at the fitness center today."

"They sent me home. Jane Willoughby is being questioned by the police." Piper flipped her ponytail over her shoulder and walked over to Callie. "I don't think Steve Willoughby wanted me there because he knows that I know you. Everyone knows now that Jane and Drew were having an affair. Steve is devastated."

She emphasized the last word with another theatrical flip of her ponytail. "I had nothing to do with you rummaging around Jane's office," she continued, her pretty blue eyes snapping with anger. "But Steve won't believe me. He thinks I let you in. I need that job, you know." Piper's cheeks were flushed with emotion.

Callie was taken aback at Piper's tone, but her temper flared. "Let the police do their job. It's really not your business what I do and anyway, it's my head on the chopping block here, not yours."

Piper stared at her evenly. "Yeah, I guess so. But I need to pay for my next trimester's tuition. How am I going to pay for that without a job?"

Callie glanced at Max who was watching this interchange with an expression that was part embarrassment, part irritation. "Piper, you'll find a job. Remember, Callie, when you said that you needed a social media person for the shop?" He added this last in a hopeful tone as he glanced at his boss.

"Yes, but that was meant to be an internship. I can't pay an additional employee right now." Callie wasn't sure she trusted Piper but she wasn't going to tell that to Max right at the moment. She couldn't stop thinking about Kitty/Minette and how she was going to tell the right people about that possible connection.

Piper's face crumpled and she sounded near tears. "I'm sorry. It's just been such a terrible day! No one likes to hear that their boss is being questioned by the police."

Max put his arm around Piper. "I know that firsthand. Now, listen, Piper." He used the gentle tones he usually reserved for the little kids who came into the shop. "Why don't you head home and relax as long as you don't have to work. I'll pick up some food and come by later." He kissed her on the cheek.

Piper sniffled. "Okay. Thanks. Sorry I burst in here like that, guys. See you, Max. Text me." She flounced out the door, her A-line skirt floating out behind her.

Max looked at Callie. "She's just upset."

"Aren't we all? Let's get this food done and then we can both go home."

Max smiled back at her. "You've got a deal." He went back to his work station, whistling, no doubt at the thought of meeting Piper later. Young love – there was nothing like it.

Max finished his tasks, cleaned up his station and waved goodbye to Callie, who was anxious for him to leave so that she could make her phone call. She didn't feel right about Max overhearing, especially because she now feared she'd been wrong about the possibility of Jane's involvement in the murder. Exhausted, she slumped against the counter and was about to dial when her cell phone rang. Hugh.

A sense of dread gripped her when she heard her ex-husband's voice, which was out of breath. "We had to bring Olivia to the hospital today. She's had a very bad asthma attack and none of her medications were working."

"No! What are they doing for her now? Is she OK?" Callie's heart clenched and seemed to stop for a minute as she waited for his answer.

"They've got her on some new medications and she seems to be improving. I just popped outside the hospital for a minute so that I could call you. She's been admitted for the night, just to be on the safe side. We don't know what triggered the attack." Hugh's voice was strained with worry.

"Sometimes the attacks just happen," Callie said. A headache began pounding just above her right eye. She picked up her purse, put it down and picked it up again, before remembering that she was looking for her car keys. Forcing herself to calm down, she finally she found her keys and gripped the cold metal tightly in her hand, wanting something to hold onto.

"What hospital?" she asked, pacing as she spoke. "I'm leaving as soon as I clean up and lock up."

"The University hospital in Madison. You don't have to run out here. Come tomorrow if that's easier for you. They've got her stabilized and I'll call you if there is even the slightest change."

"No, I have to be there. Olivia needs me."

Hugh didn't argue, to his credit. "I'm sure she'd like to have you here. She's been asking for you," he admitted. "They'll let you in her room even if visiting hours are over. I told them you'd probably be showing up tonight."

"Tell Olivia that I'll be there soon!" She hung up and looked wildly around the kitchen trying to decide what to do first.

Working so quickly that she thought she probably looked like a time-elapsed movie, Callie wiped down countertops and stored soups and stews in the shop's large walk-in refrigerator. It made a strange buzzing noise. That figured: Another piece of equipment to buy. However, that was one worry that could wait. Her daughter was in trouble and needed her. Adrenaline made her hurry even more.

She was just turning her "Come in, we're open!" sign to "Sorry, we're closed," when she heard someone come in the back door. She dashed to the back of the shop and ran smack into Jeff. The cupcakes! She'd completely forgotten the cupcakes. "Jeff, I'm so sorry but I have to go. Olivia's in the hospital and I'm closing early so I can drive to Madison tonight." Callie's words tumbled out in a rush.

"No problem," Jeff said. His eyes looked strange, almost black, as if the pupils were unnaturally dilated. Callie felt her hackles rise as he pulled his hand out from behind his back and brandished a gleaming chef's knife, holding it toward her in a courtly gesture as if he were offering her a bouquet of flowers. "You're absolutely right. It's time for you to go."

Twenty Five

Jeff took a step closer and Callie instinctively took a step back. She looked into the eyes of her old friend and was horrified by the expression in them. Jeff appeared to be in another world. He focused his gaze back on Callie and his eyes narrowed. She took another step back and he advanced another step. Their deadly dance continued until Callie had nowhere else to go. She felt her back bump against the countertop.

How close she had been to the killer's true identity, Callie thought. Close only counted in a game of darts, as Hugh used to say. If only she'd had time to call Sands. Maybe he'd be there right now, gun at the ready.

"Jeff," Callie whispered. She had to keep him talking, try to reason with him. "This isn't going to solve anything. Please. I have a daughter. Don't do this. We've been friends for so many years."

She realized that she sounded like she was babbling but she couldn't help herself. Keeping Jeff preoccupied was her only chance. She willed a late customer to knock on the door but none came. Jeff's sarcastic words rang through the empty rooms.

"Yeah, we were friends. But you were stupid, just like Minette. Falling for Drew. Anyone with eyes could see that he just used women." He gestured with the knife and Callie recoiled.

"What was it with Drew?" Jeff spat. "He had everything. Why did he have to go after other people's wives? I'll bet you didn't know that he was having an affair with Minette a couple of years ago?"

When Callie didn't answer, he gave a bark of self-mocking laughter. "They covered it up pretty well. But in the end, I know Minette

225

better than anyone, even better than she knows herself. She can't hide anything from me. They weren't nearly as clever as they thought they were. I actually think they wanted to get caught. You know, add to the thrill." His creepy laughter rang out again.

Callie felt her knees start to tremble with fear. Maybe she could talk Jeff through his pain. It was her only chance.

"I'm so sorry that happened to you," she murmured in what she hoped was a soothing manner. "What happened then?" There was one item in her purse that might possibly help her. Callie held her hands at her sides helplessly. Would Jeff notice if she put her hands behind her back so that she could search for the items with her fingertips?

She shifted slightly to the side where she thought she'd left one of her kitchen tools but Jeff was staring over her head, into a void of his own dark thoughts. Thank goodness, Callie thought, placing one hand behind her on the countertop. Her fingers touched her purse and she stopped moving as Jeff looked sharply at her.

"I thought Minette had moved on," Jeff was saying. "We were a team again, building our business, talking about having kids. And then, Drew's business started to boom while ours started to go downhill. It made me so angry. Minette got depressed. She was convinced that she was with the wrong guy." His eyes flashed and Callie glanced uneasily at the knife. It gleamed with menace, a stark contrast to her cheery kitchen. A clock ticked loudly and in the dead silence of the shop, Jeff and Callie's breathing seemed as loud as a windstorm.

"I found Minette one day at Drew's bistro after closing time," Jeff said, his words rushing out, his voice shaking. "She was so upset that she confided to me that she was still in love with him except he wouldn't take her back. He'd already moved on to Jane Willoughby."

Jeff grasped the knife more tightly and Callie saw the tendons of his arms bulge. "Another married woman! Minette just couldn't forget him. No matter how much I loved her, I couldn't make her forget him. He had to die. And then Minette and I could finally be happy together again. But as long as he was around, it wasn't going to happen."

"You killed him." Callie breathed. "I thought it was Minette."

"No way," Jeff sneered. "She'd never be able to do it." He glared at her. "I knew when you said you had spoken to Jane that something was up. Then, when I found out that Jane was being questioned by the police on a tip from you, I realized it was only a matter of time before you figured it out."

"So you were the one who attacked Lucille and me."

"Lucille talked too much. She even knew about Minette and Drew – apparently that chef she was dating just loved airing Drew's dirty laundry. It was only a matter of time before she said the wrong thing to the wrong person. Too bad I couldn't finish the job."

He went on, his voice strangely calm. For some reason, this was more frightening than if he had been screaming at her. "I knocked you out the other day hoping to keep you out of commission long enough to get out of town with Minette." Jeff sneered. "Too bad you're such a go-getter."

The knife wavered in his hand a bit before he took it in a tighter grip and held it up, close to Callie's eyes. She blinked back tears and tried not to squeal in fright.

"Don't you see?" Jeff slowly shook his head, the knife still raised, its sharp point dangerously close to Callie's face. "Minette and I can still be happy!" He smiled then, a normal smile and for a second, Jeff looked like the handsome, athletic man that Callie thought she knew.

Taking advantage of his calmer demeanor, she took another tiny step backwards. Had he seen her move? No, his moods were shifting again. He frowned. "Minette is all upset about Drew but one day she'll know it was for the best."

Suddenly, Jeff stepped closer and held the knife right in front of Callie's nose. Time was running out and Jeff's next words confirmed that.

"Unfortunately for you," Jeff said shaking his head, "you couldn't stick to your own business and keep out of mine. That's why you're going to have to die. I'm going to make it look like a suicide – you're going to slit your own wrists with this knife and die relatively peacefully or I'm going to slit your throat." Jeff regarded the knife, running his thumb lightly over its sharp edge. "I'm sticking you in the walk-in refrigerator. No one will find you until morning."

As she took in these horrible words, Callie forced herself to breathe. She held her body steady, ready for a chance to move if she could.

"Minette and I are heading out of town forever and starting over. We'll find new mountains to climb. All Crystal Bay has to offer are cheating jerks like Drew and pathetic rock climbing walls at Bodies by the Bay. Minette and I are going to travel the world," Jeff said, almost dreamily, his eyes glassy and unfocused. Callie started to tremble.

"Where is Minette?" she asked, hoping to throw him off balance.

"She's in the car, waiting for me to finish. Then we're out of here."

Callie swallowed back a lump of terror. "She knows you want to kill me?"

"That's right. She hated that you were with Drew! In fact, she's the one that tampered with your food that night." Callie blanched but Jeff just smiled.

"It wasn't Jane," she whispered.

Jeff looked at Callie with mock pity. "Minette kept trying to see Drew but he kept saying no, he was busy. Finally, she asked if she could come over on the same night you two had a dinner date. The same night, in fact, that he found out that he won Taste of Crystal Bay. She even brought him flowers!"

So those had been the mums that Callie had seen with the tags still on them.

"She added ipecac to the food out of spite?"

"Someone at Bodies by the Bay told her it was a great way to purge. Minette developed an eating disorder after Drew dumped her. The sad part is that the weight never even really came off. Poor Minette – she couldn't even do an eating disorder right. Yeah, she was angry that you and Drew had a date that night and she was jealous he was cooking for you. She thought it would be 'funny' – her words – if you both got sick." Jeff smirked, but his eyes burned with madness.

Having grasped the final item she was looking for while Jeff was talking, Callie held it tightly, steadying her feet and gathering her courage before making her move. She spoke quietly to Jeff while holding his gaze. "The affair must have been so hard on you."

"Not as hard as it ended up being on Drew. I followed her and then decided to spy on them from across the Bay, where it narrows. You can see pretty clearly into Drew's house depending on where you stand."

"You were the one at Mrs. DeWitt's! You dropped that rope that Koukla found," Callie said slowly.

"Gee, Callie. You're really on the ball. Just for that I'm going to tell you the rest of this sweet bedtime story. Your last one, you might say. After all, what are friends for?" He chuckled to himself again and Callie steadied herself, gathering courage for what she had to do next.

"I used my rock climbing gear to get into Drew's house. No sign of forced entry – nice, huh? I waited until I was sure Minette was gone before climbing in through Drew's window. He'd left it open. It was a warm night, just right for romance." He spit out the last word as if it tasted bad. "I must have been quick and clean because none of the neighbors reported seeing a thing." He smirked at his own cleverness.

"Drew thought I was there to talk. He told me not to worry, he'd never loved Minette and they weren't going to get back together. Like that would reassure me! The smug bastard. He offered me a drink as a peace offering and turned around, thinking it was settled on his word alone. That's when I killed him." Callie watched him clench and unclench his fists, perhaps reliving the memory.

"I don't like to have to kill you but at least now you know why I have to do what I'm about to do. So which is it? Suicide — because you're so distraught about Drew – or should I slit your pretty throat?"

Callie gripped the familiar objects in her hands and decided it was now or never. She raised Olivia's asthma inhaler and sprayed it into his eyes to stun him, then whipped the kitchen blowtorch out from behind her back and turned on the flame.

"Don't come any closer," she said, sliding along the side of the countertop. The inhaler hadn't done anything except surprise him, so Jeff was able to reach for her almost immediately. He growled like a bear and sprung forward, as Callie blasted her blowtorch directly into his face.

Jeff screamed and howled like an animal in a trap. He fell to his knees, the gleaming knife falling to the floor as if in slow motion. Before he could move, Callie picked up the knife and ran to the front of her shop, away from where he'd had her trapped by the counter. The sickening smell of burned flesh permeated the kitchen and Callie was horrified to see that Jeff was now on his feet, advancing towards her, his eyes filled with tears and rage, burn marks ravaging his cheeks, nose and forehead.

Callie had already leapt away from the counter. She held her blowtorch out in front of her. She was shaking and trembling now, rage replacing the fear she'd felt just seconds before. "Don't you dare take another step!" she screamed as Jeff rushed at her.

Callie closed her eyes and averted her face while she aimed the full force of the blowtorch toward Jeff's head, the knife jutting out in front of her.

Again he fell to the floor, clutching his eyes, rolling and screaming in pain. Callie looked down at the knife and saw that it was dark with blood, thankfully not her own. It appeared that as Jeff had come towards her, he'd run straight into his knife.

While Jeff lay writhing on the floor, Callie ran for the door.

"Help! Help!" she screamed as she burst through the front door of Callie's Kitchen. A couple on the sidewalk took a step back when they saw that she carried a flaming kitchen blowtorch and a bloody knife. Callie dropped them both on the ground and sank to the sidewalk. Inside her shop she could still hear Jeff screaming in agony.

"Please, can you call 911?" she asked. The girl grabbed her cell phone and punched in the numbers while her companion leaned down, asking Callie if she was all right. Taking deep breaths, Callie stood up, filling her lungs with the cool night air. "You know what? I'm great. But that guy in there? He's not so hot."

Twenty Six

"**C**heers!" said Mrs. DeWitt, topping off Callie's champagne glass. She took a quick sip and then clinked with Mrs. DeWitt and then Samantha, who was standing next to her. A few feet away, George chatted with Olivia, fully recovered, who was frolicking in Mrs. DeWitt's great room overlooking the water. Even Koukla had been invited to the bash.

Max, his hair spiky and gelled for the occasion stood next to Piper, resplendent in head-to-toe '50s vintage. They laughed and chatted with Chef Johan and Lucille, still a hot item. When he wasn't ranting about not getting paid, Johan was actually pretty nice. Lucille, always bubbly, seemed happier than ever.

Even Callie's ex-husband Hugh was there with Raine. Thankfully, Raine had restrained herself and there was no talk of her sex life. Well, at least that Callie could hear. Dozens of other guests were being served canapés and champagne in celebration of the new Taste of Crystal Bay prize winner – Callie's Kitchen. Best of all, customers were beginning to come back to Callie's Kitchen to enjoy her Greek food and home-baked treats. It looked like her dream business just might pull through.

It was two weeks after Jeff's apprehension via blowtorch and things in Crystal Bay were slowly getting back to normal. Jeff had been led away in a police-escorted ambulance that had gone straight to the hospital, but he had survived his injuries and was now being charged with Drew's murder.

Minette was distraught. Contrary to what Jeff had told Callie that horrible night, she was not a willing participant in Jeff's schemes. She had been bound and gagged in the back of the Minette's Chocolates van. Once she had discovered that he was Drew's killer, she'd tried to leave him but he'd restrained her. Minette's Chocolates appeared to be closed for good this time.

On the bright side, Olivia's health was greatly improved. The doctor had determined that an allergy had exacerbated her asthma – apparently Olivia was allergic to Raine's new perfumed soap and body wash. A completely mortified Raine had apologized graciously to everyone and thrown the products in the trash, promising to never buy them again. She wasn't so bad. Callie decided she'd visit Crystal Bay's nicest bath products store – with Olivia so the same thing didn't happen twice – and buy her some beautiful, non-allergenic replacements.

Jane hadn't fared so well. She and her husband had separated. However, Bodies by the Bay was up and running after a short hiatus.

Jane was facing an audit. It turned out that Jane had been funding "Drew" the bistro for months, using an account she had kept secret from her husband. She had been funneling funds from the fitness center into Drew's account but had cooked the books at Bodies by the Bay so that her husband was none the wiser. Drew's large bank loan was his attempt to repay her.

By all accounts, Jane was not a happy camper, particularly where Callie was concerned. Jane had hardly been willing to speak with her, but she relented after admitting that she was grateful that Callie had helped bring Drew's killer to justice. Even so, the memory of Jane's anger and despair still stung. As the party buzzed around her, Callie's thoughts went back to her recent tense meeting with a heartbroken Jane.

"I'll never forgive you for exposing me or for the fact that you got to spend time with Drew out in the open while I had to hide. But I'm happy that Jeff is going to pay for his murder. I loved Drew," Jane had said, trying to keep her voice firm but unable to stop tears from slipping down her cheeks. "He didn't deserve what happened to him."

"No," Callie whispered. "He didn't. Jane," she said slowly. "It doesn't matter now, but I have to know. Why was Drew spending any time with me when he loved you?"

"Drew didn't know what he wanted," Jane had said, blowing her nose and regaining some of her poise. An angry tone had crept back into her voice. "At first he said he was just seeing you in order to keep tabs on you and your business. I think he had an idea that you two could join forces and help each other survive the economy. He told me once that he wanted to try cooking classes together and create some "Drew" meals-to-go to appeal to the tourists and local crowd that might not otherwise visit his bistro."

Callie remembered how Jane's eyes had flashed with anger as she spoke, her voice like steel. "That's what he kept saying. But I could tell by the way he spoke about you that he was starting to like you. It upset me. I wanted him all to myself, even though I couldn't 'officially' claim him." The look she had given to Callie was full of regret. "I know he cared about you as a friend and that he respected you." Jane's weak smile hadn't reached the corners of her mouth.

"You ruined my life, but I know Drew would appreciate what you've done for him." At that point, Jane had buried her face in a tissue and sobbed. Callie had merely put a hand on Jane's shoulder and waited for her to quiet down.

"I didn't ruin your life, Jane," Callie had corrected gently. "You made some decisions that took you in the wrong direction. But I sincerely hope that you get your life back someday." Jane had only nodded at her and turned away, caught up in her own misery.

Callie's recollections were interrupted by hearing her name called. "Hey," Sam said tugging at her sleeve. "You're a million miles away." Her best friend smiled at her. "Come back to earth, because I think you're on soon."

"Here's to Callie Costas," Mrs. DeWitt's voice rang through the spacious room which was decorated with fairy lights on each window framing a stunning view of the silvery water lapping against her boat slip. Tonight the pier was as calm and still as a mirror. She held up her glass in a toast. "Congratulations on being our new contest winner, a well-deserved victory." Loud applause greeted this statement. Mrs. DeWitt nodded at Callie. It was her turn to speak.

Callie took a deep breath to steady her trembling nerves and stepped in front of the crowd. She was wearing a new, sleek black dress belted at the waist. Viv had presented her with a hot-pink "statement" necklace that added a burst of color to her outfit.

"Mrs. DeWitt and the rest of the committee, thank you for this honor," Callie was pleased to note that her voice sounded strong, confident, despite the fact that her knees were shaking. "We've all experienced a lot of loss in these last few weeks and we've seen some of our dearest friends become the victims of tragic events." The crowd's chatter had stilled and she felt many pairs of eyes gazing at her.

"I am thrilled to accept the cash prize, but I have an announcement. I am donating half of the prize to start a scholarship at the Crystal Bay College's Business School. I want all students to have the opportunity to get to do what they love, just like I've been able to do." She smiled at her father, whose eyes twinkled back at her, lifting his glass even higher.

She glanced at Mrs. DeWitt, who nodded encouragingly. "It will be an annual scholarship, named after my father, who taught me everything I know about food, life and being a good businessperson – and about being a good person, in general. It will be named the George P. Costas Business School Grant."

The crowd cheered and Olivia jumped up and down, beaming at her grandfather. George beamed back and Viv embraced him. Even

Koukla gave out a little yip at his feet, so George let part of a canapé drop from his hand to the floor, where Koukla quickly inhaled it.

Callie said "Thank you," once again and then went to hug her father. He was smiling broadly, but tears shone at the corner of his eyes. Callie knew that he would never let them fall, no matter what.

"What a gift," he said, holding his daughter at arm's length.

"You deserve to have a scholarship in your honor, Dad. Especially after all you've done for me."

"I meant...." George struggled to stay in control. "What a gift it is, to have a daughter like you."

This time, Callie struggled not to cry. She dabbed at her eyes while Grandma Viv and Samantha joined their little group.

"Congratulations my darling," Viv said, kissing Callie on the cheek. Sam followed suit. "I'm so proud of you, Callie. Especially because you never got arrested," Sam said ruefully. "Come to think of it, I take it back. You didn't make my job all that easy." The group laughed together.

Viv regarded them all with a fond look in her eye. "Well, this has been delightful. Good news always helps to erase the bad. Still, I think we've all had enough excitement for a while, don't you think?" she said, smiling down at Olivia who was stuffing canapés into her mouth. She looked taller every day and her appetite was becoming impressive.

"Yes. Definitely." Callie sipped her champagne gratefully. "I'm ready to move ahead with my business. Less excitement sounds like a good thing." They all stood, chatting and enjoying their champagne until a tap on the shoulder and a familiar, sexy, sandpapery voice made Callie turn around.

"Hello. Callie?" She turned and saw Detective Sands, as ill at ease as a schoolboy.

"I didn't know you were invited!" Callie blurted it out before she realized how rude she'd sounded. "I'm sorry, I'm just surprised. I haven't seen you since, well, the whole incident with Jeff. It's nice to see you," she finished, realizing how much she meant it.

"Hello, Detective Sands," George said graciously. Then: "Ladies. Let's go get some food. I think I see macaroons," George said. He winked at Callie.

"Yes!" Sam said, winking as well.

"I LOVE macaroons. Let's go!" Samantha looked at Sands, smiled at Callie and then herded the group toward the dessert table. Viv couldn't resist peeking over her shoulder. Callie watched as she gave Sands a nod of approval. What was going on?

"Very nice to see you, too," Sands replied, apparently deciding to ignore the little drama that had just played out before him. He was dressed in a tailored jacket over a white shirt and jeans. Overall, Callie thought he looked very handsome.

"Congratulations. You must be very proud." He grinned at her.

"Thanks," Callie said, with a genuine smile. She was touched that he'd shown up at her party and was now feeling almost too shy to meet his eyes. "Forgive me for what I said before. I'm glad you're here."

"Me too," Sands said, looking down at her with a grin. His hazel eyes sparkled at her and he took her hand, clasping it briefly. "I know you've been through a lot. I was only doing my job."

"I know," Callie said, with a small smile. "And I'm glad that Drew's killer has finally been found."

"So," Sands cleared his throat. "What will you do with the money?" In all the chaos, he was the first person who had really asked her that.

"I have so many plans!" Callie was unabashed in her enthusiasm. "New ovens, to replace the old ones, first of all. I'm having Piper work on social media, part time. She quit working at Bodies by the Bay and I can afford to pay her a basic salary. General maintenance, like a new coat of paint. Things got a little beat up in there, as you know."

"I do," he said gazing down at her, just a hint of a smile on his lips now. Callie could smell the clean, linen scent of him. When had he gotten so close? Her heart began to pound, but for once, she didn't mind.

"You know, I never did get to have a meal from Callie's Kitchen," he said with a sparkle in his hazel eyes.

Callie laughed. "That's true. But I'm happy to remedy that situation whenever you're ready."

"Excellent," Sands replied. "I have just one request: no crème brûlée."

"Oh, you don't like it?" Callie raised her eyebrows.

"I love it. I just don't want you anywhere near me with a blowtorch." He took both of her hands this time and held them tightly. His touch was warm and comforting.

"No problem," she said, her voice cracking.

"Good. Then it's a deal?"

Callie nodded.

"Let's seal it then," Sands said. And he kissed her.

THE END

Recipes from Callie's Kitchen

Loukoumades

Delicious Greek doughnuts, George's favorite.

For the doughnuts:
5 cups flour
1 tsp salt
1 package yeast (active dry yeast)
Water as needed
Oil for frying (Callie uses canola oil)

For the syrup:
2 cups sugar
1 cup honey
1 cup water
Cinnamon for sprinkling on top

Sift the flour and salt together in a large glass or ceramic bowl and create a well in the middle. Dissolve the yeast in 1 cup of the water and pour into the flour. Mix together gently. Add more water slowly, just enough to create a sticky batter, not too thick or thin. To test, if you can pull some batter without it breaking off, it's the right consistency.

Beat this mixture for two minutes with an electric mixer and then cover the bowl with a towel. Set in a warm place until the dough doubles in bulk.

When the dough is ready, make the syrup: Place the sugar, honey and water in a saucepan and bring to a boil, cooking until it reduces enough to make syrup that is easily pourable but not too runny. Keep warm on the stove while the *loukoumades* fry.

Heat the oil in a large, deep pot. Using a small ice cream scoop or two teaspoons, scoop out the risen batter into a ball and drop it into the hot oil which should be hot enough that the batter should rise to the top but not brown too quickly.

Cook, turning a few times with slotted spoon, until the puffs are golden. Remove them from the oil and place on a plate covered with paper towels to drain.

Pour syrup over the puffs and sprinkle with cinnamon. Serve at once.

Makes about 6 dozen *loukoumades*.

Callie's Greek Chicken Stew
Aka "Kota Kapama"

A Callie's Kitchen customer favorite.

To serve four:

2 lbs boneless skinless chicken breasts
1 large onion, diced
1 tsp minced garlic
1 tbsp tomato paste
1 large can crushed tomatoes – 28 oz.
1 bay leaf
1 or 2 cinnamon sticks (to taste)
A good glug of red wine (optional)
Olive oil, butter

Melt 2 tbsp butter in a large skillet, then add olive oil. Season the chicken generously with salt and pepper and brown on both sides in the oil. Remove chicken and place in a Dutch oven.

Drain most of the oil from the saucepan until you have about two tablespoons. Sauté the onions and garlic, then add them to the Dutch oven with the chicken along with the remaining ingredients. Simmer for about an hour and 15 minutes or until done. Before serving, strain out bay leaf and cinnamon sticks. Excellent served with rice or roasted potatoes.

George's *Spanakopita* (Greek Spinach-Cheese Pie)

Spanakopita normally requires butter only, but Callie lightens her *spanakopita* as her father taught her, by using a mixture of melted butter and olive oil to brush each pastry sheet. She also uses a low-fat feta cheese since it's so flavorful, but of course, regular is excellent, too.

Ingredients:

Six 10 oz. packages of chopped frozen spinach thawed and drained of excess liquid (but not too dry)

1 bunch scallions (green onions), chopped, white and pale green parts only

Dash of garlic powder

5 large eggs, lightly beaten

3 cups of reduced-fat feta cheese, crumbled (George will use sheep's milk feta imported from Greece if he can find it, but living in Wisconsin, he also enjoys the wonderful, locally produced feta cheese.)

2 sticks unsalted butter, melted and mixed with ½ cup extra-virgin olive oil + more olive oil if needed

1 regular-sized package of phyllo dough sheets, sometimes called "pastry sheets." (Phyllo dough sheets are found in the frozen foods section of most supermarkets, near frozen pie pastry and the like. George likes to use Athens Foods brand. NOTE: When you get home from the store, be sure to place phyllo pastry in the refrigerator, NOT the freezer so that it can thaw. George always repeats this instruction to Callie, every time she makes it.)

Salt and freshly ground pepper to taste.

1 tablespoon fresh dill chopped (or 1 tsp. of dried dill, but George prefers fresh – he says it tastes better.)

Preheat oven to 350 degrees F.

Prepare the phyllo: Phyllo pastry bakes up delightfully light and flaky, but the sheets are very thin and can dry out quickly. So here's how George makes sure that his phyllo stays nice and fresh: Take a clean tea towel and wet it, then wring out most of the water. Place your phyllo sheets on a cookie sheet with a rim. Place waxed paper directly over the phyllo, then place the damp tea towel over the paper. Lift up the wax paper and tea towel only when you are ready to take the next sheet and then quickly replace it.

In a large mixing bowl, toss together the spinach, onions, dill and garlic powder. Add the feta cheese and eggs, mixing lightly but thoroughly until well combined. Pour half of the melted butter over the top, season with salt and pepper, and mix again. It should not look too "liquidy."

Brush a 10 x 15 inch pan with butter. Place about half of the phyllo sheets (usually about 10) into the pan, brushing each thoroughly with melted butter (don't forget the corners) before adding the next one. Each sheet needs to be thoroughly coated with a thin layer of melted butter.

Add spinach-cheese mixture and spread evenly in the pan. Repeat phyllo sheet process until you have used them all.

Trim any overhanging phyllo dough from pan using kitchen shears, then score the pie into squares (about halfway down, for easier cutting later) with a sharp knife. Bake at 350 degrees F for about one hour, until the top is golden brown. Let cool slightly, then finish cutting and serve.

Yield: About 15 generous squares of *spanakopita*.

Mini Greek Yogurt Coffee Cakes with Streusel Topping

Have ready a 12-cup muffin tin. Grease and flour the pan well or spray with a baking spray that contains flour.

Preheat oven to 350 degrees F.

For the cake:
2 cups all-purpose, unbleached flour
1 tsp baking powder
1 tsp baking soda
Pinch salt
½ cup (1 stick) unsalted butter, softened
2 eggs
1 cup granulated sugar
1 cup Greek yogurt, either 0% or 2% fat. Callie likes to use the Fage brand Greek yogurt, available at most supermarkets.
1 tsp pure vanilla extract

Streusel topping:
4 tbsp cold butter, cut into small cubes
½ cup dark brown sugar
2 tbsp flour
2 tsp cinnamon
Combine all streusel ingredients with a biscuit cutter or two knives until the mixture looks like coarse crumbs. Set aside.

Make the cake batter:

Sift together flour, baking powder, baking soda and salt in a medium bowl. Cream the butter and sugar in an electric standing mixer on medium speed until light and fluffy.

Add eggs one at a time until well combined. Beat in the vanilla extract.

Gradually add flour in thirds, alternating with the Greek yogurt and ending with the flour.

Fill mini-Bundt cake pans or muffin cups about 2/3 full and sprinkle each with streusel mixture.

Bake for 20 minutes or until a toothpick inserted in the center of one of the cakes comes out clean.

Let cool in pan on wire rack for at least 10 minutes. Loosen each cake using a spatula or butter knife; let cool until you can comfortably lift each cake from the pan. So as not to disturb the streusel topping, it's best not to dump the cakes upside down, but to gently lift them out upright.

Makes about 18 mini coffee cakes.

My Big (Low) Fat Greek Salad

The perfect light and healthy dish for warmer weather. Add some grilled chicken and you have a complete meal, especially with warm pita bread on the side. Serves 4.

Ingredients:

1 bunch romaine lettuce leaves, washed and dried

2 tomatoes cut in quarters

1 red onion, thinly sliced

1 seedless cucumber (sometimes called an English cucumber), sliced

1 cup feta cheese, crumbled

½ cup black Kalamata olives (if not pitted, be sure to warn your diners to look out for the pits)

2-4 anchovies for top of salad (optional)

1 tsp dried oregano (Greek oregano is good; found at many well-stocked supermarkets)

1/2 cup olive oil

¼ cup freshly squeezed lemon juice or red wine vinegar

Kosher salt and freshly ground pepper to taste

Tear the romaine lettuce in bite-sized pieces and make sure that you discard any limp outer leaves. You want the crunchiest, greenest parts of the lettuce.

In a large salad bowl, whisk oil, vinegar or lemon juice, salt, pepper and oregano. Add lettuce, vegetables, cheese and olives; toss until lightly coated with dressing. Garnish with anchovies if using and serve immediately.

Crème Brûlée Cupcakes

You will need a small kitchen blowtorch to make the caramelized frosting for these cupcakes, which is really a version of a rich pastry cream. You can use your broiler but the blowtorch is easier. Just be careful!

For the cake:
1 cup all-purpose flour
1 tsp baking powder
½ tsp salt
1 cup granulated sugar
4 large eggs
6 oz. unsalted butter, softened
½ cup buttermilk
2 tsp pure vanilla extract

Preheat oven to 350 degrees F. Put paper liners in the muffin pan. Sift the flour, baking powder and salt in a medium bowl and set aside.

In the bowl of a standing mixer, beat butter and sugar until light and fluffy. Add eggs one at a time until well blended. Add vanilla extract.

Alternate flour mixture and buttermilk in thirds, beginning and ending with the flour.

Bake for 15-20 minutes, until pale golden on top. The cakes should spring back when you touch them with your finger.

Frosting Ingredients:
1 cup whole milk, slightly warmed in a saucepan
1 tsp pure vanilla extract
3 large egg yolks
2 oz. unsalted butter

¼ cup granulated sugar, plus additional sugar for topping

2 tbsp all-purpose flour

In a large bowl, beat the egg with the sugar until creamy, and then add the flour. Add warmed milk and whisk until smooth. Pour into the saucepan you used to warm the milk and gradually whisk over low heat until the custard thickens. (It should coat the back of a wooden spoon.) Remove from the heat and stir in butter and vanilla. Let the custard cool; you'll want to put a piece of wax paper or parchment on top so it doesn't form a skin. Refrigerate until very cold; you don't want the frosting to be too runny.

Spread the pastry cream on top of each cupcake and sprinkle generously with additional granulated sugar. Use your kitchen blowtorch (or broiler) to caramelize the sugar until golden brown. Serve immediately or chill and serve when cold.

Makes 12 cupcakes.

Acknowledgements

So many people helped make this book possible. I'd especially like to thank the following:

Linda Reilly, for her warmth, astute suggestions, encouragement and enthusiasm for this project.

Linda Rodriguez for her wonderful online mystery writing classes, gentle voice of encouragement and excellent writing tips.

Kathleen Bleck, for her intelligent feedback and thoughtful suggestions that helped improve the story, as well as her willingness to read an early version of this book.

Loretta Nyhan – author, friend, book cheerleader, wise guru – she helped me not to feel like such a "Sassenach" in the often confusing world of publishing.

Renee Barratt for her beautiful book cover design and professionalism. You made my vision come to life!

Sisters in Crime, The Guppies and The Cozy Gups for the tireless ability to answer the questions of a newbie author and the uplifting words. The same goes to the crew at Midwest Mystery Writers of America – thanks for your support of aspiring writers.

My family, friends & LGP cohorts – thanks for the stalwart support of everything I do.

And last but not least, my husband and loving tech-support guy, Jim Kales, who makes everything possible and who believes in me even when I don't. Thanks for tolerating my Masterpiece Mystery addiction and for always being willing to watch just one more episode.

To all of you not listed here who have helped, supported and encouraged me in this sometimes crazy journey – thank you!!!

About the Author

Award-winning writer and blogger Jenny Kales worked for years as a freelancer, but fiction writing has always been a dream and *On the Chopping Block* is her debut mystery novel. Kales' marriage into a Greek-American Midwestern family inspired The Callie's Kitchen mysteries, featuring Calliope Costas, food business owner and amateur sleuth. The setting of the story, "Crystal Bay," is inspired by a favorite family vacation spot - Wisconsin's beautiful Geneva Lakes. Ms. Kales is an avid reader, cook and baker and she's addicted to mystery TV, especially anything on Masterpiece Mystery or BBC America. She lives just outside of Chicago with her husband, two daughters and a cute but demanding Yorkshire terrier, and is hard at work on the next novel in the Callie's Kitchen Mystery Series. Visit the author's web site at *www.jennykales.wordpress.com*. To keep up with author news, giveaways, recipes and other fun stuff, sign up for a FREE seasonal newsletter at *tinyurl.com/huv5pof*.

Preview of Book 2
Spiced and Iced

**Enjoy the first chapter in the next installment
of *The Callie's Kitchen Mystery Series*!**

"**W**hy does *anyone* think it's a good idea to have their bridal shower right before the holidays?" grumbled Natalie Underwood, her long red curls bouncing pertly as she rushed about the room. Her slim figure, decked out in a short, sleek dress and dark-colored tights seemed to bristle with consternation as she straightened silverware and adjusted the festive Christmas centerpieces in The English Country Inn's waterfront dining room.

"Because they enjoy making everyone as stressed out as they are?" Calliope Costas responded, but with a smile. Her friends and clients called her "Callie," but her Greek father normally stuck with "Calliope."

As the proprietor of Callie's Kitchen, a Mediterranean meets Midwest from-scratch meals business, she'd had her fair share of demanding clients. But customers were customers. Anyway, Callie knew she was more able to tolerate self-absorbed brides now than she used to, now that she had a new special someone in her own life.

As the two women chatted, Callie was rushing alongside Natalie, placing mini boxes of her famous Greek snowball cookies, aka, *kourabiethes*, at each place. The inn had its own chef, but occasionally

Callie contributed an extra sweet treat to events at the inn at the host's request. To celebrate the season, Callie had spiced the treats with ouzo, the flavorful Greek liqueur, and had placed a fragrant clove in the center of each cookie. She wished that Natalie would eat a cookie – maybe the combination of booze and melt-in-your-mouth texture would cheer her up.

"Okay, that just about does it." Natalie straightened a final centerpiece and glanced out the huge expanse of windows overlooking Crystal Bay's namesake waterfront. She leaned forward a bit, squinting at the view. Callie kept placing boxes of cookies at each place. If anyone was out there, it had to be a duck who had forgotten to migrate: who else would brave the 15-degree temperatures?

The day was a bit overcast, but nothing unusual for Wisconsin in mid-December. The lake looked icy and gray, but even the lack of sun couldn't take away from its beauty. So far the month was unusually cold, even for Crystal Bay. Unlike previous years when warm temperatures prevented the water from icing over completely, it looked like this year the bay and surrounding waterways were experiencing an early freeze. The ice fishermen and ice skaters would have a field day.

Inside, the airy dining room glowed with soft Christmas lights and so many fresh pine boughs and tiny white fairy lights that it felt like walking through a winter forest. Large windows framed the pleasant vista of Crystal Bay. Delightful. Callie inhaled the pine-scented air deeply before turning to Natalie once more.

"Anything else that I can do to help right now?" she asked.

The young woman shook her head. "Not that I can think of." Natalie was, by all accounts, exceptionally good at her job as the head of events at The English Country Inn, a Crystal Bay mainstay for the last 40 years. The midsized boutique hotel was situated directly on the water, making for charmingly picturesque views. The interior décor reflected its namesake with inviting floral sofas and wallpaper, plush carpet and warm paneling.

The inn was also famous for a spectacular English-style Victorian tea service, presented only at Christmastime. Locals and tourists alike flocked to partake of the tender cucumber tea sandwiches, rich, flaky scones and spicy gingerbread. Callie had planned to attend the tea event with her grandmother, Viv and her 10-year-old daughter, Olivia. She was even toying with the idea of inviting the British-born detective she was seeing. Would a detective enjoy a tea party?

Callie glanced again at Natalie who appeared to be white with fatigue. "Natalie, come on. Let's sit down for a minute. You look run off your feet."

"I can't," Natalie responded firmly. "You're sweet to worry about me but there is just so much to do."

"Let me help you then. I need to go back to work soon, but I can stay a little longer. Why not take advantage?" Callie smiled.

Natalie smiled back, but weakly, so it seemed to Callie. "Thanks," she said with a sigh. "Maybe I will take a short break. This particular bride is not my favorite and I really can't let my feelings show."

"Oh?" Callie asked, handing over one of the *kourabiethes*. Natalie dropped into a chair with another gusty sigh and munched glumly on the cookie.

"I'm surprised you don't know the story," she said. "These are good by the way. A little spicy, but buttery."

Callie smiled. At least her *kourabiethes* hadn't lost their ability to cheer people up. "Thanks. Now – what story are you talking about?"

"Well, this is the <u>second</u> bridal shower I've planned for the bride. At the first one, she and some of her relatives got, shall we say, a little too argumentative and the groom ended up ditching her."

"I didn't know that." The bride, Lexy Dayton, was a regular customer at Callie's Kitchen, and she had insisted that the Greek cookies be on the menu at her bridal shower. "That's terrible. Poor Lexy!"

Callie offered, reluctant to criticize a loyal client – and Greek cookie lover.

Natalie rolled her eyes at Callie. "I can't say I blame her ex. The Daytons appear to be ever-so-elegant on the surface, but they know how to wreck a party. Believe me. In any case, Lexy blames me for her relationship gone awry. Logic is not her strong suit."

"I'm inclined to agree. Why on earth would she have her bridal shower at the inn if she blames you for ruining her last engagement?" Callie asked, raising her dark eyebrows.

Natalie finished her second cookie before answering. "The Daytons are loaded, so they really could afford to have the shower anywhere. Though, I suppose this setting makes sense to them. Apparently, Dayton brides have been fêted at The English Country Inn since forever and they are intent on keeping the tradition alive. I only hope that the groom doesn't dump Lexy today. I could lose my job!"

Natalie slumped back in her chair and frowned at her beautifully manicured fingernails. "To make matters worse, I went to high school with Nick Hawkins, Lexy's new groom. He had a crush on me way back when, but I think he's forgotten about it. Not Lexy, though. She's probably got a spreadsheet of every woman that Nick ever glanced at."

Callie laughed. "Oh, Natalie. No wonder you're tense today! Don't worry so much. Everything looks beautiful, the food will be delicious and you can just cut them off early if they hit the bar too often. Hopefully, the Christmas Spirit will help too."

Natalie stood up, smoothing her navy dress, accented with a flowing scarf, tied into a loose bow. To Callie's eyes, the dress looked like an expensive designer number that Callie had drooled over online. Was it Kate Spade? Either it was the real deal or a very convincing knock-off. Natalie must be doing well for herself if she could purchase *that*. Callie could only afford to dream of such clothing.

"You're probably right. And thanks for talking," Natalie seemed a little more calm and some color had come back to her attractively freckled face. "If you're sure you don't mind, I think I will ask you to do something for me. Will you see if the coat check person is here? The guests are arriving any minute and I forgot to do something."

"Of course," Callie agreed, inwardly relieved to be given such a minor task. She had been up early and was feeling tired.

"Thanks for all of your help today," Natalie smiled at Callie before lowering her voice to a near whisper. "I know you probably wouldn't but, please, don't repeat my story about the Daytons."

"No worries, here," Callie responded. "We've all dealt with bridezillas."

Natalie giggled and started walking quickly down the hallway. "See you in a minute," she called over her shoulder.

Callie checked her watch and strode to the lobby to look for the coat check person. She didn't see a soul, not even the concierge, Melody Cartwright.

Perhaps Melody wasn't working today – she was the type to have a lot of irons in the fire. Besides working part time at the inn, the forty-something Melody ran a tea party business for children and was about to have her first book published – it would include tea party tips and recipes. Callie thought the book sounded wonderful. There was even talk of her being a guest on a national talk show. Melody was Crystal Bay's closest thing to a celebrity these days.

"Melody!" Callie called, but no one answered. She headed back near the coat check area and was relieved to see a young woman standing behind the half-door.

"Oh. Hi there. I'm helping out today for the Dayton shower and Natalie Underwood just wanted me to check to see that you'd arrived," Callie explained.

The young woman nodded and smiled. "Well, let her know I'm here and I'm ready when the guests are." She smoothed her long blond hair back from her face. "Is everything okay? Natalie usually checks in with me personally before an event."

"Oh yes, everything's fine," Callie said, relieved that her tasks were nearly finished. Her assistant, Max, was working but she needed to get back to her shop for a pile of food prep. "Natalie is just really busy today. I'm Callie Costas, by the way."

"Kayla Hall," the coat check girl said, extending her hand. "I know you – you run the Greek food business downtown. It's really good."

"Thanks!" Callie felt herself blush a little at the praise. "You look familiar to me, too. I hope you can come to Callie's Kitchen again soon. We've got some great Christmas goodies. I even decided to do Kringle this year."

Kayla's eyes lit up at the mention of the classic Danish pastry, a Wisconsin Christmas tradition. Callie was about to elaborate but stopped when she noticed that Kayla suddenly looked strained, a forced smile painted on her face.

"Welcome to The English Country Inn," Kayla said perkily to someone who stood just behind Callie. "May I check your coat?"

Callie stepped aside for a tall, model-thin woman in her mid-fifties with a short, chic gray haircut. Without a glance at Callie, she handed a fur coat across the door to Kayla. She didn't look as if she ate much Christmas Kringle but looks could be deceiving. Callie had learned that sometimes the thinnest people had the best appetites.

"Thank you," the woman addressed Kayla in a brisk tone. Her voice was deep and resonant, like a newscaster. She was wearing a bright red jacket and matching pencil skirt that set off her athletic build. Her Christmassy outfit was set off with dangling earrings in the shape of small, sparkly snowflakes.

Abruptly, she turned to Callie. "Are you working the Dayton bridal shower? I need to speak to someone about the seating."

Ah. The famous Dayton mother of the bride. She certainly appeared to be elegant and put together. Callie tried to imagine her in the type of family brawl that Natalie had described and failed.

"I'm not the event planner, if that's what you mean," Callie began, but the other woman cut her off.

"I know that. Natalie Underwood is the event manager." The Dayton woman took a step closer, enveloping Callie in a cloud of expensive perfume that smelled like the *La Vie Est Belle* Callie's best friend Sam had gifted to her at her last birthday. *Life Is Beautiful.*

However, this woman appeared to be thinking just the opposite about life, at least at the moment. She glared at Callie and started tapping her foot. "Do you work for Natalie? I need to go over a few things. But perhaps Natalie would be the best person for me to deal with."

Anxious to get back to her own place of business, Callie decided the best thing to do was be gracious. "I'm sure she would be able to assist you. I just provided a few treats from my food business, Callie's Kitchen. Your daughter may have told you."

"Oh yes, Callie's Kitchen." She didn't look as if she thought much of her daughter's taste in food providers. "All right, then. Please see if you can find Natalie. The guests should be here in half an hour and I want everything to be perfect."

Getting a sympathetic glance from Kayla, Callie attempted to soothe the nervous mother of the bride. "Of course you do. I'll go look for her right now."

Grateful for an excuse to leave this woman's towering and intimidating presence, Callie scooted off in the direction she'd last seen Natalie. There was no one in sight but a few housekeeping workers and they had no idea where Natalie – or Melody Cartwright, the concierge – had disappeared to.

Callie started to sweat. The last thing she wanted was a confrontation with Mrs. Dayton who, despite her polished appearance, became somewhat overbearing once she spoke. Natalie was in for an interesting afternoon.

Finally, one of the bellboys took pity on Callie and directed her to Natalie's office, situated near the kitchen, where succulent odors of roast chicken were wafting through the doorway. Her stomach rumbled but this was no time for food.

"Natalie," Callie said, knocking on the closed office door. "The mother of the bride is looking for you and she seems a little tense."

The door swung open but instead of Natalie, it was Melody Cartwright who emerged from the office. "Hello, Callie," she said. "I was looking for Natalie, too."

"Oh!" Callie was startled. "I wondered where you were. The Dayton party is arriving and you might want to get out there, pronto. The mother of the bride had some things to discuss with Natalie and she looks like she means business."

"Oh my," Melody said, a frown creasing her forehead. "The Daytons want a perfect event, that's for sure. Where can Natalie be?"

Perfect. There was that word again. Despite enjoying the fee that came with supplying food for an event, Callie was glad she wasn't running this show. Everyone seemed a bit too uptight and combined with what Natalie had shared about the Daytons, the event had all the potential of a reality TV episode, complete with overturned tables and hair-pulling.

Melody ran a hand over her smooth dark hair, pulled back in a low bun. She looked conservative, but sophisticated, quite a different look than when she dressed up as a princess or a fairy for the children's tea parties she hosted. Melody pulled her ivory blouse more securely over her hips and smoothed her black trousers as she started down the hallway.

"If you're finished, you can feel free to go," she called over her shoulder to Callie. "I'll find Natalie. Thanks for your help!" Melody disappeared around the corner.

Callie let her breath out in a whoosh and headed back to the dining room to collect her coat and any stray cookie boxes. She heard a hubbub of voices in the lobby and realized that the guests would be entering the dining room any minute. No need to stick around for the bride – leave that pleasure to The English Country Inn.

As she re-entered the dining room, the windows framed a winter wonderland of white, fluffy snowflakes that descended gently from the sky. The scenery was certainly holding up its end of the bargain. Hopefully the calm winter scene would pacify any edgy guests – or hosts.

Callie located her belongings and looked out the window once more. The snow was really coming down now, a harbinger of slippery roads. Instead of taking a chance on running into Mrs. Dayton again, Callie decided to go out the dining room door that led to the patio, a popular spot in warm months. It was closer to the parking lot, anyway, she rationalized. She put on her coat and braced herself for the cold.

As she stepped outside, Callie felt some of the stress lift from her. Snow was a pain to drive in, but a white Christmas was so romantic and this year she would have someone to share it with. Gazing out at the water and inhaling the cold, head-clearing air, Callie relished the chilly beauty of the scene, but a flash of color in the water near the large boathouse attached to the hotel caught her eye. Squinting, she took a closer look.

Just visible through the fluffy white wall of snowflakes was a burnished orange blob. That was odd. Did somebody drop something in the water? Callie was ready to shrug it off and head for the warmth of her car, but something made her take another look. A prickle of apprehension made the hairs on the back of her neck stand up.

Slowly, Callie started walking toward the object. It was slow going. The snow was starting to become slippery and ice patches were already on the ground. The falling snow was starting to obscure the ice patches, making them even more dangerous.

Callie stumbled a bit and with a struggle, righted herself before she fell. She glanced longingly back towards the parking lot, but her curiosity was getting the better of her. She felt silly and vowed to head back to the car if she slipped one more time. For all she knew, it was a stray buoy, left behind when the piers were taken up and stacked like Tinker Toys for winter storage.

Cautiously now, Callie stepped closer. From this vantage point, it was clear the item wasn't a buoy. *What was it?* The colors sharpened as she got closer. Callie started to quicken her pace, slipping a bit, but focused now. The outlines of a human body were now coming into view. Callie caught her breath in a gasp. An icy sensation began at her scalp and continued to her toes.

Forgetting the dangers of the ice and new-fallen snow, Callie made a beeline to the water's edge and the unidentified object floating in it. What she saw made the back of her scalp tingle and her stomach lurch. She screamed.

Natalie lay face down in the water. The thin ice must have broken when she fell, revealing the icy depths underneath. Callie shuddered and shrieked, tears springing to her eyes and momentarily blinding her. *No. Not again. Please.* She wiped her streaming eyes with a mittened hand and forced herself to look again.

Natalie's beautiful hair fanned out like seaweed. The back of her head was a bloody mass and the ends of her long, coppery locks were already starting to become covered with a fine coating of powdery snow.

Cautiously, Callie leaned down and nudged Natalie, loudly calling her name to no response. With one huge push, Callie turned the event planner over and then fell back onto the patio. Freezing water splashed onto her jeans and her hands felt like they'd been dipped inside a flash-freezing machine.

Natalie floated with her arms outstretched in the frigid water, her long designer scarf speckled with blood. Her normally rosy, freckled face was now grayish white and her wide-open eyes were glassy and devoid of the spark of life.

Made in the USA
Lexington, KY
27 June 2019